GHOSTS of EMPIRE

GEORGE MANN

GHOSTS
of EMPIRE

TITAN BOOKS

GHOSTS OF EMPIRE

Print edition ISBN: 9781783294183
E-book edition ISBN: 9781783294190

Published by Titan Books
A division of Titan Publishing Group Ltd
144 Southwark Street, London SE1 0UP

First edition: October 2017
10 9 8 7 6 5 4 3 2 1

A CIP catalogue record for this title is available from the British Library.

Printed and bound in the USA.

What did you think of this book? We love to hear from our readers. Please email us at: readerfeedback@titanemail.com, or write to us at the above address.

To receive advance information, news, competitions, and exclusive offers online, please sign up for the Titan newsletter on our website:

WWW.TITANBOOKS.COM

To the crew at Titan, for all of their recent help and support.

ONE

His heart was thumping in time with the cadence of his pounding feet.

Every step jarred his body. His lungs burned. His head was swimming with the exertion. He'd been running like this for over a mile, and he knew he wouldn't be able to keep it up much longer.

The air was thick with rain, stinging his eyes, causing his suit to become sodden and clinging. Around him, the city was slowly giving itself over to the encroaching night. Streetlamps blinked on, bright and unreal, making the slick pavements gleam like the glassy surface of a river. The rain had driven all but the most stubborn pedestrians to seek the shelter of their homes, pubs and favorite restaurants, and even the roads were desolate, with only the occasional specter of a car drifting through the spray, surrounded by wisps of phantasmal steam.

He'd considered trying to flag one of them down, to commandeer it, but he knew the best way to lose his pursuers was to head for somewhere crowded, somewhere they might be seen. The man who had sent them would not wish to draw attention.

He risked a glance over his shoulder. They were rounding the bend, running side by side, eyes fierce and intent. Their paws made no sound as they bounded along the pavement, and their ears were pricked, their muzzles drawn back into ferocious snarls. Through their ghostly flanks he could trace the outlines of the nearby buildings, and in their wake they left a mesmerizing trail of swirling particles, dust motes of pure, golden light. He'd never seen anything quite like it; the way the Russian had simply *folded* them into existence with a gesture of his hands, as if drawing them from the air itself.

They were getting closer. He turned his attention back to the road, forcing his weary muscles to keep moving. If he could just make it a little further, he was sure he could shake them off…

It had all started in a house in Belgravia. He'd been there posing as a "fixer for hire", offering his services to a conglomerate of Russians who'd put out word in the wrong kind of circles that they were looking for someone to take on a job. He'd been softening them up for weeks, inveigling himself into the fringes of their operation, trying to earn their trust. So far, he'd been unable to establish precisely what they were doing in London, but he'd hoped that, tonight, they would finally reveal their hand.

In the event, they had—just not quite in the manner he'd intended. They'd had another agent waiting for him, a freelancer by the name of Sabine Glogauer, who'd identified him without a moment's hesitation. It was a typical downturn of luck— he'd been certain he was close to winning the contract and discovering their plans, but instead he'd found himself facing a rival—and worse, a rival whom he'd crossed on more than one occasion, and who'd been only too happy to twist the knife. Now, he supposed that the whole encounter had probably been contrived as a test of *her* loyalty, rather than his. The Russians must have been on to him from the very start. They'd certainly been prepared to kill him upon Sabine's confirmation of his true identity.

Thankfully, he'd had a good deal of practice diving through sash windows. So now he was here, barreling down the rain-soaked streets, a pair of spectral hounds in hot pursuit, stinging fragments of glass still buried in the tender flesh of his face and hands.

He skidded around a bend in the road, his feet slipping on the slick paving slabs. He lurched, jarring his back, but carried on, splashing down a narrow alleyway between a dress shop and an abandoned theater. His breath was fogging now, his hair dripping water into his eyes. Every muscle was protesting. His gun was a dead weight in his pocket. He'd already tried loosing off a few shots at the beasts, to no avail; the bullets had passed clean through their intangible bodies, pinging off the brickwork behind them. Somehow, he imagined, their jaws would prove far more corporeal if the creatures were to catch up with him.

He sidestepped a heap of discarded wooden crates, ducking out of the way at the last minute, and winced as his ankle turned over on the wet cobbles. He went down, falling to one knee, clawing at the wall in desperation. His fingertips came away raw and bloody. He forced himself up, roaring with the exertion, breaking into a hobbling run that sent shooting pains up his shin. He could sense the creatures behind him, closing in, and there was absolutely nothing he could do.

He felt the thud of one of them against his back, and he was carried forward under the weight of it, sprawling to the ground, striking his chin against the cobbles. He rolled, bringing his arms up to try to fend it off, but the other one was on top of him too, its jaws snapping at his forearms, tearing fabric and flesh.

He felt warm blood mingling with the rain, running down the inside his shirtsleeves. He kicked, but his boots could find no purchase upon the spectral creatures, eliciting only a spray of golden particles with each intended blow. They dispersed in the rain, before coalescing again a moment later.

This can't be it. Not here. Not like this.

He fought frantically to protect his throat as one of the hounds sank its teeth into his shoulder, but he was impotent, with no way of fighting back against these strange, nightmarish beasts.

As unconsciousness descended, he thought he sensed another presence in the alleyway—a looming, shadowy figure, standing over him—and the scent of fresh dew and tree sap filled his nostrils. Then blackness overcame him, and the last thing he felt was the fangs of one of the creatures biting deep into the flesh and muscle of his thigh.

"Oh, this really isn't good enough. Can you imagine what they'd say in New York if someone served *this*?" Gabriel Cross lifted his spoon and allowed a trickle of pale soup to drain back into the bowl before him. He dropped the spoon with a clatter, and craned his neck, looking for a waiter. "I mean, I can't even tell what it's supposed to *be*."

Donovan sighed, and pointedly took another sip from his spoon. Gabriel was growing bored. He'd adopted his most asinine persona—the errant playboy—and was making flippant pronouncements in order to stir up some distraction. The two elderly ladies at the neighbouring table were already pulling faces and muttering behind their serviettes—it wouldn't be long before one of the other diners complained, and then things would escalate, and an indignant Gabriel would end up bickering with the waitstaff. Donovan had seen it all before.

It was, he knew, a result of the time they'd spent cooped up inside the airship during their long transatlantic voyage, and the relative sobriety of London. Gabriel was having a difficult time relaxing. He'd confessed as much in the hotel bar, late the previous evening—he missed scudding about over the rooftops of New York; missed the freedom of donning his hat and coat and transforming himself into the Ghost. That other persona— that solitary figure of vengeance—was the *real* Gabriel, Donovan had decided, and being forced to bury that part of him for so long was beginning to have repercussions.

London, it seemed, was as sleepy a city as a holidaymaker could wish for, certainly amongst the society circles in which Gabriel—ostensibly a rich bachelor—seemed to move. Take the Savoy, for example: opulent, unnecessary, and completely boring in every way.

There'd simply been no call for Gabriel's particular breed of vigilantism, either during the crossing, or in the three days since their arrival. If there *was* clandestine activity going on throughout the city, it was being comported in that peculiarly British way—politely, and without causing any disagreement or upset to others.

Even Ginny, whom Gabriel had brought here for a period of convalescence following her recent trauma in Cairo, had little need of his attention—she was recovering well, and enjoying the sightseeing; as resilient a woman as Donovan had ever known.

Consequently, Gabriel was making his own entertainment— and doing so at the price of his dining companions' embarrassment.

"Oh, let it go, Gabriel. It's not worth causing a fuss," said

Ginny. She put a dissuading hand on his arm, and her pretty face, framed by her fashionable bob of blonde hair, creased in an expression that was more annoyance than concern.

"It's the Savoy, Ginny. Of course it's worth making a fuss." Gabriel leaned back in his chair and regarded them each in turn, from Ginny, to Flora, to Donovan. There was a questioning look in his eyes, as if he were searching for an ally, or else daring someone to tell him to behave.

"Well *I* like it," said Donovan, "but then I don't have quite as refined a taste as you." He set his spoon down. "Except when it comes to women," he added hastily, with a quick sideways glance at Flora. She was sitting on his left at the round table, her expression unreadable. He decided he'd probably got away with it. He pushed his empty bowl away from him. He was dying for a cigarette.

"Well, let's hope the main course is palatable, at least," said Gabriel. He rubbed his chin distractedly, and Donovan saw Ginny heave a sigh of relief. "Afterwards we can take a stroll along the embankment, if you like? Assuming the rain has let up."

"I'd like that," said Ginny. She, too, pushed the remains of her soup across the table, and Donovan realized she'd hardly touched it. Perhaps that was Gabriel's game. He realized he must have missed something; that Gabriel had evidently been making such a fuss about the soup because he'd seen that Ginny wasn't eating it, and was trying to save her the embarrassment. So it had been a small act of chivalry, rather than contrived rebellion. Perhaps England suited Gabriel better than he realized.

Donovan smiled, and took a gulp of water. Even that tasted

different from the water in New York. Maybe it was something to do with all the rain.

Gabriel was looking to the door, his brow furrowed. There was an empty place set between him and Donovan — supposedly reserved for their guest, who had yet to show his face.

"I really think we should have waited for your friend," said Flora, touching Donovan's arm. Her fingers felt cold through his shirtsleeve. She nodded in Gabriel's direction.

"We waited an hour," said Donovan. "They wouldn't have been able to hold the table much longer. I guess something must have come up. Work, most likely."

"I thought you said he worked for the British government?" said Flora.

Donovan nodded. "Yes, but he doesn't keep regular hours."

"Like someone else I know." She awarded him a knowing smile.

Donovan reached for his cigarettes, pulling one from the crumpled packet and offering them around. Gabriel took one and pulled the ignition tab, causing its tip to spark in the low light. Donovan dropped the packet on the table. He was nearly out. Soon he'd have to buy some English cigarettes, and resort to lighting them by hand. He couldn't understand why the people here had such a fondness for outmoded technology, like matches. Perhaps it was something to do with the ritual. Or the fact that many of them still seemed to smoke pipes.

"Strange that he hasn't sent word," said Gabriel, through a pall of smoke. "He seemed so effusive on the phone."

"You know what it's like," said Donovan. "He's probably lost track of the time. There'll be an apologetic note at the hotel in the morning, and we'll make alternative plans. It's not like we're in a hurry."

Gabriel nodded in agreement, but Donovan could sense his disquiet.

"Tomorrow, then," said Donovan, to the table at large. "What do you say to the Tower of London?"

"I think that's a splendid idea," said Ginny. "I'll brush up on all the grisly details in my guidebook this evening."

Donovan laughed.

"Then you can be our tour guide," said Flora. "I want to hear about all the kings and queens who lost their heads. All the scandal and gossip."

There was a commotion by the door, a collective intake of breath from the circling wait staff and nearest diners. Donovan, frowning, peered over Ginny's shoulder as she twisted in her seat, trying to see what was going on. "If it's gossip you're after, it seems we're in the right place," he said.

People were getting out of their seats, their faces creased in appalled concern. They began to migrate to the entrance, forming a small crowd around the dining-room door and obscuring his view. He guessed someone unexpected must have arrived, given the response—perhaps a celebrity or minor dignitary. That would certainly make the most sense… and yet the looks on people's faces told a different story.

Donovan glanced at Gabriel, who was slowly rising from his seat, his cigarette abandoned and smoldering in the ashtray.

"Gabriel? What is it?"

"I think…" he muttered, but the rest of the sentence was lost when a figure lurched through the gathered throng, taking a series of juddering steps toward their table.

Donovan got to his feet, circling around protectively before Flora.

The shambolic figure took another step toward them, and Donovan could see now why the ripple of shocked incomprehension had passed through the other diners. The man was steeped in blood, which soaked what remained of his shredded suit, staining the front of his shirt a deep, wine red. He had suffered what appeared to be a terrible mauling, as if from a dog or big cat. Puncture marks from thumb-sized teeth still glistened with dribbling blood, spilling more of the stuff down his chest and arm with every thumping beat of his heart. His hair was dripping from the rain, and blood had been smeared across his left cheek.

"What the..." started Donovan, stopping short as the man came to a jolting halt before them. He looked woozily from Donovan to Gabriel, and the hint of a delirious smile pulled at the corners of his mouth.

Donovan's eyes widened in horrified recognition—he *knew* this person. "*Rutherford?*"

"Sorry I'm late," croaked Peter Rutherford. "Hope I didn't spoil dinner." He raised his hand, as if to mop his brow, and then his eyes seemed to lose focus, his legs went from under him, and he collapsed onto the carpet in a bloody, trembling heap.

TWO

"Give me room! Get all these people back. And fetch me
something I can use to bind his wounds."

Gabriel was on his knees beside the prone Rutherford,
while Donovan was trying to clear a space, urging the crowd of
gawking diners to keep back. They seemed reluctant to comply,
either through shock, or because they were simply unwilling to
relinquish their view of unfolding events. He supposed it was
hard to blame them—it wasn't every day that a man staggered
into a society restaurant dowsed in his own blood.

While Donovan stood guard, Ginny rushed over to one of
the unoccupied tables and yanked the white tablecloth from it,
sending cutlery and empty wine glasses clattering to the floor.
Flora hurried to help her, and together they began tearing the
tablecloth into long strips. Another woman from the crowd
came forward to assist, and soon they'd fashioned a series of
makeshift bandages, which they passed to Gabriel, who set
about binding Rutherford's wounds.

Rutherford was in a horrific state. He'd lost so much
blood the color had drained out of his face, awarding him a
pale, ghostly aspect. His eyes had rolled back in their sockets,
displaying their disturbing milky-white sclera, and a thin line
of stark red blood was trailing from the corner of his mouth.

It dribbled slowly down his cheek as Donovan looked on. His breathing was coming in short shallow gasps, and Donovan could tell that he was exceedingly close to death. Blood burbled from multiple wounds in his arms, chest, and legs.

Donovan hoped Gabriel knew what he was doing. He supposed if there was anyone in the room who'd taken a beating before, it was Gabriel. Donovan had grown used to seeing his friend nonchalantly tending his own wounds—or else stoically ignoring them while he carried on with the fight at hand. Hopefully he could do enough to keep Rutherford alive until professional help arrived.

What Donovan couldn't fathom, though, was the manner of creature that had inflicted such grievous wounds. It wasn't as if there were wild beasts roaming the streets of London. Had it been rabid dogs?

"There," said Gabriel, rocking back on his haunches. "That should staunch the bleeding, for a few minutes at least." He looked up at Donovan. "Has anyone sent for a doctor?"

Donovan glanced around, searching for a response. A murmur rumbled through the crowd, before one of the waiters stepped forward. "We've called for an ambulance," he said. He was a tall, thin man in his late twenties, and seemed to be the only one of the staff who hadn't recoiled in panic. His hands were clasped so tightly before him they were starting to turn white, and he was trying desperately not to look down at the bloody mess of the man by his feet. He spoke in a clipped, formal accent as he stood behind Gabriel. "I presume you know this man?" he said to Donovan.

Donovan gave him a withering stare. "Of course we know him. He was supposed to be our dinner companion. He's a friend."

The waiter nodded. "The ambulance should be here shortly." He took a deep breath, and then turned to address the crowd of diners. "Ladies and gentlemen, if you'll please accept my apology for any upset. I would recommend you all now return to your seats to make way for the ambulance crew. We'll have this matter resolved in just a moment, and service will be resumed."

Another murmur passed through the crowd, before it began to slowly disperse. People drifted toward their seats, still gawping openly at the scene unfolding on the floor in their midst. Donovan looked at the waiter in disbelief. What was it with these people and their inherent deference to authority figures? Was it the uniform? Or perhaps it was simply the fact the man had apologized to them, as if accepting responsibility for everything that was happening. That was another thing he'd noticed since arriving here in London—everyone seemed to have a habit of apologizing for things that weren't their fault.

Gabriel was still hurriedly tightening makeshift bandages around Rutherford's left shoulder, right thigh and both forearms. He nodded sharply in acknowledgement without taking his eyes from his work. Rutherford was barely breathing. Donovan was beginning to think it was already too late. It was going to take a miracle to keep him alive, and even if they did, he'd never be the same again. "Gabriel—can I do anything to help?"

"Just keep a look out for the ambulance. All we can do now is hope."

Donovan willed them to arrive quickly.

"What's all this about, Felix?"

He turned to see Flora at his elbow. The initial surge of adrenaline had clearly begun to wear off, and he could see she was trembling now, finally comprehending the horror of what she was seeing. She put her hand to her mouth. "That poor man."

Donovan put his arm around her shoulders and pulled her close. "I don't know. Remember I told you he worked for the British government?" He lowered his voice, wary of being overheard. "He's an agent with the Secret Service."

"A spy?" said Flora.

"Of a sort," said Donovan. "I think whatever's happened to him, it must be connected to that."

"But why come here? He should have gone straight for an ambulance. Surely someone in the street could have helped him? Why come and find you like this?"

Donovan watched Gabriel applying pressure to a seeping wound in Rutherford's side. "I think that's the pertinent question," he said. Why *had* Rutherford forced himself to make it to the Savoy?

The murmuring of the diners suddenly rose in pitch, and Donovan turned to see two medics hurrying in through the main entrance. They were carrying a stretcher, and were dressed in matching black and white uniforms. They were bedraggled from the rain, hair plastered to their foreheads. They bustled over to Gabriel's side, shooing him out of the way.

"I bound his wounds as best I could," said Gabriel. "He appears to have been mauled by an animal, although I'm damned if I know what could have caused this much damage."

"Alright, sir. Thank you for your assistance. We can manage from here," said one of the medics, without even turning to properly acknowledge Gabriel, who was still kneeling on the carpeted floor, blood dripping from his hands. He looked for a moment as if he was about to reproach the man, but then sighed, and reached for a torn fragment of tablecloth, upon which he set about wiping his hands.

As the two men lowered the stretcher to the floor and began gently lifting Rutherford onto it, Gabriel walked over to join them. Behind him, Ginny was watching and listening, her expression unreadable.

"I'm going with him to the hospital," said Gabriel. "I'll meet you back at the hotel."

Ginny stepped forward, hoisting her handbag onto her shoulder. "I'll come with you."

"No," said Gabriel. He glanced around to ensure no one was close enough to overhear. "We're not sure what he might be mixed up in yet."

Ginny narrowed her eyes. Donovan sensed an undercurrent of frustration, as if she thought Gabriel was mollycoddling her. "You *know* I can look after myself."

Gabriel shook his head. "Of course I do. It's not that. I just don't think it's a good idea for us both to get involved. If whoever came after him realizes they didn't quite finish the job, then they might try again. I'm going to make sure he gets to the hospital safely, but if I'm not back by morning, I'll need you to come find me."

Ginny gave him a dubious look. "So this *isn't* just about you trying to be the hero?"

Gabriel laughed, his face a picture of mock hurt. "Who, *me*?"

Ginny rolled her eyes.

"Just be careful, Gabriel," said Donovan. "God knows what Rutherford's got himself embroiled in. His… *associates* might not take too kindly to a foreigner sticking his nose into their business, let alone the people—or *things*—that did this to him."

Gabriel nodded. "Don't worry. I'm not going looking for trouble. We're on vacation, after all." He grinned, but his concern for his friend was evident in his voice. "I just need to make sure he gets to the hospital."

Ginny nodded. "Alright. If he comes round, tell him we're thinking of him."

"I'll do better than that," said Gabriel. "I won't leave until we've made alternative arrangements for dinner."

St Bartholomew's Hospital was an imposing Georgian edifice that, to Gabriel, resembled a stately home more than a famed medical institution. He felt utterly dwarfed by the towering, slab-like structure, the balconied roof, and the grand entrance arch. He could imagine lavish horse-drawn carriages trundling back and forth on the paved forecourt; long, gloomy galleries lined with austere portraits of long-dead nobles; musty libraries and gilded drawing rooms. It had the air of some royal estate that had been co-opted during the war and never handed back by the surgeons.

The ambulance had taken only a few minutes to speed through the slick, empty streets, and now, standing in the rain, watching the two ambulance men unload a still unconscious Rutherford from the rear of the vehicle, Gabriel couldn't help but wonder if he'd done the right thing. Donovan had been right—whatever government agency Rutherford worked for weren't going to take kindly to his interference. And yet... what had compelled Rutherford to stagger through the streets to keep his appointment at the Savoy, half delirious and suffering from potentially fatal wounds? Why hadn't he made for the nearest holophone box or flagged down a ride to the hospital?

He'd been trying to tell them something. His appearance in that distressed, wounded state had been a message of some kind, and Gabriel could only conclude that his old sparring companion had meant to ask him for help. To what end… well, he supposed he was going to have to stick around to find out.

Gabriel followed the medics inside, keeping his head bowed against the incessant rain.

His initial impressions of the place couldn't have been further from the truth. Inside, the hospital reeked of carbolic, and was functional and clean, with tiled walls and polished wooden floors. There was nothing of the grandeur of the outer shell of the building evident, here, aside from the tall sash windows; it was clinical and functional, and bustling with activity.

Doctors, nurses and porters buzzed about the place like worker ants, criss-crossing each other's paths, shouting commands to one another as they attempted to prioritize those patients with the most grievous injuries. Patients crowded in the small entrance lobby, some of them seated on low wooden chairs, others pacing, others still crowding on the floor, their backs pressed against the walls. One man was nursing a bloodied nose; another held his limp arm in a makeshift sling, while a woman was attempting to corral two small children, one of whom had a large, purple welt on the side of their head.

The ambulance men bearing Rutherford's stretcher were waved straight through to what Gabriel took to be an operating theater, through a set of heavy wooden doors and along a narrow passageway. They hurried through while a porter held the doors open for them. He was a cherubic man in shirtsleeves and waistcoat, who peered myopically at Gabriel through a pair of thick spectacles, and then held up his hand up in warning as Gabriel attempted to follow behind the stretcher.

"I'm afraid I cannot allow members of the public into the operating theater," he said. His accent was thick and regional, and unfamiliar to Gabriel.

"I'm not a member of the public," said Gabriel. "I'm the one who brought him in. I bound his wounds at the restaurant before the ambulance arrived." He held up his hands, showing the man the dark, ingrained blood. It had clotted beneath his fingernails. He was going to have to scrub them clean when he got back to the hotel.

"I see," said the porter. "Are you a member of the patient's family?"

"I'm a *friend*," said Gabriel.

"Then I'm going to have to ask you to take a seat in the waiting area," said the porter. "This way." He released the door, which swung shut on well-oiled hinges, and beckoned for Gabriel to follow.

Gabriel glanced back at the door, unsure whether to push his luck. "Listen, it's important that I stay with him. He'd want me to be there."

"I dare say," said the porter, "but the rules are there for a reason, sir, and we need to give the surgeons room to work." He offered what Gabriel presumed was supposed to be a sympathetic smile. "They'll do what they can for your friend. There's nothing more you can do now. Please, this way."

Gabriel bristled at the man's patronizing manner, but he supposed it wasn't worth making a scene. He'd managed to get Rutherford to the operating table—that had been his goal—and now he'd have to leave it to the doctors to do their work. He'd know more in a couple of hours, if Rutherford was able to pull through.

He followed the porter to a small side room, just off the main thoroughfare. There was no one else waiting inside. "In there, sir. Take a seat, and as soon as there's any news about your friend, I'll let you know."

"Thank you," said Gabriel. "Look, before you go—is there anywhere I can clean up? A restroom?"

The man's lips twitched in a smile at Gabriel's colloquialism. "Yes, sir. Just across the hallway, you'll find a gentleman's *lavatory*." He emphasized the last word, as if to make a point.

"Thanks," said Gabriel, refusing to rise to the jibe. He watched as the man turned his back and strolled away, whistling tunelessly.

He glanced around the waiting room. It was a small, featureless box of a room, lined with uncomfortable-looking wooden chairs, and a small coffee table heaped with the previous day's newspapers. On the wall, a painting of Queen Alberta loomed down at him, severe and unattractive in her gilded crown. A single window looked out onto the driveway, where he could see the ambulance still parked, its rear doors hanging open. The two ambulance men who'd helped Rutherford were standing off to one side, both smoking cigarettes beneath a glowing streetlamp. He heard the sound of wheels churning pebbles, and watched as a black van skidded abruptly to a halt beside the ambulance, its headlamps flickering in the gloom. A blonde woman and two men in suits alighted from the vehicle, and headed for the main hospital entrance.

With a sigh, Gabriel wandered out into the hallway. The restroom was just where the porter had indicated, and he ducked inside, heading straight for the sink. The soap was hard and perfumed, and reminded him of the stuff he'd been forced to use during the war—when he'd been lucky enough to get hold of any. It proved largely ineffective at removing the ingrained blood, but it would do until he could get back to the hotel and take a proper soak in the bath. He dried his hands on a paper towel, and ambled back into the hallway, wondering how long he was going to have to wait for news.

There was some commotion going on, further up the hallway. The porter was engaged in a fracas with one of the suited men Gabriel had seen getting out of the van just a moment earlier. He was a burly sort, tall and broad with dark hair, and was physically restraining the porter, holding him back against the wall as the smaller man bellowed and squirmed in his grip. It didn't appear as if the man in the suit was about to strike him— more that he was preventing the porter from scurrying away from some disagreement.

Gabriel couldn't help but smile—it was only what the porter deserved. He'd clearly turned his patronizing attitude on the wrong man.

Behind them, the wooden doors opened, and the blonde woman, along with the other suited man—this one slightly smaller, with close-cropped sandy hair—came hurrying out, pushing a trolley bearing the prone form of what appeared to be a patient.

As they hurried down the corridor, the man holding the porter released his grip, and the porter slid to the ground, rubbing his chest.

Something didn't feel right. Acting on instinct, Gabriel stepped out into the path of the oncoming trolley.

Cursing loudly, the woman leaned left, swerving the trolley to avoid a direct collision. "Get out of the way!"

Gabriel looked at the man on the trolley. He could see the hastily made bandages he'd tied around Rutherford's wounds were still in place. What the hell were these people trying to do? Were they the ones who'd tried to kill him? What other possible reason could they have for snatching him from the operating table?

"Where are you taking this man?" he demanded, moving further into their path.

"What's it got to do with you?" snapped the sandy-haired man.

"I'm the one who brought him in. He needs urgent help. From a *doctor*."

"You were at the Savoy? Then you have our thanks," said the woman. "We'll see to it he's well looked after. Now get out of our way."

"I can't allow you to take him from this hospital," said Gabriel.

"Like hell you can't," said a voice to the right of him. He turned, directly into the fist of the burly man who'd been causing the porter so much grief just a few seconds earlier. Gabriel staggered back, striking the wall, momentarily dazed by the sheer force of the blow. His jaw was smarting. It had been a blow intended to drop him, and he lurched unsteadily, his vision swimming. He raised his fists, ready to defend himself against a second blow that never came—the three newcomers were already making off down the corridor, running at full pelt, the wheels of Rutherford's trolley rattling across the porcelain tiles.

Groggily, Gabriel staggered after them. Behind him, he could hear the porter calling for help.

He burst out into the night, just in time to see the woman leaping up into the passenger seat of the van, just as the driver gunned the engine and it roared to life, churning up a slew of stones as it shot off at speed. Abandoned on the driveway was the overturned trolley that had, only a few moments earlier, borne the unconscious Peter Rutherford.

Cursing, Gabriel ran a hand over his face, and then gave chase.

THREE

onight, the sky was a wash of deep, inky blue—ominous and
foreboding. Gray clouds gathered on the horizon like a pall
of smoke, and rain lashed the windowpanes, drumming on
the roof tiles as if calling him out, demanding his attention. In
the distance the stuttering rooftops of Westminster formed a
jagged, irregular horizon, like spurs of broken glass.

He could sense something gathering, out there in the
darkness. Something bleak and strange; something *unwelcome*.
The avatar knew it, too; that was why it had broken free of
its shackles, striding out into the night in search of whatever
festered out there amongst the dank alleyways and shadow-
draped lanes. He only hoped it might survive the night.

Roland Horwood turned away from the window, allowing
the drape to fall back into place. He felt unsettled, unable to fall
into his usual evening routine. He'd eaten, but had abandoned
the small meal of ham and boiled potatoes halfway through,
distracted by the sounds from outside and the itch of uncertainty
at the back of his mind. He'd tried numbing the anxiety with a
generous glass of red wine, but still it gnawed away at his gut,
and he felt jittery, as if his body wanted him to keep pacing.
He'd even considered going out there to look for it, but he
knew that was a fool's errand; it could be anywhere within a

ten mile radius by now, and he was hardly a proficient tracker.

He crossed the room and clicked the wireless on, but the weather was interfering with the signal, and try as he might, the only sound he could extract from the thing was a burr of static, which only added to his agitation, his sense of sudden isolation. Mostly, he adored living out here, away from the mad rush of the city, from the filth and the bickering and the lolloping ground trains that rolled through the streets, threatening to crush everything in their path. He supposed that was probably a metaphor of some kind, but he was too on edge to find any humor in it.

He imagined the state of his garden once the storm had blown over. It would take him days to put everything back in order—not least to work out what he was going to do, now that the avatar had gone. What if it didn't return? What if it *did*? Perhaps he'd been a trifle naïve. He should have considered all of these possibilities. He should have *planned*.

Horwood flicked off the wireless and returned to the window. There was still no sign of it, out there in the storm. It had been, what, three hours? Maybe more. He hadn't seen it leave, but he'd found the evidence of its passing when he went outside to check on it—the torn branches and scattered leaves, the strange impressions in the mud, the cavernous hollow where it had stood.

A sudden gust caused raindrops to drum loudly against the pane, only inches from his face, and he leapt back, nearly losing the glasses from the end of his nose. He pushed them back into place with his index finger, then smoothed his shirtfront in embarrassment, despite the fact he was alone.

With a sigh, his heart hammering from the sudden shock,

he crossed the room and dropped heavily into his armchair by the fire. The logs he'd piled in the grate earlier that afternoon were still a little damp, and they smoldered and crackled as he warmed himself. He knew there was nothing he could do. Worse, though, he felt he had a sense of what was coming, of what would be needed in the days to come, and through his carelessness, he'd jeopardized it all. He thought he might have played a part in it, somehow, found a way to protect the things he held dear, but now he was left wondering whether everything he'd done had been for nothing.

He picked up his empty wine glass. He supposed there was always the rest of the bottle. He'd regret it in the morning, but for now, it might help. He sloshed another large measure into the glass, and then drained it, gulping it down, willing it to do its work. It warmed the back of his throat, almost causing him to splutter.

The billowing wind brought another dash of rain against the window. He looked round, craning his neck, but there was nothing to see. This time, he would force himself to stay where he was, to put it out of mind.

If it hadn't returned by the morning, then he'd have to start checking the newspaper reports, maybe take a trip into the city.

He heard the rustle of movement, of feet stirring gravel, and lurched to his feet, upending his wine glass over his trousers. He ignored it, allowing the glass to roll away across the carpet, leaving a stain on the cream pile as stark and uncoordinated as spilled blood.

He returned once more to the window, cupping his hands against the reflection of the gas lamps, pressing his nose up against the cold glass.

There! Something moved. He frowned, squinting, trying to make it out.

There was a thud against the glass beside his head, and, slowly, he stepped back. It was a hand, formed from knotted growths of willow branch and ivy, its fingers splayed. Slowly, it slid away, and he watched it go, listening to the howl of the wind. It was followed by a loud *crunch*, as something heavy thudded to the gravel, and he knew at once that it was back, and in need of him.

Horwood glanced around, looking for his coat, but he must have left it upstairs, or in the back room, and there wasn't time to go searching for it. He stumbled to the front door, sliding the chain from the catch and pulling it open. The wind whipped the rain up into his face, causing him to splutter as he staggered out. After the cosy glow of the fire, the chill air caused his teeth to chatter, and he hugged himself as he ran across the driveway, kicking up stones with every footfall.

It was there, lying on the ground like so much damp kindling. It had slumped onto its side, its face buried in the crook of its arm, and it was unmoving.

Huge chunks had been taken out of its torso, and its thigh, and its other arm was missing from the elbow down. As Horwood got closer, dropping to his knees before it, he could see where the vines were trying unsuccessfully to knit themselves back together, to maintain their form.

"Oh no, oh no," he muttered, as he ran his hands over its flank, feeling the twigs respond, the ivy curling around his fingers. "What have you done?"

The avatar stirred, emitting a sorrowful sound reminiscent of a deep, plaintive sigh.

Shaking his head, Horwood got to his feet, wiping the rain from his eyes. "There's still time," he said. "Hold on. I know what we have to do."

FOUR

At this time of night, London seemed utterly forlorn, and yet utterly spellbinding, too.

It was dissimilar to New York; not simply in the crazed, organic layout of its streets, or the ornate splendor of its buildings, but in its *texture*, too, in the way it felt, and smelled. It was as if Gabriel could feel the weight of history bearing down upon him, reminding him of his own insignificance. He knew most people wouldn't understand, but for him, a man who'd spent so long soaring above the rooftops of Manhattan, memorizing every nook and cranny, London was like some strange, archaic puzzle he was yet to fully understand. Its heart beat to a different rhythm.

He leaned forward in his seat, watching the city flit by as the car hissed down the ancient streets, crooked like gnarled fingers. Rain lashed the windscreen, making it difficult to discern anything beyond a few yards ahead. Everything seemed muted and softened, and even the streetlamps seemed to have difficulty puncturing the shadowy mantle that had settled over the city. The taillights of the van in front were their only beacons, guiding them on. Toward what, Gabriel could not be certain.

The taxi driver was a short, muscular man in a waistcoat and cap, with tattoos spiraling up his forearms and a burr of unshaven growth over his lower face. When he noticed Gabriel looking, he turned and smiled, and Gabriel noticed his two front teeth were missing.

"So, what's your game, then? It's a miserable night to be chasing after people in an unmarked van." His missing teeth gave him a pronounced lisp.

"It's a friend," said Gabriel, in as non-committal a tone as he could muster. He'd hailed the taxi outside the hospital just moments after he'd witnessed the three suspicious figures—the woman and two men—bundling Rutherford's unconscious form into the back of the van, and he'd given the driver directions to follow behind it at a safe distance.

The driver nodded and turned his attention back to the road. The spray from the van was reducing visibility even further, and they were forced to hang back, allowing the van to pull ahead of them a short way.

"Don't lose them," said Gabriel. He was beginning to wish he'd brought his full rocket boosters with him. It would have been a simple matter to follow the van from overhead, even taking into account the torrential weather. Although, he supposed, walking around with two fuel canisters strapped to his calves wasn't entirely in keeping with the dress code at the Savoy.

He reached inside his jacket and his fingers brushed reassuringly against the butt of his modified Luger. At least he'd had the foresight to bring that with him from the hotel— along with a handful of other concealed tools of his trade. He had a sense he might yet have need of them.

"Right-o," said the driver, a moment later. Gabriel felt the car slow as the driver eased the brakes on, and they sloshed through a puddle of standing water to draw up to the curb.

He kept the windscreen wipers going, ticking across the screen like a metronome, so that Gabriel could peer out at the scene unfolding ahead of them.

The van had come to a stop outside a three-story house. It was an old, well maintained building on the end of a terrace, the brickwork painted in stark white, with a set of stone steps leading up to the front door, and what appeared to be an iron staircase around the side, presumably leading down to a basement. He guessed the house must have been at least a century old, probably more.

"Where are we?"

"Bloomsbury," said the driver. "Close to Russell Square."

Gabriel nodded, and leaned forward, trying to make out what was going on outside. The woman had already left the van and was rapping on the front door of the house, while the two men were unloading the prone Rutherford from the rear of the vehicle.

Rutherford still appeared to be unconscious, and the men were staggering under the burden. Gabriel only hoped that his friend wasn't already a literal dead weight—that they hadn't allowed him to die in transit, or worse, finished him off with a quick bullet to the head. He supposed they'd be unlikely to go to all of this trouble if he *were* dead; more likely they were keeping him alive in the hope of extracting information from him. That gave Gabriel hope that he'd be able to intervene in time, and try to get Rutherford to safety.

Of course, he had no idea what Rutherford had gotten himself mixed up in—only that the man had proved a stalwart ally back in New York the previous year, and that Gabriel felt a certain sort of kinship with him, after fighting elbow-to-elbow against a common foe. He owed it to Rutherford to do whatever he could to help.

He returned his attention to the house. Someone had answered the door—an elderly butler or valet—and was now hurriedly waving the men to the side entrance, while stepping aside to allow the woman to enter via the front door.

Gabriel watched the two men stagger down the iron staircase, their faces creased with strain, their hair plastered to their scalps by the incessant rain. There was little to distinguish them—they both wore formless black suits and dark woollen overcoats; outfits designed, Gabriel knew, to blend in easily in a crowd. These were men who were used to moving unseen amongst the multitude.

They reached the bottom of the steps. Rutherford's arms flopped uselessly by his sides, blood mingling with rainwater, running down his sleeves and dribbling from his fingertips. A moment later the men disappeared from view.

The front door had closed behind the woman, and suddenly the street was deserted once again. The house might just have been any other in the quiet square, its inhabitants taking shelter from the inclement weather.

Gabriel sat for a moment, contemplating his next move. Everything was still, silent, save for the drumming of the rain on the roof of the cab. The driver gave a polite cough. Gabriel could sense him fidgeting nervously in his seat. He wondered what the man thought about the scene that had just unfolded before them.

"So, you getting out here, guv, or you want me to take you back to your hotel or something?"

Gabriel fished in his pocket for some coins. He examined

them for a moment in his palm, and then shrugged and handed them over to the driver. He still had no idea what the strange denominations meant. "Forget you ever saw me," he said. "Forget you saw any of it."

The man looked at the heap of coins in his cupped hands. "Whatever you say. I've not seen nothing."

Gabriel opened the door and stepped out into the torrential downpour. The raindrops stung his face, and within seconds they were already trickling down the back of his neck, soaking into his collar. Beside him, the car engine coughed, and then the cab reversed, swinging into a side street, before turning and sloshing away into the night.

Without the steady beams of the car headlamps, the square took on a rather more sinister aspect, and all of a sudden Gabriel felt cold, tired, and homesick. He'd brought Ginny here to recuperate from their recent troubles in New York, and Donovan to get him away from the clutches of a gang lord known as the Reaper, but suddenly they seemed like distant problems, half a world away.

Right here, now, he was facing a choice. He could still turn and walk away; jump in another cab and be back at the hotel within half an hour, curled up with Ginny, pretending like none of this had ever happened. Did he really want to get embroiled in whatever was going on here between the British Secret Service and whoever had taken Rutherford inside that house? Did Ginny and Donovan deserve that?

He knew they didn't, but also that there was never really any choice. He couldn't walk away and leave Rutherford to die, no matter the circumstances, or the odds. If there was a chance to save him, Gabriel had to take it.

He decided the direct approach would be best. Turning his coat collar up, he hurried across the road, splashing through the runnels of surface water that were threatening to merge into a stream.

He took the steps two at a time, and then huddled in the small open porch, brushing the rainwater from his shoulders. He thumped on the front door with the edge of his fist and stood back, his shoulders hunched against the rain.

He heard footsteps from the other side—the *click-clack* of heels on a tiled floor—and then a key was turned in the lock, and the door opened inward to reveal the butler he'd seen earlier.

He was a thin, aged man, probably in his eighties, with a balding pate that still clung resolutely to a few neat wisps of white hair, which he'd swept back from his temples and tucked behind his ears. He had leathery, liver-spotted hands, and his lips were thin and pale. His eyes, however, were bright and alert, and he narrowed them, peering suspiciously down the length of his Napoleonic nose. "Yes?" he drawled.

"Oh, hey, sorry to bother you. Miserable night, isn't it? I don't know how you guys put up with it."

The butler glowered at Gabriel, but said nothing.

"Look, thing is, my car's broken down around the corner, and I'm stuck out here in the rain. I know it's a liberty, but I saw your lights were on, and wondered if I could make a call? I just need to speak to my hotel, see if they can't sort something out." Gabriel offered his best charming grin.

"I'm sorry, sir, but it's rather inconvenient at the moment. Perhaps if you were to prevail on Mr. Laughton, next door?" The butler began to close the door. Hurriedly, Gabriel shoved his foot in the way.

"Now, look here, what's a chap to do? I'll pay, if that's what you want?" He reached into his pocket and took out his wallet. The butler made a sour expression, as if Gabriel had made some kind of vulgar faux pas.

"That really won't be necessary, sir. I'm sure Mr. Laughton will be only too glad t—" He stopped suddenly at the sound of a man screaming from deep within the bowels of the house.

So Rutherford *was* still alive, and being tortured, by the sound of things.

The butler coughed. He looked sheepish.

Gabriel leaned forward over the doorjamb, trying to get a look into the house. The décor was elegant, if a little shabby. There was nothing to suggest it wasn't an ordinary residence in a well-to-do area of town; nothing, that was, apart from the screaming. "Is everything alright? Look, if I can help in any way…"

The butler stiffened. "It's just the hounds, sir. They probably sense the presence of a stranger, and are growing uneasy." He started to close the door, pushing Gabriel back. "Now if you'd kindly excuse me, I should attend to them. Mr. Laughton will be more than forthcoming, I'm sure."

Gabriel considered his options. He could easily overpower the butler and force his way inside, but in doing so he'd undoubtedly raise the alarm and bring the others running. Far better that he allow the man to think his ploy had been successful, to back away and then see if he could enter the house via the side entrance, down below.

"Alright, alright!" said Gabriel, holding up his hands in mock surrender. "A guy can tell when he's not wanted. Sorry to have troubled you. Thanks for nothing."

He stepped back, and saw the evident relief on the butler's face as the man hurriedly closed the door. He heard the chain slide across the lock, and then footsteps disappearing down the hall.

The rain brushed the back of his neck like icy fingers.

So, his supposition had been right. They'd brought Rutherford here in an effort to extract information. Well, he'd have to see what he could do about that.

Gabriel backed away from the house and down the steps, and then, with a quick glance up at the windows to ensure he wasn't being observed, slipped around the side of the house and down the iron stairwell. The metal was cold to the touch, and slick with rainwater, which was pooling in the small lobby area below.

He splashed down before the door, drew his gun, and listened.

He couldn't hear anything on the other side of the door. Cautiously, he tried the handle. It was unlocked, but secured by a bolt on the other side. He'd either have to risk putting his fist through one of the small glass panes, or give the door an almighty shove to try to force the bolt away from the frame.

Neither option was particularly appealing. As the Ghost he might have kicked the door aside and gone in weapons blazing, but as Gabriel, he was ill-prepared for a fight. He'd have to choose his moment carefully.

He took a sodden handkerchief from his pocket and wrapped it around the butt of his gun, weighing it in his hand. Then, pressing his ear up against the door, he waited, arm raised, until he heard Rutherford issue another scream, and then tapped sharply at the glass, careful to coincide the noise of the shattering pane with the cries from inside.

The resultant hole was just large enough for him to get his hand through.

Hurriedly, he reached in, wincing as the jagged glass nicked his wrist, and fumbled for the bolt, sliding it free.

The door yawned open.

Inside, it was dark, the only illumination coming from a narrow, tiled passage that appeared to lead deeper beneath the main house. There was clearly an extensive basement level here, which Gabriel assumed shared the same considerable footprint as the house above.

He slipped inside, closing the door carefully behind him while avoiding the fragments of broken glass on the floor.

The room was tiled white, floor and ceiling, and smelled of carbolic. It reminded him of the hospital. There were three plain wooden chairs, a small, mismatched occasional table, a trolley — evidently designed for ferrying unconscious or immobilized victims to and fro — and a bizarre, ungainly contraption in the corner that had the shape and form of an eight-foot tall man.

It was, Gabriel presumed, a medical automaton of some kind. Its chassis had been constructed from a series of brass struts and complex ball sockets to resemble a humanoid skeleton, only unlike a human being, the machine was equipped with a pair of secondary arms that had been affixed to additional shoulder joints in its back. These additional arms terminated in an array of vicious-looking medical implements — scalpels, drills and syringes.

The machine's torso had been paneled with sheets of polished, beaten brass, and housed — Gabriel presumed — the mechanisms that powered it.

It was standing in the corner, deactivated and still. He eyed it warily, half expecting it to stir in his presence. Its face was a blank polished mask, with two inset glass lenses that clearly served as its eyes. They gleamed in the low light, and left Gabriel with the unsettling impression that the machine was watching him.

He stuffed the handkerchief back into his pocket and readied his gun. He could hear the low mumble of voices coming from somewhere along the passage. He presumed that was where he'd find Rutherford.

The challenge was going to be getting him out of there. He wasn't going to be much help in a fight, and the likelihood was that Gabriel was going to have to carry him. That narrowed their options. There were at least three of the enemy agents—the woman and the two men—plus whoever had already been in the house. He could discount the old butler, but the others we're most likely trained agents, and were likely to put up a good fight. They were on home turf, too, with all the advantages that offered.

He was going to have to put them down, quickly and efficiently, and then effect the extraction. Without his rocket canisters he was going to be slow, too, so locating the keys to the agents' van was also a priority. He'd taken the precaution of strapping on a pair of small ankle boosters beneath his suit, but they wouldn't be enough to give him any proper lift, especially with the additional weight—they were designed simply to give him an advantage if he found himself cornered, enough to surprise his attacker and allow him to get away.

He crossed the room, heading toward the mouth of the passage, but stopped short, sensing motion from the corner of his eye. Was there someone else in the room? A guard he'd missed during his initial sweep, waiting in the darkness to shoot him in the back?

He turned quickly, brandishing his Luger, but the room remained empty. There was no one lurking in the shadows behind him. He caught his breath. He was clearly feeling jumpy.

And then the automaton moved its head, and Gabriel almost cried out in surprise.

The lenses in its mask swiveled, spinning in their mounts. The head turned, creaking loudly in the otherwise silent room. It was *looking* at him. Cogs whirred, and the machine adjusted itself, in a gesture that made it look as if it were flexing its shoulders, stretching as if roused from a long slumber. It took a tentative step forward, its heavy foot thudding on the tiles.

Gabriel took a step back, keeping his gun level.

The machine straightened up, raising its lower left arm and opening and closing its fist, so that the scalpel blades glinted in the reflected light. It took another thunderous step toward him.

The thing was *huge*. It lurched closer, and Gabriel kept pace with it, wary that its strangely elongated arms might lash out at any moment. A single blow from the scalpel-encrusted fist would be enough to put him down, permanently.

Hissing steam escaped from a series of vents on the machine's back, and trunk-like pistons in its thighs sighed with every step. It was backing him into the opposite corner.

He quickly weighed his options. There was still time to duck down the passage in search of Rutherford—but then the thing might come after him, and hemmed in from both directions, he'd have little to no chance of making it out alive. Even if it didn't pursue him, there was every chance he'd have to come back this way to make it out, only to find his escape route blocked.

He was going to have to stop it. He hefted his gun, taking aim for its head, and then hesitated. If he fired it now, he'd bring the other agents running, and lose the element of surprise. The odds were already against him.

He cast around for anything else he could use as a weapon. There was nothing but the wooden chairs. They were hardly going to stop a machine of this size. His only hope was to get behind it, see if he could find a way to damage the vents on its back, or thrust something into its internal mechanisms to jam them. If he could slow it or deactivate it somehow, he could buy himself some time.

The automaton lurched forward suddenly, taking two successive steps, and then swung out with both of its right arms. Instinct took over, and Gabriel threw himself to the ground, hitting the porcelain tiles hard, and rolling. The machine's foot came down where his head had been a moment earlier, and he scrabbled hurriedly to his feet, the heels of his hands smarting from the impact. He'd lost his gun in the fall, and he searched for it desperately, before realizing it had skittered across the floor to the other side of the room. If he made a run for it now, he'd be leaving himself exposed to those flailing scalpels.

Elsewhere in the house he heard Rutherford screaming again. He was running out of time. He had to stop the machine, and he had to do it *now*.

It was coming at him again, this time jabbing at his chest with a fist of dripping syringes—filled, he presumed, with some manner of deadly toxin. He leapt back, almost colliding with the gurney he'd seen earlier. He felt his way around it, swinging it between himself and the machine to form a makeshift barrier. The machine's eyes spun as it tracked his every movement, the scalpel fingers of its right hands twitching nervously.

Gabriel backed away, his hands held out to either side, searching for one of the chairs. His fingers struck something hard, and he twisted and grabbed it, swinging the chair up before him and wielding it as a lion tamer might, warding off the mechanical man with his makeshift wooden shield. It wouldn't withstand a direct hit, but it might fend off a glancing blow and give him time to recover his Luger. He might yet need the explosive rounds he'd planted in its chamber.

He jabbed forward with the chair, attempting a feint, but the machine only responded by chopping down with its upper right arm. Gabriel's arms juddered under the force of the impact and the chair sheared in two, sending splinters showering into the air, and causing him to stagger back, face averted. All that was left in his hands were two broken spurs. The machine stomped forward, crushing the remains of the seat underfoot, and Gabriel kept pace with it, circling out of its reach.

He glanced at the splinters of wood in his hands. The stake on the left still seemed relatively sturdy. He saw the machine coming in, swiping two of its arms in a wide circle aimed at taking his head from his shoulders—and dived. He struck the floor by its feet and half rolled, half skidded across the tiles. He leapt to his feet, the wooden stakes still clutched in his fists. He was behind the thing, now, and as it started to turn, he thrust one of the stakes down through the frame of its left leg, wedging it so that it interfered with the movement of the piston.

The machine stumbled, and then raised its leg, trying to shake the wooden baton free, but it was firmly stuck. Confused, the machine slammed its foot down upon the tiles, and then raised it again, as the piston misfired noisily, steam hissing as the pressure began to mount.

Hurriedly, Gabriel grabbed the remaining stake in both hands and thrust it into one of the vents on the machine's back, leveraging it with as much strength as he could muster, until he felt the satisfying crack of internal gears. The machine emitted a shrill whine as the cogs in its lower left shoulder failed to find purchase, and the limb swung uselessly idle by its side. That, then, was the syringes out of commission.

Gabriel stepped back, edging toward his discarded Luger. If he could stay behind the machine, maybe he could find a way to disable its other arms. He glanced across the room at the nearest chair, and the mess of splintered wood upon the ground. If he could fashion another stake…

He looked up just in time to see the machine was pivoting at the waist, its legs remaining firmly planted on the tiles as it twisted its torso through a hundred and eighty degrees, swinging around with its two right arms outstretched in a wide, windmill attack.

Realizing that he was already too late to avoid the blow, Gabriel threw himself back, narrowly avoiding the swinging scalpels but taking a glancing blow to the shoulder.

He went down, lifted from his feet by the force of the blow, thudding hard into the tiled wall and sliding, dazed, to the floor. He blinked frantically, fighting back the tide of dizziness and nausea that threatened to overwhelm him. If he blacked out now, he was as good as dead.

With a roar, Gabriel forced his legs to move, propelling him out of the way of a second blow that cracked the tiles where he'd been slumped, sending plumes of dust billowing into the air.

He landed heavily on the floor, inches from his Luger. Blearily, his head throbbing, he snatched it up, brandishing it at the machine, his aim wavering. There were eight explosive rounds in the magazine—enough, he hoped, to bring the thing down.

It was lumbering forward, dragging its inert leg, readying itself for another strike.

Gabriel couldn't wait any longer. The noise of the fight had probably already alerted the others to his presence. He squeezed the trigger.

The first explosive round detonated like a thunderclap in the small, tiled room, punching a hole through the machine's upper right shoulder, and spraying hot, glowing fragments against the wall behind it.

The machine, momentarily forced back by the ferocity of the blow, came on again. Gabriel fired again, this time opening a smoldering cavity in its chest. A third whistled past its head, blackening the tiles behind it.

The stench of cordite was sharp in Gabriel's nostrils as he slid back, keeping his weapon level. He could barely believe that the thing was still going. It was shambling now, its internal mechanisms grinding, its movements jerky and imprecise. Its scalpels still flashed, however, deadly and intent, as it pulled its arm back, readying itself for the killing blow.

Gabriel fired again, and kept on firing until the weapon stopped discharging in his hand. The roar of the detonating rounds left his ears ringing, the flare of the explosions causing flashing stains upon his retinas.

The machine, its upper half now nothing but a twisted hulk of malformed brass, took one final step, and then toppled forward, slamming into the tiles by Gabriel's feet. Black smoke curled from the wreckage, causing him to hack and splutter.

Gabriel dragged himself away from the carcass of the ruined machine, until his back was pressed against the nearest wall. Then, wincing from a sharp pain in the side of his head, he held onto the wall as he dragged himself to his feet. He was still feeling dizzy from the blow he'd taken, and he knew with utter certainty that the fighting was far from over.

Running footsteps sounded in the passageway. He pressed himself back against the wall, still clutching his Luger.

The footsteps skidded to a halt on the threshold of the room.

"Jesus!" exclaimed a woman. "Look at it."

"Careful," replied a man, levelly. "Whoever did this might still be in there, and they've come prepared for a fight."

So there were two of them. Gabriel's luck was still with him — for now.

"Alright. You take the right, I'll take the left," said the man. Two figures slipped into the room. Gabriel tensed. The man was coming in his direction. He traced the man's outline through the pall of smoke.

Not yet. Gabriel fought down the impulse to act. The man took another step toward him. His head was turned in the other direction. Gabriel couldn't really get a good look at him, but he guessed it had to be one of the men he'd seen unloading Rutherford from the van earlier. He was carrying a gun.

He took another step forward, turning his head — and Gabriel leapt out, swinging the butt of his Luger, and clubbed him across the side of the head.

He went down hard, wailing in pain, but Gabriel was already on the move, circling around the broken remnants of the automaton, his eyes fixed on the woman. She'd seen him move, heard her colleague go down, and she was tracking him with the barrel of her gun as he moved.

"Who are you?" she said. "What do you want?"

Gabriel didn't respond. He figured his continued silence might unnerve her and throw her off balance.

"Answer me," she insisted, "or I'll shoot."

"You're going to shoot whether I answer or not," he said, his voice level.

She squeezed the trigger and he ducked to the left. The bullet ricocheted off the wall and rattled harmlessly down the passageway.

"Come out where I can see you, with your hands up."

Gabriel smiled. If he did, he'd be riddled with bullets in seconds.

The smoke was beginning to clear. A minute or two longer and she'd have a clean shot. It was time to make a break for it. If he could get to Rutherford, maybe he could find a route out through the house.

He turned, straight into the path of a fist.

Gabriel stumbled back, as the man came at him again, going low with a second gut punch. Gabriel doubled over, dropping his useless gun and shielding his face with his hands as the man raised his knee, trying to catch Gabriel before he had chance to straighten up. Gabriel twisted, swinging back, connecting with the man's ribs. The guy was made of stern stuff—Gabriel had given him a hell of a whack around the head with the Luger, a drop that would have put a lesser man down for an hour.

The man came in with another swing, and Gabriel feinted left, before ducking right, causing the man to punch the wall and howl painfully as his knuckles crunched against the tiles. A swift knee to the man's balls caused him to drop to one knee, and Gabriel used him as cover, stooping to sweep up a fragment of the broken automaton to use as a makeshift blade.

He pressed it against the side of the man's throat as the woman circled them both, her gun brandished at arm's length.

"Drop it," she said.

Gabriel pressed the metal shard a little more firmly into the man's flesh, until it pricked the skin, drawing a glistening bead of blood. He tried to twist his head away, but Gabriel kept the pressure on. "I don't think so," he said. Slowly, the man raised his arms in surrender.

"I *will* shoot you," said the woman.

Gabriel heard footsteps from the passage behind him. He didn't dare turn to look, but he knew the game was up. There was no way he was going to make it out of here alive, not now. He'd failed Rutherford, and he'd failed Ginny, too.

"Gabriel. Stop this. *Now*." The voice was instantly familiar, if a little weary. "And you, Regina. Lower your weapon."

"Rutherford?" He twisted to look. Rutherford was standing in the mouth of the passageway, leaning heavily against the wall. He looked exhausted. His hair was mussed and damp with sweat, and there were dark rings beneath his eyes, but the color had already begun to return to his cheeks and his eyes were bright and alert. He was wearing a loose-fitting bathrobe, patterned in green paisley. "It's alright, Gabriel. They're *friends*."

Gabriel glanced from the man to the woman, and then cautiously lowered the metal shard. He took a step back, giving himself room, just in case the others decided to ignore Rutherford and come for him again. "They don't *seem* very friendly."

"You *know* this man?" said the woman.

"Yes. His name is Gabriel Cross," said Rutherford. "He and I have an understanding."

The woman made a dismissive noise, but she lowered her own weapon, sliding it back into a holster on her hip. The man was still down on his knees, rubbing his throat. He didn't look at all happy about the sudden shift in circumstances. Gabriel could see his jaw working back and forth as he ground his teeth in frustration.

"Gabriel helped me out in New York last year," said Rutherford. "I owe him my life. We'd arranged to have dinner tonight while he's holidaying over here, that's all."

"Does dinner often involve blowing up expensive equipment and attacking members of the British Secret Service?" said the man, finally getting to his feet. His voice was a dry croak.

"British Secret Service?" echoed Gabriel. "So you're…?"

"Yes," said Rutherford. "We're colleagues."

"Then why did you bust him out of the hospital like that? He needed medical attention. And what's with all the screaming?" Gabriel locked eyes with Rutherford, searching for any hidden message, any sign that the man was in trouble and was stalling for time, but all he received in return was a weak smile.

"We'll explain," said Rutherford. "Over a nice, calm cup of tea."

"Alright," said Gabriel, as he wearily dropped the metal shard to the floor. "Now that's much more like the British welcome I was expecting."

FIVE

"You're with the CIA, I presume?" said the woman, whom Rutherford had introduced as Regina Richards. She was attractive, in a fiery kind of way. Her sharp blue eyes kept flitting from Rutherford to Gabriel; he could see she was far from comfortable with the situation. She was sitting directly across from Gabriel, her legs folded, her hand within easy reach of her weapon. "We're going to need to see your papers."

They were sitting in a drawing room on the ground floor, and the butler whom Gabriel had encountered on the doorstep earlier was—somewhat reluctantly—serving them hot tea in little china cups. The room had a sense of faded grandeur about it; it had once been plush and welcoming but had faded over decades of use. Despite the valet's best efforts to keep the dust at bay, there was little he could do about the worn carpets and faded leather of the armchairs. Gabriel imagined that little had changed here since before the war, as if this relic of another era was somehow being held together by the sheer willpower of the butler alone. It was utterly at odds with the gleaming modernity of the medical equipment below stairs. Or at least, it had been, until Gabriel had emptied eight explosive rounds into it.

The other agent, whom Gabriel now knew to be called

Hargreaves, was standing by the door, leaning against the wall, thick forearms crossed over his chest. He hadn't taken his eyes off Gabriel since they'd left the laboratory area below, and Gabriel could tell he was spoiling for another fight. It wasn't just his throat that had been injured, Gabriel mused, but his ego, too.

"Not exactly," said Gabriel, with a quick glance at Regina. He sipped hesitantly at his tea. It was pungent and unsweetened. He still wasn't entirely sure how far he could trust these people. He was, after all, a foreign national—and an American at that—who had managed to involve himself in a Secret Service operation. More than that, though, he couldn't shake the feeling that he was only seeing a part of the picture. Rutherford had chosen to involve him in this by coming to the Savoy. He still had to ascertain to what end—and he'd have to wait until he could get some time alone with Rutherford to do it.

"Gabriel is more of a… lone operative," said Rutherford, with a grin. "But he's on the side of the angels. I can vouch for him."

Hargreaves pointedly cleared his throat.

"A lone operative?" said Regina. "So you're unsanctioned?"

"I work with the police department," said Gabriel. "I get things done."

Regina nodded, but he could see she wasn't entirely placated.

"Listen, do you mind if I smoke?"

"Go ahead," said Regina.

Gabriel reached into his jacket and saw Hargreaves bristle. He smiled playfully, and slowly withdrew his silver cigarette case. He flipped it open and offered them around. Rutherford eyed them enviously, but shook his head.

Gabriel placed one calmly between his lips and pulled the

ignition tab. He drew heavily, and then allowed the smoke to stream in ribbons from his nostrils. The others watched him with interest. He had the sense of being on trial, and supposed that, in a way, he was.

"You're going to have to come with us," said Hargreaves, after a moment. "We're taking you in."

"I don't think so," said Gabriel. He took the cigarette from between his lips and flicked ash into the half-empty teacup. "I followed you here to ensure my friend's safety. I know nothing of your operation, and I don't want to get involved." He glanced at Rutherford. "Whatever's going on here has nothing to do with me. All I want is a half-decent steak and the company of an old friend."

Hargreaves stepped away from the wall, unfolding his arms. "I'm afraid it's not that simple. You're an unauthorized foreign agent operating on British soil."

"I'm a New Yorker on holiday," said Gabriel, but he could already see the way things were going. They weren't going to give him a choice in the matter, and Rutherford was in no position to intercede. "Anyway, that can wait—you still haven't explained what we're all doing here." He looked to Rutherford. "You should be in the hospital. Your injuries…"

Rutherford leaned back in his armchair, causing the ancient leather to creak. "This place… it's where we bring any agents who are injured in the field."

"So they can report in before they die?" said Gabriel. "That seems a bit cold, even for Brits. Takes 'stiff upper lip' to a new kind of extreme."

"No. We bring them here to be *healed*," said Rutherford. "The man who runs this place, he's a surgeon."

"Rather more than a surgeon, actually," said Regina. "We call him 'the Fixer'. He has certain… methods at his disposal. Ways of accelerating the healing process. He probably saved Rutherford's life. Those wounds weren't inflicted by any normal animal."

Gabriel frowned. He'd sensed something odd about the wounds back at the Savoy. "What do you mean?"

Someone entered the room, and Rutherford turned to see the third agent, the other man he'd seen at the hospital, standing just inside the doorway.

"I think we've heard enough," said the man. "Don't you?"

"Boyd. You've put in the call?" said Regina.

"Yes. Absalom is expecting us." He glanced at Gabriel. "*All* of us."

Gabriel shot a glance at Rutherford, who gave an almost imperceptible nod. At least this way, Gabriel supposed, he might be able to find out a bit more about what was going on—and keep a watchful eye on Rutherford at the same time. "Alright," he said, holding out his wrists in mock surrender, his cigarette drooping from his bottom lip. "I guess you'd better take me in."

It was still raining. The van's tires hissed over the slick asphalt. Gabriel sat in the back beside Rutherford, hemmed in by Hargreaves, who'd made a point of sticking close to him as they'd left the house. He had the sense that Hargreaves was looking for the opportunity to pay him back for the beating in the basement. Gabriel would have to be on his guard—the man might be British Secret Service, but it didn't mean he was above personal vendettas or reprisals.

Despite the thawing of the post-war tensions between Britain and America, many — on both sides of the Atlantic — still harboured deep misgivings. Not least Queen Alberta herself, who seemed intent on sabotaging her government's attempts at peace, by insisting on a hard-line stance, continuing to refer to the American people as "upstart colonists", "separatists" and "traitors".

It wasn't unusual for agents such as Hargreaves — so deeply indoctrinated to defend his country against external threats — to adopt a similar hard-line approach. He clearly didn't approve of Rutherford's trust in, or friendship with, an American such as Gabriel. Not least, Gabriel imagined, because he had threatened to slit the man's throat with a rusty blade. Whatever the case, despite Rutherford's assurances, Gabriel was very much aware that he'd effectively been taken into custody by British agents, and was currently being transported — most uncomfortably — to a more secure location for questioning.

"Hang on, what's that?" said Regina. She was sitting in the front passenger seat, straining against her seatbelt as she leaned forward, peering out of the windscreen and into the inky blackness beyond. It was late, and the road ahead looked utterly deserted.

"What's what?" said Boyd, from behind the wheel.

"That light, up ahead. Didn't you see it? It kind of... flickered in the road."

Boyd shrugged his shoulders. "Are you sure you didn't take a knock to the head back there as well?"

Gabriel felt Hargreaves stiffen in the seat beside him, unappreciative of the jibe. Rutherford remained silent, slumped on Gabriel's other side, his head resting back against the seat. Behind them, something rattled in the empty storage compartment of the van.

Gabriel peered between the front seats, searching the road as it swam toward them out of the darkness. "There!" he said, a moment later. "I saw it too. A sudden flash of pale light; a circle, with a bluish tinge."

"That was different. The first one was on the other side of the road. Boyd, I think you'd better slow down."

Gabriel felt Boyd step on the brakes, dropping the speed of their approach.

"It's probably just some malfunctioning streetlamps, damaged by the storm," said Boyd.

"No, it looked more like..." Regina trailed off, as a glowing blue circle appeared in the air before them, about a hundred yards further down the road. It was about the size of a car wheel, and contained a second, concentric ring, along with a five-pointed star, and a series of unfamiliar symbols.

"...a symbol," finished Gabriel.

Boyd pulled the van to a sudden halt, rocking them all forward in their seats. As they watched, the brilliant light of the symbol began to fade, while a series of similar, smaller circles appeared in the air around it.

"What is this?" snapped Hargreaves impatiently. "Can't we just go around them?"

As Gabriel watched, more symbols began to appear, flanking the others. These were vivid reds and greens, describing further intricate patterns in the air. He felt his pulse quicken. He'd seen Astrid studying similar eldritch symbols back in her abandoned church in New York, or scrawled onto slips of paper and placed inside the shells of animated golems. There was something particularly *otherworldly* about what he was seeing. "There's something wrong," he said. "Go back, quickly. Those symbols… they're unnatural."

"*Unnatural?*" said Boyd. "What do you mean? Look, if you know something about this, then you—"

He was cut off, suddenly, by a shrill howl from outside, as the van was buffeted by a sharp gust of wind, which threatened to tip the vehicle over onto its side.

"What the hell?" said Rutherford. He was suddenly alert, peering around Regina's headrest, trying to see what was going on.

Boyd had slammed the gearbox into reverse and was hastily gunning the engine, backing away from the strange lights at speed, but the howling gale was now pummeling the side of the van in a relentless barrage, causing it to rock dangerously on its axles.

"Boyd!" shouted Regina. "You're going to tip us over!"

"It's not *me*," barked Boyd, fumbling the pedals.

For the second time that night, Gabriel wished he'd been more prepared. If he'd brought his goggles, he might have been able to get a better idea of what they were up against. Instead, he was forced to squint into the darkness, searching for any clue as to who was behind the mysterious lights. They were still swirling in the air, but now he thought he could just make out the silhouettes of people moving amongst them. "It's an ambush!" He leaned forward, stabbing in the direction of the lights with his finger. "Look. There are people there, amongst the lights."

"He's right," said Regina. "There are at least four, maybe five of them. Someone knew we were coming."

"It's the Russians," said Rutherford. "I've seen this before. The hounds that attacked me..."

Russians. So that's what this was about. Russian operatives were here in London, and they had some kind of axe to grind with Rutherford, or other members of the British Secret Service. And Gabriel had gone and wound up in the middle of it all.

"Russians, I can deal with," said Hargreaves, reaching for his holster. "Magical lights, not so much." He drew his gun and checked the safety catch. "Stop the van, Boyd."

"I've got a better idea," said Boyd. He hit the brakes, shoved the stick shift into first, and slammed his foot to the floor. The engine screeched, and the van shot forward like a loosed bullet.

"Are you sure this is a good idea?" said Regina, bracing herself against the dashboard.

"Hold on!" said Boyd, by way of response, as the vehicle careened across the wet road, windscreen wipers still battling the downpour, ethereal wind still threatening to send them crashing into one of the nearby houses. Boyd battled the steering wheel, intent on seeing his missile strike home.

As Gabriel watched through the windscreen, one of the circles of light began to break apart, teasing itself into wispy tendrils that seemed to billow in the air, like it was being disturbed by the breeze. The figure behind it—now partially lit by the backwash of light—drew back his hand, and then punched forward, and the light seemed to obey his command, surging out to meet the van, growing in scale and magnitude as they screeched along the road toward it.

"Incoming!"

They struck the ribbons of light as if entering a strange,

warping tunnel, and the whole van seemed to *shift* suddenly, twisting onto its side as it shot forward, its wheels lifting entirely from the ground.

They came down hard on their side, the steel frame buckling and screaming as they continued to scrape across the asphalt, hot sparks and fragments of broken glass peppering their exposed hands and faces. Gabriel grasped for Boyd's seat, trying desperately to hold himself steady as his weight shifted, crushing Rutherford and causing the seatbelt to bite painfully into his upper chest and neck. Beside him, he heard Hargreaves grunt in pain.

They skidded for another twenty or thirty yards, before coming to a sudden, screeching halt. The engine was still burring, the front wheels spinning but finding no purchase. Gabriel could smell burning. He heard Regina calling to Boyd, but didn't register Boyd's response.

Carefully, he pushed Hargreaves off of him—noting the streaming blood from under the man's left eye, where a fragment of glass had buried itself in the soft flesh of his cheek—and twisted in his seat, jamming his foot in the foot well.

"Rutherford?"

Rutherford looked up at him, pained and disorientated. "I'm sorry, Gabriel."

"You can worry about that later," said Gabriel. "Are you hurt?"

"No. I'm alright, I think." He winced, reaching for his side and the site of his recently repaired wounds.

"Boyd's dead," said Regina. Her tone was matter-of-fact. Gabriel watched her draw her gun and undo her seatbelt. She was bleeding from a gash on her forehead, and another on her arm. The blood was trickling down across her knuckles, dripping onto her pants. "Hargreaves?"

"I'm alright," he said. "The door's buckled, but I think I can get out through the window."

Regina twisted around, fixing Gabriel with a glare. "*You*. Stay here with Rutherford until we're back."

She dropped forward out of her seat and began wriggling through the misshapen aperture left by the shattered windscreen. Hargreaves, on the other hand, had planted his boot firmly on Gabriel's thigh, and was using him as a platform to gain height as he tried to worm his way through the window. Gabriel gritted his teeth and decided the jagged shards that still jutted from the window frame and were currently raking Hargreaves's chest were probably payment enough.

Outside, he could hear footsteps. He watched Regina's feet disappear through the hole. Seconds later, he heard the report of gunfire as she snapped off a round. Hargreaves, who had now managed to haul himself up through the window so that now only his waist and dangling feet were inside the van, gave a sudden cry of alarm, and opened fire too, loosing three shots in quick succession.

There was a soft thud as, presumably, his assailant hit the floor.

Seconds later, Hargreaves had scrambled up and out, sliding across the ruined body of the van and dropping to the ground.

Gabriel felt a hand on his arm. He turned to see Rutherford looking up at him. "Get out there," said Rutherford. "They need you."

Gabriel gave a curt nod. This wasn't his war. He didn't owe these people anything. Worse, he was unprepared for a battle of this kind. But he couldn't stand by while the other British agents got themselves killed. Besides, it was a case of self-preservation. If the Russians did manage to finish off Regina and Hargreaves, Gabriel was in no doubt they'd come for him and Rutherford, too. They wouldn't want to leave any witnesses.

He heard a noise just outside the van; the scrape of a boot on wet asphalt. He motioned for Rutherford to remain silent, while he scrambled forward between the two front seats, until he was resting against the dashboard, close to the hole through which Regina had previously disappeared.

He glanced over at Boyd. The man was slumped forward in his seat, the belt straining to hold his weight. He'd bashed his nose on the steering wheel, and it was spread awkwardly across his face. Dark blood streamed down his chin, soaking the front of his stark white shirt. One of his eyes was swollen and bruised, and Gabriel could see that his left arm had been broken, his fingers mangled.

Gabriel reached over and felt inside the front of Boyd's jacket until he located the man's holster, and then quietly slid the gun free. He weighed it in his fist, popped the chamber, and saw that it was loaded and full. "I guess you won't be needing this," he mumbled, beneath his breath.

The footsteps outside were now coming around the front of the van. Gabriel could hear both Regina's and Hargreaves's weapons discharging further down the road. It had to be one of the Russians.

Gabriel pressed himself flat on his back, angling his shoulders toward the hole. He raised the gun, clutching the butt in both hands. He took a deep breath.

"Cover your face," he said, just loud enough for Rutherford

to hear, before reaching inside his jacket and yanking a thin
cord stitched into the inner lining.

The tiny rocket canisters strapped to his ankles ignited with
a roar, and suddenly he was surging forward, sliding out on his
back through the hole, his jacket shredding on the wet road. He
squeezed the trigger, unleashing a hail of bullets at the hooded
figure who was lurking just outside the ruined vehicle, causing
them to jerk suddenly and fall back across the van's hood. The
three symbols of light that had previously surrounded them
dimmed, and then faded to nothing.

Gabriel rolled onto his front, and then leapt to his feet, his
back screaming in pain where the uneven road had scraped
his skin through the torn remains of his suit. He scanned his
surroundings swiftly, trying to get a measure of the situation.

Up ahead, Regina had ducked behind the low front wall of a
garden and was taking pot shots at two further hooded figures
that were lobbing what appeared to be waves of pure, fiery light
in her direction. The ghostly missiles were bursting harmlessly
upon the grass behind her, dissipating into the air—although
Gabriel suspected that if any of them struck their intended target,
the effects would be entirely different. A third was leveling some
kind of weapon at her—a large gun, adorned with glowing sigils,
which projected a withering ethereal fire, translucent and blue.
Where it struck the wall, all the plant life in the vicinity blackened
and crisped, while the fabric of wall itself remained unmolested.

Hargreaves was standing over a fourth hooded figure, smoke
curling from the end of his gun. Raindrops were spraying off
his head and shoulders, plastering his hair to his face. He looked
up to see Gabriel watching, and nodded once, before taking off
down the road to lend his support to Regina.

Gabriel watched him go, and then turned his attention to the dead body, still sprawled across the van's hood behind him. He stumbled over, keeping his gun raised. He could see now that it was definitely a man, and Gabriel nudged him in the ribs with the nose of the gun. He didn't appear to be breathing. Cautiously, keeping the gun pressed against the man's chest, he reached down and yanked the hood back, revealing the face.

The man was pale, with stark blue eyes—still open wide in shock—and dark hair that was thinning around the temples. He wore a long, wiry beard, and his cheeks were crudely tattooed with circular symbols that mirrored those he had conjured from thin air. His gray robes were crude and simple, and tied at the waist with a white cord. He must have been around thirty years of age, and was undoubtedly dead.

Where had these people come from, and how had they known the van would come this way, at this particular time? And what the hell kind of magic were they using that could flip a couple of tonnes of speeding metal?

Gabriel stepped back from the corpse, and it slid to the ground by his feet, crumpling into a heap.

Behind him, the battle was still raging. Hargreaves was now on the opposite side of the road, his back pressed to a wall in the mouth of an alleyway. Regina was still raining bullets on the two hooded figures, which were deflecting the projectiles with sweeping hand gestures, as if their strange elemental magic had granted them invisible shields.

Gabriel decided to even up the odds. He crossed the road, keeping to the shadows, heading for the same alleyway as Hargreaves. Maybe if he could loop around behind the hooded figures, he'd be able to catch them off guard.

He stopped short, however, as the air before him suddenly *crackled* to life, as if with a discharge of electricity.

He fell back, watching in awe as a large circle of fizzing blue light formed in the air before him, as if someone were tracing it with his or her finger. The circle hung there, complete for a moment, before strange, dancing symbols began to appear around its inner edges, followed by a second, smaller circle containing a pentagram.

He raised his gun, his finger on the trigger.

Seconds later, another hooded figure seemed to simply *fold* out of the glowing circle, sliding into existence where before there had been nothing but empty space. The figure glanced up at Gabriel, and he saw burning malevolence behind the eyes, sigils tattooed upon the cheeks, a long, dark beard, flecked with gray.

Gabriel pulled the trigger and felt the gun kick as the bullet left the chamber. The hooded man, however, simply raised his hand and shimmered for a moment, before appearing again two feet to the left. Behind him, the crackling circle of light—a portal of some kind, Gabriel could only presume—began to burn itself out, fading away to nothing.

Gabriel swiveled and fired again, but once again, the hooded man raised his hand and seemed to somehow temporarily discorporate, shifting himself to the right, allowing the bullet to ping harmlessly off the wall on the other side of the road. This time, Gabriel noticed that he was surrounded by a halo of the same crackling light as the portal. The hooded man murmured something in Russian, and behind him, more portals began to fizz open.

Gabriel flicked his wrist, flipping the gun with a single, smooth motion, so that he was holding the still-hot barrel, effectively turning the butt into a deadly cosh. With a growl, he launched himself at the Russian, swinging the gun, bringing it down in a wide arc toward the man's head.

Gabriel's aim was true, and the gun struck the man across the forehead—only meeting no resistance as his hand passed straight through the man's now spectral head, causing Gabriel to overbalance, staggering forward so that his entire body burst through the ghostly form of the man. The light crackled painfully over Gabriel's flesh, blinding him with its sudden glare, and then he was out the other side, and the man was shoving him forcefully between the shoulder blades, so that he continued to overbalance and tumbled to the ground, bashing his elbow and knee and rolling onto his back. At some point during the fall he'd lost the gun.

Panicking, he pushed himself back, away from the oncoming Russian, his boots skidding across the slick road. The man was forming new, complex interlocking circles in the air before him.

How could Gabriel even begin to fight an enemy who could make himself discorporate, or manipulate the very air around him into a weapon? He'd caught the other one off guard when he'd shot out from inside the wreckage of the van. This one didn't seem to be letting up his defenses for even a second.

Gabriel scrambled to his feet, but the man shoved at the air, and a force like a bolting horse struck Gabriel in the chest, expelling the air from his lungs and bowling him backwards. He struck the sidewalk hard, pain lighting up his chest. He groaned, rolling onto his side. Nearby, the Russian was readying himself for another attack.

Gabriel gulped for breath, but couldn't catch it. The air was growing thin. His lungs were burning. He watched, as the

Russian stirred reality before him with a wave of his hand. It was *impossible*. However this strange hooded magician was doing it, he was stealing the very air from Gabriel's lungs.

Blackness limned the edges of his vision. He reached for his throat, desperation causing the muscles to spasm. He was going to die here, on a quiet street on the outskirts of London, away from all the people he cared about, from the city he loved. He thumped at the ground, trying to stop his body convulsing.

And then the air was suddenly flowing again, and the Russian was lying on the wet concrete by Gabriel's feet, blood streaming from an exit wound in the side of his head. It mingled with the rain, swirling away into the gutter.

Gabriel, dragging air into his deprived lungs, looked up to see Hargreaves standing a few feet away, his weapon still trained on the dead magician.

Gabriel nodded, unable to speak, and clambered to his feet, searching the road for Boyd's gun. He found it a few feet away, and scooped it up, wiping the butt against his damp suit.

He heard running footsteps and pivoted, raising his gun, to see Regina hurtling down the road toward them. Her jacket had been singed, and there was an angry red streak across her right cheek, but otherwise she looked unharmed. Russians were stalking along the road behind her, eldritch symbols dancing all around them.

"Go!" she bellowed. "Get Rutherford and get out of here. He knows where to go. Get him to safety, and get him to Absalom."

"I can't leave you here to face them alone," said Gabriel, levelly. More portals were crackling open around them.

"Who said anything about staying here to face them?" said Regina. She turned and squeezed off another shot. "We'll rendezvous later at the safe house. Now *go!*"

Gabriel glanced over at the wrecked van, and then back at the hooded figures marching toward them, arms raised. Portals of light were crackling open all around them.

Hargreaves was hurriedly reloading his gun, backing away. "Go! We'll cover you."

He turned and sprinted for the overturned vehicle, gunfire barking loudly behind him. The police would be here soon—at least one of the local residents would have called them—and he hoped the Russians would be gone before they arrived. If nothing else, Regina had been right about that—they needed to draw the enemy away before anyone else got hurt in the crossfire.

He skidded to a halt, almost sliding into the roof of the wrecked van. He hauled himself up to the shattered window through which Hargreaves had previously wriggled free. "Rutherford! Come on!"

He peered down into the vehicle, but there was no sign of anyone in the back seat. "Rutherford! Where are you?"

He craned his neck. Boyd's corpse had been disturbed—his pockets searched—but there was no one in the front seat, either. Was he too late? Had one of the Russians already dragged Rutherford out into the street?

He dropped back to the ground, glancing around. Aside from the bundled corpses of the Russians they'd killed, there was nothing else in the road, and no sign of Rutherford.

"Rutherford!" he hissed, trying to keep his voice low enough not to draw the attention of the other combatants, who presently seemed intent on Regina and Hargreaves.

He heard a spluttering cough from around the other side of the van. He raised his gun and circled slowly around the back of the vehicle. His boots splashed in the gutter water as he mounted the sidewalk and peered cautiously around the back wheel.

Rutherford was on his knees, sodden, rain pattering over his shoulders. He was hunched over the corpse of a hooded figure—another bearded man—who'd been repeatedly stabbed in the chest, judging by the torn robes and still-bubbling wounds. Rutherford was still holding the bloody knife.

"Come on!" said Gabriel, stepping out from behind the rear end of the van. "Time to go."

Rutherford looked up, narrowed his eyes, and then clumsily got to his feet, wincing at the pain in his side. He wiped the knife on the corpse's robes, and tucked it into his belt. "Come on. I know where to go." He clapped Gabriel on the shoulder. "I need a drink."

SIX

The safe house didn't *look* particularly safe.

They'd trudged across London for close to an hour, keeping to the back streets and alleyways to avoid running into any civilians or police patrols that were still out at this hour. Gabriel had lost all sense of time, but as they'd entered the Limehouse district he'd noticed the sun was beginning to show itself above the crenulated tops of the buildings. Soon, the city would stir, and the streets would be filled once again with the noisy bustle of people and machines.

He was cold, weary, wet and smarting—and Rutherford had been forced to stop twice to catch his breath, still suffering from the after-effects of whatever mysterious treatment he'd received at the hands of the Fixer. They both knew he should have been resting, but time was a luxury they didn't have— they were both intent on reaching the safe house before Regina and Hargreaves, assuming either of them had survived the encounter on the road.

The safe house itself was in a narrow side street that stank of faeces and rotten food. It was quiet, save for the sounds of a crying baby, a shrill warble coming from deep inside one of the adjoining houses. Rainwater formed runnels down the soot-stained sides of the buildings, collecting in filthy channels that ran parallel to the cobbled lane, where it sloshed along like a foetid stream, eventually swirling down the open grates to the sewers below. The conditions here were as bad as Gabriel had ever seen, reminding him of many of the slum tenements of Hell's Kitchen—where people were forced by circumstances to eke out a paltry existence, surviving hand-to-mouth, terrified of their own neighbours and the mob bosses who served as their landlords.

Rutherford approached the heavy wooden door. Green paint—which had once been applied liberally—was now flaking off, and the door carried no nameplates or number. The downstairs window had been boarded over with thick, stained planks, and the whole place had an air of desertion about it. Rutherford tried the handle, but the door was locked.

"Hold on," he said. He crossed to the boarded window, pulled the knife from his belt, and set to work on the mortar around one of the half-bricks, worrying at it with the tip of the blade. It crumbled easily, and a moment later he'd worked the brick free, revealing a small hollow, from which he extracted a key. He slid the brick back into place and returned to the door. A moment later and he had it open. They both ducked inside, locking it behind them.

Gabriel was relieved to get out of the rain, despite the primitive surroundings. Rutherford crossed immediately to the far wall and lit the gas lamp with a box of matches he found on the sideboard beneath, igniting everything in a warm yellow glow.

The door opened directly into a living room, of sorts. It smelled damp and disused, and rodents had left their spoor scattered about the bare floorboards. A fireplace had already been built up with wood, and four mismatched armchairs had been placed in a circle before it. In the far corner, in an alcove beside the chimney breast, a holotube terminal and a telephone sat on a small table. A door, standing ajar, led through to what Gabriel presumed to be a kitchen. Behind him, a narrow set of stairs led to an upper floor.

"Just give me a minute, and I'll light the fire," said Rutherford.

"I can do that," said Gabriel, taking the matches from him. "You find us that drink."

Rutherford nodded and wandered through into the kitchen while Gabriel set about starting the fire. A few minutes later the wood was crackling as the flames took hold. Gabriel removed his sodden jacket and draped it over the back of one of the chairs, before collapsing into another. The warmth of the fire prickled his cold skin, and he sank back into the embrace of the soft armchair, suddenly lethargic. He started when, a moment later, Rutherford reappeared from the kitchen bearing two glass tumblers. Rutherford crossed the room, smiled appreciatively at the fire, and then handed one of the glasses to Gabriel, before slumping into another of the chairs.

"Well, bottoms up," he said, before knocking back his head and draining the glass.

Gabriel followed suit, shuddering as the cognac hit the back of his throat. "Nice place you've got here."

"It hasn't been used in years," said Rutherford. "The Service maintains a number of them around the city, for occasions such as this. Disposable addresses, rendezvous points, boltholes. By tomorrow it'll be cleaned out and a family from one of the nearby slums moved in." He ran a hand through his hair, then sighed.

"So are you going to tell me what the hell is going on?" said Gabriel.

"Yes, I suppose I owe you that much. I'm sorry to involve you in all this, Gabriel. That was never my intention."

"All of *what*?"

"The Russians."

"I gathered that much while one of them was trying to choke me to death with eldritch magic," said Gabriel. "But why? What are they doing here?"

"That's what I'm trying to find out," said Rutherford. He looked weary, as if the burden of it all had finally become too much to bear. "They've been operating on British soil for some months, working out of a house in Belgravia. The word around town was that they were looking to hire someone for a job—to secure some prized information—so I was assigned to go undercover, to put myself up for the job and find out what it was they were after."

"And?" prompted Gabriel.

"Well, that's the thing. The meeting was earlier on this evening, before I was set to meet you for dinner. A last-minute thing. I'd put out word in the right circles, and received an invitation to the house… the sort of invitation I couldn't refuse."

"You went in alone?"

"I didn't have much choice," said Rutherford. "Not without blowing my cover. But there was someone else there, a woman named Sabine Glogauer, a freelancer. It was a trap. She confirmed my real identity the moment she saw me."

"A trap?" echoed Gabriel. He reached over for his jacket, pulled out his cigarette case and flipped it open. Thankfully, the cigarettes inside were still dry. He lit one, and then tossed the case over to Rutherford.

"I shouldn't, you know. Not after…" he shrugged. "Sod it."

He took one, and dropped the case on the arm of his chair. Gabriel watched him light it, then draw gratefully on the aromatic smoke.

"You were saying...?" said Gabriel.

"I think they were expecting me," said Rutherford. "And by that I mean—I think they'd known who I was all along. They'd lured me there to kill me, to send a message to my superiors. Someone had tipped them off."

"This Sabine woman?"

"I don't think so," said Rutherford. "She was there to confirm my identity, and no doubt she's the one they've hired to complete this mysterious job."

"Then who?" Gabriel leaned forward in his chair, warming his hands before the fire.

"That's just it," said Rutherford. "There were only a handful of people who knew. And now, after that attack on the van back there, I'm almost certain."

"You think it's an inside job," said Gabriel.

Rutherford nodded. "Someone in the Service is working with the Russians. They tipped them off about my real identity, and they set us up for the ambush this evening, when they realized their damn hounds hadn't finished the job."

"And that's why you came to *me*," said Gabriel. It was all becoming clear—the reason Rutherford had gone to such extremes to reach the Savoy. If he'd called it in to one of his team, they might have sent the Russians instead. On top of that, he wouldn't want to alert whoever was responsible that he was on to them.

"As I said, I'm sorry for dragging you into this. I... well, look, I didn't have anywhere else to turn. If I'm going to figure out what's going on here, I'm going to need to work in the shadows, and there's no one better equipped for that sort of business than you." He took another drag on his cigarette, and looked Gabriel straight in the eye. "Will you help me?"

"I'm here, aren't I?"

Rutherford laughed. "Yes, I suppose you are. It's not much of a holiday, though."

"Yeah, well, I've never been one for kicking back and enjoying the weather," said Gabriel, with a grin. "So what's next?"

"I need to work out how deep this goes," said Rutherford, "and get to the bottom of what the Russians are doing here in London. Stop them, if necessary."

"Not to mention what powers they're drawing on," said Gabriel. "If we're going up against them, we need to know how to *fight* them."

Rutherford was staring into the fire. He looked haunted. "What they did back at that house, the way they just folded the light to create those creatures…" he trailed off.

"The hounds you mentioned?"

Rutherford nodded. "Yes. For a while there, I really thought the game was up."

"We can't do this alone. Not with forces like that involved."

"There's a man I know. An old friend. He's something of an expert in these matters."

Gabriel nodded. "I can make some calls, too. And Ginny might be able to help, even if it's just holding them off for a while."

"Ginny?"

"Long story," said Gabriel. "Let's just say she's changed somewhat since you last met."

"Alright," said Rutherford. He flicked the butt of his cigarette into the fire. "Although she always was pretty handy with those pistols."

"What about the others? Regina and Hargreaves. If they made it out alive, there's every chance they're going to show up here looking for you. Can they be trusted?"

Rutherford sighed. "I don't know. I don't think *anyone* can be trusted. Not until we know more about what the Russians are planning. One thing's clear, though. They're here in force. It's worse than we imagined."

"It always is," said Gabriel. "But it sounds to me like we start with this Sabine woman. If we can get to her, we can find out what the Russians were after."

"Agreed," said Rutherford. "Although she's not going to be easy to find." He rubbed the back of his neck, winced, and then stood, putting his hand out for Gabriel's empty glass. "Another?"

Gabriel nodded. "Yeah. Thanks. But then I'm going to have to get back to the hotel and check in with the others." He frowned. "What about you? You can't stay here. If there really is someone on the inside working with the Russians, none of the safe houses are secure. And you can't even think about going home."

"It's alright," said Rutherford. "I've another place nearby. A place no one knows about. I've always been big on insurance policies."

Gabriel nodded. "Another drink, and then we move."

Rutherford started toward the kitchen. There was a rap at the front door. He froze.

After a moment, they heard someone scraping at the brickwork by the window, and then the newcomer returned to the door. "Rutherford. It's me, Regina. Let me in."

Rutherford glanced at Gabriel. He narrowed his eyes.

Gabriel could tell what he was thinking. Slowly, he got to his feet and crossed to his jacket. He pulled Boyd's gun from the inner pocket, checked the safety, and positioned himself behind one of the chairs.

He glanced at Rutherford, signaling he was ready.

Rutherford put the glasses down on the fireplace and walked to the door. "Are you alone?" he said.

"Yes, I'm bloody alone," came the irritated response. "And I'm cold, wet and bleeding. Open the damn door."

Reluctantly, Rutherford turned the key in the lock and opened the door, holding it before him like a shield.

"Thank you," said Regina, as she staggered in, dripping water onto the floorboards. She looked half-drowned. Her hair had shaken loose from its ponytail, falling in uneven strands down the side of her face, and she was sporting a fresh black eye and bloodied lip. She glanced at Rutherford, then Gabriel, and then shrugged. "Well, this is a warm welcome," she said.

"Were you followed?" said Rutherford, as he shut the door behind her.

"What do *you* think?" she snapped. "Look, I don't know exactly what's going on here, but I could do with a shot of whatever I can smell on your breath, and a seat before the fire."

"Alright," said Rutherford. "I'll see to it." He reclaimed the two glasses from the fireplace and disappeared into the kitchen while she removed her coat and stood before the fire, a small puddle forming around her feet.

"Are you really here on holiday?" she said, casting Gabriel a sideways glance. He'd already slipped the gun back into his belt, and he dropped back into his seat, keeping a watchful eye on her.

"I *was*," he said. "Although I admit, it's not been the most relaxing break. And dinner tonight was a terrible bore."

Regina laughed, and hooked her loose strands of hair behind her ear. "Well, I'm sorry for trying to kill you back there at the Fixer's house. And thanks for your help." She paused. "We're still going to have to take you in, though."

"That can wait," said Rutherford. He crossed to the fire and handed them both their drinks. "Gabriel's not going anywhere in a hurry, and we need to deal with these Russians." He leaned against the back of the nearest chair. "What happened to Hargreaves?"

"We split up," said Regina. "He's gone straight to Absalom. With Boyd dead and that palaver in the street, we needed a cleanup crew, and someone suppressing the news outlets to stop word getting out."

Rutherford nodded. "Well there's no point staying here. Gabriel's going back to his hotel. This doesn't have anything to do with him. We can pick him up when all this is over for a debriefing session with Absalom. There are more important matters to attend to."

Regina looked as if she were about to protest, then relented.

"We can trust him, Regina. It's okay."

She nodded her assent.

"Good," he said. "I'm heading home for a bath. Then we'll rendezvous with Absalom this afternoon."

"You can't go *home*," said Regina. "You're a target."

Rutherford glanced at Gabriel. "Alright. I'll get a room in a hotel. I need to rest up, let the Fixer's compounds do their work. You should go home, too, get some sleep."

"He's right," said Gabriel. "For what it's worth. You were great out there, but you've taken a beating. We all have. If you're planning to take on those Russians again, you're going to need all the strength you can muster."

"I thought this didn't have anything to do with you?" she said, her tone barbed. Gabriel held up his hands in mock surrender, and she sighed. "I'm sorry, it's been a long night."

"Right," said Gabriel. "That I can agree with."

Rutherford downed the remains of his brandy and reached for his jacket. "Come on. Don't get comfortable. Let's go."

"Alright," said Regina. "You're right. A couple of hours sleep, and then we meet back at the office to work out what the hell we're going to do."

"Exactly," said Rutherford.

Gabriel stood, and crossed to the other armchair, reclaiming his cigarette case. He slid his arms into his still-wet jacket. "Good luck. Both of you." Regina was shaking out her coat. He put a hand on Rutherford's shoulder. "You know where to find me when you need me to help out with this Absalom business."

Rutherford nodded. Together, they walked to the door. Outside, the rain had finally abated. Gabriel leaned in and pulled Rutherford into a brief embrace. "I'll trail her for a mile or so, see where she goes. Call me at the hotel this afternoon," he whispered, before releasing him and stepping back. Regina was behind them now, still looking somewhat bedraggled.

"You too," said Rutherford. He turned to Regina. "See you later."

She nodded as she stepped out into the street, pulling the door shut behind her.

Gabriel watched as she turned and headed off down the street. Then, with a quick glance at Rutherford, he set off behind her.

SEVEN

Gabriel couldn't remember ever seeing a sight quite so welcome as the entrance of the Clarington Hotel, as he pushed through the revolving doors three hours later, stepping into the lobby and garnering the appalled stares of the milling guests. Even the footman, to whom he had spoken the previous evening before heading out for dinner, offered him an almost comical double take, before registering his distinct disapproval. Even so, it did little to dispel his sense of relief.

The hotel had only been recently completed, and still retained a polished gleam of elegance and fashionable modernity. Sweeping curves, gold paneling and carousing statues by a bubbling fountain gave the place a glamorous appeal—not least because it had already become renowned as a haven for popular jazz singers and rich out-of-towners, people who wished to paint the town red while courting the lens of the daily newspapers. Gabriel, of course, had been keeping something of a lower profile.

He'd followed Regina all the way to what he presumed to be her apartment building in Kensington, before doubling back to Chelsea and the hotel. Regina had walked swiftly and pointedly, avoiding the main thoroughfares but otherwise taking a relatively direct route from the safe house. If she *was*

Rutherford's mole, she wasn't giving anything away. Not yet, at least.

He couldn't help wondering what had become of Hargreaves, however. Had he really gone directly to this "Absalom" character, or could he have given Regina the slip for a more sinister purpose? He supposed anything was possible, but he made a mental note to remind Rutherford to remain vigilant around the other man.

He felt his stomach growl at the wafting scent of bacon and eggs as he crossed the hotel foyer, making for the elevators. It was nearly eight o'clock, and many of the other guests were coming down to breakfast, dressed in their impeccable morning suits and elegant daywear. He smiled at them gleefully as he drew their stares.

The elevator attendant—a young man in a smart red jacket with brass buttons—held the door for him, noticeably wrinkling his nose as Gabriel entered the confined space. Gabriel leaned against the rail, and began dusting ingrained muck from the front of his jacket. His sleeve was torn, the fabric hanging loose at his elbow.

"Can I help you, sir?"

Gabriel looked up, and smiled. "Seventh floor, please."

The attendant eyed him suspiciously, finger hovering over the button. "Um, well, are you *certain*, sir? I mean to say: is everything quite alright?"

Gabriel's smile broadened into a grin. "It will be, when I'm soaking in the tub with a Bloody Mary," he said.

The attendant looked dismayed at the very thought. Without another word, he averted his gaze and thumbed the button. He stood facing the doors as the indicator dial ticked away the floors, and refused to make further eye contact with Gabriel for the duration of the ride, not even to encourage a tip as Gabriel bundled out into the lobby on the seventh floor.

As the doors shut behind him, Gabriel caught sight of himself in a mirror. He supposed that, in his present state, he didn't much look like he'd be worth hitting up for a tip. In fact, he looked like he'd spent the night in an alleyway amongst the detritus and the trash—bedraggled, filthy and bruised.

With a shrug, he set off along the corridor toward his suite. An elderly woman was emerging from her room a little further along the passageway, but when she saw Gabriel coming, she quickly retreated, disappearing back into her room and hastily closing the door behind her. He hurried past, rounded the corner, and fished in his pocket for his room key. Thankfully, he hadn't lost it while he'd been rolling around in the street the previous night. He located the door to room 321, turned the key in the lock, and went in.

"Gabriel!"

The relief on Ginny's face was palpable the moment he walked through the door. She was sitting on a sofa in their hotel suite, and she jumped immediately to her feet, running over to throw her arms around his neck. She squeezed him so tightly that he had to prise her off in order to breathe. Then, as if suddenly registering the condition of his clothes, the swollen lip and livid bruise on his cheekbone, she stood back, still gripping him tightly by the shoulders. She looked him carefully up and down, her face creased in concern. "Where have you been? When you didn't come back last night we tried the hospital, but they told us Peter had been discharged. It was all I could do to stop Felix setting out on a manhunt. Heaven knows you can look after yourself, Gabriel, but you might have sent word." The words spilled out in a sudden cascade, as if seeing him had somehow released a pressure valve.

"I'm sorry," he said, breaking free of her embrace and heading over to the drinks cabinet, where he splashed a large measure of brandy into a glass. He leaned against the wall, and downed it. The alcohol burned his throat as he glugged it down. "I was busy."

"Busy?" He could sense that Ginny's concern was threatening to bubble over into frustration. "Look, how's Peter?"

"He's okay," said Gabriel. "Despite everything. His people took him to some 'fixer' guy, who patched him up. I'm not sure how they did it, but he walked out of there with just a few aches and pains."

Ginny was frowning. "But those wounds…"

Gabriel nodded. "Believe me, he looked almost as good as new."

"And you were there all night?" There was no accusation in her tone; she'd long ago reconciled herself to Gabriel's unconventional lifestyle and irregular hours.

"No." He reached for the bottle and poured himself another large measure of brandy. "Look, Peter's in trouble. When we left the safe house, the car was ambushed. We were attacked in the street."

"By whom?"

"By Russians."

"*Russians?*"

"Yes. And they were wielding some kind of strange energy, opening these glowing portals in the air…" He trailed off, peering into his glass. Even now, it seemed unreal.

Ginny seemed to be taking it in her stride. He supposed that was only to be expected—being possessed by a shard of an Ancient Egyptian goddess had given her a somewhat broader perspective than most. "And where's Peter now?"

"Safe," said Gabriel. "We managed to get away. But there's trouble brewing here, Ginny. Those Russians—they're dangerous, and they're after something. Rutherford is caught right in the middle of it."

"And so are you. That's what you're going to say next, isn't it? That whoever these Russians are, they know who you are, now. That you're not sure if we're safe here anymore, that maybe Felix and Flora and I should get out of here, head to Paris or Amsterdam for a few days while you stay behind to help Peter. That you can't leave a friend in need, no matter how dangerous it might be." She walked over to him, took the brandy bottle out of his hand, and took a long draw from it, before putting it back on the cabinet and wiping her mouth with the back of her hand.

"Well... I..." Gabriel stammered. "I guess so, yes."

"Well you know what you can do with *that* idea," said Ginny. She met his gaze; there was fire in her eyes.

"Listen. I know we're supposed to be here on vacation. To get some rest. And I'm sorry. It's just I can—"

She waved him quiet. "I mean you're damned if you think I'm running away. And I know Felix will feel the same. Peter is *our* friend, too. So if he needs help, then we're *all* damn well going to give it to him."

Their eyes locked, and for a moment he felt he could feel the power behind her stare, the tempest within, stirring, willing him to defy her. Then a smile cracked on his lips, and he saw the corner of her mouth twitch, too, and suddenly they were both laughing at the absurdity of it all. Still laughing, he stepped closer, took her in his arms, and kissed her.

"You need a bath," she said, a moment later, pushing him away.

"Funny enough, I was just saying that to the guy in the elevator…" he said, making for the bathroom. "Give me half an hour, and then we'd better get Felix here so I can tell you both what's been going on."

"Alright," said Ginny. "I'll lay out some fresh clothes. And, Gabriel?"

"Yes?"

"I'm glad that you made it home."

"Russian wizards?"

Donovan was sitting in one of the armchairs by the window, a cigarette dangling from his lower lip. He was eyeing Gabriel from across the room, with an expression that seemed poised somewhere between the incredulous and the downright weary.

Beside him, Flora perched quietly on the edge of a chaise longue, taking everything in. She knew, of course, about the events that had taken place back in New York, of Ginny's possession by Sekhmet and the rise of the Circle of Thoth—but Gabriel wasn't entirely sure what she'd made of it all. That said, after years of being married to an NYPD cop, she was hardly unaccustomed to living with uncertainty and drama.

"*Really*, Felix?" said Gabriel. He was pacing the room in a red silk dressing robe, sipping from another glass of brandy. His hair was still mussed and damp. "After everything we've seen together, after all that we've encountered, you're going to question *this*?" He stopped before the window, parting the curtains with the edge of his hand and peering out at the busy street below. Cars and buses streamed by, stirring puddles of rainwater; pedestrians bustled along the pavements; everything seemed normal, sedate, undisturbed—aside, that was, from his raging headache and the fact his left hip hurt every time he moved. Gabriel knew, though, that somewhere out there, amongst the rows of crooked chimneys and cobbled lanes, the parks and pavilions, the men who had attacked him last night were planning their next move. He took another swig of his brandy.

After taking his bath, he'd returned to the main suite to find the others waiting for him, brimming with questions. Evidently, Ginny had sent for them and provided a brief precis of what he'd already told her. Now she, too, was sitting quietly on the bed, processing the rest of what he'd had to say. He'd given them a blow-by-blow account of everything that had happened since he'd left them in the restaurant the previous evening— the hospital, the fight with the automaton, the ambush and subsequent rush to the safe house. He wondered if Donovan was going to be quite so forthright as Ginny in pledging his assistance to Rutherford; they had, after all, traveled halfway around the world in order to get some respite from the mess that was awaiting them back home.

"God, no," said Donovan. "I've seen enough in my time to know that if you tell me you were ambushed by light-wielding wizards, I should believe every word of it. I'm just amazed at our capacity to find trouble wherever we go. We're supposed to be here on *vacation*."

Gabriel laughed. "Believe me, I know. And my aching limbs

are telling me exactly the same thing. Look, there's no need for you to get involved. Enjoy your rest."

Donovan leaned forward in his chair, taking his cigarette between his thumb and forefinger and sprinkling the ash into the porcelain tray on the coffee table. "You know that's not going to happen, right?"

Gabriel glanced at Flora, to see the corner of her lip curl in amusement. "Well, it's about time you brought me on one of your little adventures."

Donovan glanced at her, frowning. "Now hold on a minute…"

Flora looked at him expectantly. "Go on…?"

"Well, it's not safe," blustered Donovan.

"Exactly," said Flora. "So for once I'll be able to keep an eye on you." She turned to Gabriel. "So what's the plan? How do we help this friend of yours?"

Gabriel caught sight of Donovan's helpless expression, and downed the end of his brandy to hide his amusement. "The key has to be this 'Sabine' character, the woman Rutherford met at the Russian's house in Belgravia. Apparently she's a lone agent, a sword for hire, and for some reason the Russians needed her. If we can get to her, perhaps we can find out what they're up to."

"What about the house itself?" said Ginny, causing all of them to look round. "It seems a logical place to start. We might be able to pick up the trail from there."

Gabriel shook his head. "Too risky. They'll be watching the place. And if they've any sense, they'll have already cleared out. The address is compromised." He shrugged. "Besides, it's the first place the British agents will go. Rutherford still doesn't know which of them he can trust, and they seem intent on bringing me in for a 'debrief'. I'd rather keep out of their way."

"Alright. So this Sabine woman," said Donovan.

"Glogauer, Sabine Glogauer."

Donovan waved a hand, as if the details were the last thing on his mind. He peered at the end of his cigarette, and then flicked another heap of ash into the tray. "We're talking about a needle in a proverbial haystack. People like that—they know how to lose themselves in a city like this. Not to mention, we're on *her* territory. It's not like it's a case of going bar to bar asking if anyone knows where she is." He took a draw from his cigarette. "If we were back home I'd get uniform on it, send them out to scour the city with a description. But there are four of us," he gave Flora a quick sideways glance, "five if you include Rutherford. We don't even know where to start looking."

"That's just it, Felix. We're not going to go looking. We're going to get her to come to *us*."

Donovan frowned. "And how do you propose we do that?"

Gabriel let the curtain drop, casting the room back into shadow. Still holding his empty glass, he leaned against the back of an empty armchair. "Look, Rutherford says this woman is a known agent for hire. So I say we put word out that we're in the market."

"You mean we *hire* her?" said Flora.

"No. That's how we get her to stick her head above the parapet, to lure her in. We contrive some tantalizing job, get word out around London that we're looking to hire someone with the right sort of reputation, and then we reel her in and get some answers out of her."

"I'm not sure about this," said Donovan. "The word will already be out amongst the Russians that Rutherford's working with an American man. It's too risky. If either of us puts ourselves out there like that, we're liable to get ourselves killed."

"I'll do it." Gabriel turned to see Ginny slipping down off the side of the bed. She walked over to stand before him. "Felix is right. It can't be either one of you. It's too suspicious. But you can use me as the bait. She won't expect a woman from New York to have anything to do with Peter or the Russians."

"No," said Gabriel, bluntly. "You've been through enough. I know you want to help, Ginny, but I can't let you put yourself in harm's way again. Besides, what could you possibly want with a hired gun?"

"To have my rich American husband succumb to an 'accident' abroad?" she said, with a look that left Gabriel in no doubt which of them she'd already cast in that particular role. "And besides, you know I can look after myself."

"I think perhaps you should listen to her," said Flora, reaching over to put a hand on Donovan's arm to silence his inevitable protest. "It sounds like a viable story: a pretty young woman who's trapped in a loveless marriage to a rich heir. She's been looking for a way out—she can't afford a divorce, which will ruin her—and now she's found herself in a foreign city, where people might ask fewer questions... To someone like this Glogauer woman, that must surely seem an attractive prospect; a quick, easy assassination, with a big pay check waiting at the end of it. All she has to do is make it look like an accident, or a street mugging gone wrong."

Gabriel found himself looking at Flora through new eyes.

"It makes sense," said Ginny, from beside him. "Look, don't get me wrong—I don't *want* to do this. I'm not overjoyed at the idea. But if we're going to make this work, it needs to be a credible story. You and Felix would both arouse too much suspicion."

"They're right," said Donovan, with a sigh. He crumpled the remains of his cigarette into the ashtray. "It does make sense. Not that I like it."

Gabriel turned to Ginny. "Are you sure?"

She chewed the corner of her lip for a moment, in a disarming manner that made Gabriel want to sweep her up in his arms, and then nodded, her decision made. "Yes, I'm sure."

"Alright. I'll talk it through with Rutherford when he calls. He'll know what to do about putting the word out. It might take a couple of days."

"And what do we do in the meantime?" said Donovan.

Gabriel grinned. "I don't know about you, but I'm going to get some sleep. It's been a damn long night." He walked over to the sideboard and placed his glass beside the near-empty brandy bottle. "Why don't you take in some of the sights like we were planning. The Tower of London, the British Museum... You might not get another chance. I get the feeling things are about to get a whole lot busier around here."

"Alright," said Donovan, heaving himself up out of the armchair. "We'll check back this afternoon, when you've spoken to Rutherford." He glanced at Ginny. "You coming?"

She shook her head. "No. I think I'd rather stay here. But you go and have fun."

Donovan mumbled something incoherent as he crossed to the door. Flora offered Ginny a wan smile, and then they were gone.

Ginny waited until the sound of their footsteps had disappeared down the hall, then crossed to Gabriel, slipping her hand inside his dressing robe, running her fingers over the silvery scars on his chest. They were cold against his bare flesh.

"You don't have to protect me, you know."

"We protect each other," said Gabriel. "More than you know."
He pulled her closer, and kissed her hard upon the lips.

EIGHT

"That's the address Rutherford gave us," said Regina.

She was standing in the shadow of a sweeping terrace of four-story houses, their facades rendered in smooth white plaster, remarkably unblemished by the foul air of the surrounding city. She supposed that wealth had its advantages.

Neat rows of iron railings divided the entrance to each property, and tall sash windows looked out upon the street below. Everything looked peaceful, well maintained, and quiet. It was growing dark now, and there were no other people in the street.

She turned on the spot, taking in the surrounding buildings. Similar rows of houses were arranged around a small area of managed parkland, which formed a communal square for the local residents. Somewhere, she mused, for the nannies to bring their charges. It was all terribly exclusive, and an order of magnitude above what she could ever dream of affording on her Service salary.

Perhaps more pressing was the fact the house in question wasn't particularly sheltered from view; an interested party in any one of the surrounding terraces—not to mention the park itself—could easily have the property under observation. She couldn't help but wonder why—or how—the Russians had secured the use of a building here. How did it fit into their plans? What were they hoping to achieve? She supposed it was a universal truth that fewer questions were asked about people with money, so perhaps it was simply that: in choosing such an exclusive address, they were elevating themselves above suspicion. Either that, or the location itself had some significance she was yet to discern.

The whole matter was alarmingly opaque, and Absalom had proved little to no use either, listening dispassionately as they'd delivered their report that morning, before sending them on their way. And then Rutherford had failed to turn up, and a cursory check of his house suggested that neither he, nor any uninvited guests, had been back there since the previous day. He was out in the cold, and no one seemed to know exactly where. She had half a mind to try to track down the American. Even if he wasn't able to point them toward Rutherford, she'd at least have the option of bringing him in, and perhaps currying a little favor with Absalom for her trouble.

"Where *is* Rutherford?" said Hargreaves. "You don't think he went and got himself into *more* trouble after you saw him at the safe house, do you?"

Regina shook her head. "No. He said he was going to get a room in a hotel, get some rest. I wouldn't be surprised if he's still there, sleeping it all off. After everything he went through yesterday..." This, of course, was the most likely answer. His wounds *had* been grievous. Perhaps they'd have to give him the night, and then if there was still no word tomorrow...

Hargreaves grimaced. "The state of those wounds." He paused. "Have you ever had to, you know, pay a visit to the Fixer?"

"Once or twice," said Regina, with a shrug. In truth, she'd

had reason to suffer his ministrations on four separate occasions over the years, and even now, the ghostly remembrance of the pain from those nights still haunted her from time to time. No matter the miracles he might work, no matter that many of them owed their lives to the man, no one survived an encounter with the Fixer psychologically unscathed.

Hargreaves shuddered. "Well, here's hoping I never need to cross his path. At least not on the operating table."

Regina had returned to observing the house. There was no evidence of any habitation inside. The curtains were partially drawn, but she'd seen no flicker of movement from within. No one had come or gone since they'd arrived, and no lights were on, despite the dull quality of the evening light. "Which way do you want to go in?"

Hargreaves seemed to consider his response. "We can try round the back, but the houses around here are well fortified. It may be difficult to scale the wall."

"Well, the front door is out. It's too exposed."

"Agreed. And remember, this is supposed to be a reconnaissance. In and out, and report back to Absalom. We need a good escape route if it looks like things are going down the drain."

Regina pointed at one of the lower sash windows, which had been hastily boarded over with irregular-edged planks of wood. Beneath it, on the pavement, tiny fragments of shattered glass still sparkled where they caught the light from the nearest streetlamp. "We could take a leaf out of Rutherford's book."

Hargreaves grinned. "Not likely. I suggest we go in through the basement. We'll probably have to force the door, but I'm not anticipating any resistance. If they've any sense they'll have already cleared out and moved on. Even if they'd succeeded in seeing Rutherford off last night, the place would still be compromised. We get what information we can, and we move on."

Regina nodded. "Alright. Let's go."

Together they crossed the road, Hargreaves keeping a watchful eye on the house, Regina scanning the road around them. It was eerily quiet.

"Clear," she said, as they approached the house, boots crunching on the broken glass.

Hargreaves stepped around the railing, and onto the iron treads of the steps leading down to the basement. She followed after him, feeling for her gun in the back of her waistband. She drew it, hefting it, reassured by the weight of it in her grip.

There was nothing but detritus down in the lobby area at the bottom of the steps—the decaying remnants of newspapers, a dead pigeon, food wrappers that had blown in from the street above. The door to the cellar was peeling, red paint blistered and curling. The handle was rusted and brittle. It didn't look as if it had seen recent use.

Regina provided cover, while Hargreaves crept forward and tested the handle. It was either locked, or rusted shut. He glanced at her, motioning for her to step back. He levelled his gun, and for a moment she thought he was going to shoot the lock, but then, with a sudden, unexpected jerk, he kicked out at the door. His boot connected, and the wood around the lock burst with a splintering crack. The door yawned inwards, revealing a dark void beyond.

Without glancing back, Hargreaves edged cautiously into the basement of the house, weapon trained before him, left hand cupping the right. He went left, and Regina followed, darting right, adopting the same pose, slowly rotating her shoulders to cover the shadowy void before her.

The room smelled of damp and mildew. She edged forward, peering into the gloom, waiting for her eyes to adjust. It was almost unnaturally dark, as if the shadows themselves were slithering around to smother all traces of light.

She had little sense of what else might be in the room, other than her and Hargreaves. She could hear him breathing—the soft whistle of air escaping through pursed lips. He was tense. She couldn't blame him.

Her foot struck something and she danced back, lowering her gun. When it didn't move, she dropped into a crouch, trying to discern what it was that she'd almost tripped over. It was a coal scuttle, long abandoned and dusty.

"You okay?" whispered Hargreaves.

"Yeah, fine. It was just a—" She stopped suddenly short at the sound of scuffing feet.

"What? What is it?" hissed Hargreaves, urgently.

"There's something here. Something else in the darkness." She stood slowly, her heart pounding. She passed her gun in a wide arc through the darkness, but still, her eyes were refusing to adjust to the dim light. She could hear that breathing again, whistling in the shadows, but this time, she knew that it wasn't Hargreaves. It was coming from somewhere up ahead.

Another scuffed footstep. And then a deep, ferocious snarl. "Watch out!" She squeezed the trigger of her gun, jolted by the sudden recoil. Light flared. Her nostrils filled with the stench of cordite. Close by, Hargreaves was saying something, urgently, but her ears were ringing.

GEORGE MANN

And then she was falling backwards, wildly waving her
hands before her to fend off the massive brute of a dog that
had leapt at her out of the shadows. The sheer momentum of
it carried her over, and she struck the floor hard, knocking the
breath from her lungs.

The beast was a hulking mass of muscle and sinew, and its
jaws were only inches from her face. She could feel the spittle
flecking her cheeks as it barked. Somehow she'd managed to
get her hands around its throat as they'd gone down, and she
jammed her elbows against the ground, trying her best to pin it
in place. She wasn't going to be able to hold it for long.

Panicking, she fought for breath. "Har... Har..."

"I can't *see* you!"

The dog shifted, raking her stomach with its hind legs. She
cried out in pain. It rolled its head to the side, then jerked its
body, trying to squirm loose. She squeezed her thumbs into
the soft tissue of its throat, felt her nails break the skin, but she
knew it was already too late.

And then the dog jerked. Once, twice, and a third time, and
she felt it go limp in her grip. Trembling with adrenaline, she
heaved it off, shoving it to one side. She started to get to her feet,
but lurched away when she felt something brush her shoulder.

"It's alright. It's me."

"Hargreaves." The air was beginning to flood back into her
lungs.

"Are you hurt?"

"No... I... a little. But I'll be fine. How did you know where
to shoot?"

"I didn't."

"You could have—" she started, but he interrupted.

"I figured you'd rather that than be mauled to death by a rabid dog."

She sighed, wiping sweat from her brow. "Well, yes, I suppose you're right. Thanks."

"You would have done the same."

"I lost my gun."

"No matter. Follow me. We need to get out of this cellar."

Regina reached out and put a hand on his shoulder, and together, they edged forward into the darkness. After a moment, Hargreaves stopped abruptly. "This is the wall. If we follow it along… here! It's another door." He dropped his shoulder as he felt for the handle, and then slowly stood back as he pulled the door open toward them.

The sudden light from the small chamber on the other side stung her eyes. The cellar had clearly been subdivided, and this secondary room had, at some point, been used for the storage of tools and equipment. A single electric bulb, hanging on a wire from the ceiling, lit the room. Against the far wall, a staircase led up to the floor above.

Regina glanced back at the room behind them. The light from the doorway didn't extend across the threshold. There was nothing but thick, swirling gloom. "We need to watch our step," she said, as Hargreaves crossed the room toward the staircase. He was keeping his gun trained on the doorway above. "There's something not right about this place."

"There's something not right about *any* of this," said Hargreaves. "Now, find yourself a weapon amongst those tools, and let's get this over with. I don't want to spend any more time here than necessary. He put his boot on the first tread, and started up toward the floor above.

NINE

It was cold by the embankment that evening, with a frigid wind blowing in off the Thames, ruffling Rutherford's hair and stirring the lapels of his jacket. He shivered, and folded his arms across his chest, wishing he'd thought to procure an overcoat. He'd have to see to that in the morning. At least, he mused, the rain had abated, and his clothes had had time to dry. Despite a long soak in the bath at the out-of-the-way bed and breakfast place he'd visited, however, he still felt grimy and tired.

He leaned against the stone barrier, watching the dark swirl of the water, the twinkling, reflected lights of the city. Above, the clouds looked smoky and dull, the moon a vivid slash in an otherwise featureless sky. The only sounds were the slap of lapping water against the hull of a nearby boat, and the distant hiss of traffic.

He pulled a crumpled cigarette from the crushed packet in his pocket and lit it with a match, flicking the burning fragment over the barrier, so that it tumbled down toward the water, winking out of existence as it kissed the cold surface.

His wounds ached with a dull, throbbing pain. It would be some time before his strength fully returned, but until then, at least he was mobile. At least he wasn't dead. He'd been in worse scrapes, and he'd see his way out of this one, too.

He heard the scuff of a shoe from behind him, and resisted the urge to turn around. "You're late," he said, blowing smoke from the corner of his mouth, before reluctantly adding, "sir."

"And you're bloody well supposed to be laying off the smokes until you're better," said Major Absalom. "Doctor's orders. I've seen the report." Rutherford smiled as Absalom came to a stop beside him, resting one hand against the barrier. "But since you're at it, lend me a match, will you? This pipe's not going to light itself."

Rutherford tossed the book of matches over. Absalom struck one and turned his back on the river, sheltering himself against the wind as he slowly stirred the embers of tobacco back to life. Moments later he was wreathed in its pungent smoke.

"He wasn't best pleased about the mess your friend made in his basement, either. That's all in there, too, along with a requisition order for a replacement automaton." Absalom chuffed thoughtfully on his pipe. "I hear Hargreaves was rather taken with him, too. Especially when the blighter had his hands around his throat." He chuckled, evidently enjoying the image.

"You've talked to Regina, then?" said Rutherford. He turned to regard his superior officer. Absalom looked every part the aged establishment hero—close to retirement, with rheumy eyes, stiff white whiskers stained yellow with pipe smoke, a tangled white beard and a balding pate. He'd fortified himself against the weather with a black woollen overcoat, and wore a red scarf curled around his neck. The briar pipe dripped from the corner of his mouth, and smoke twisted lazily from his nostrils. He was a big man—almost as tall as Rutherford, and twice as broad.

He'd been a boxer in the navy, by all accounts—or at least

that was what Rutherford had been able to glean from the ladies in the typing pool; Absalom wasn't known for being talkative, particularly when it came to the misdemeanors of his own youth. Ever since Rutherford had known him, the major had been quietly cultivating an air of mystery. The ladies in the typing pool, however, were a resource that no agent left untapped—with their keen ears and sharp wits, Rutherford was only surprised that Absalom hadn't got them doing field work.

He took the pipe from the corner of his mouth and stabbed at Rutherford with the end of the stem. "She was most perturbed that you failed to make the rendezvous this morning."

Rutherford sighed. He'd decided against going in, choosing to send a coded message to Absalom from the hotel instead, urging him to meet, here, now. Anything else seemed too risky. He still wasn't clear exactly what was going on, or whom he could trust amongst his fellow agents. He'd spoken briefly to Gabriel on the telephone, and together they'd concocted a hasty plan to entrap Sabine Glogauer the following night. He'd already put out the necessary feelers. "You understand why."

Absalom frowned, revealing a series of deep-set lines in his brow. "I'm not certain that I do," he said. His voice was a dry rumble, which threatened to crack at any moment. "But I know *you*, Peter, and I want you tell me what the hell is going on."

Rutherford finished his cigarette and pitched it into the water after the match. "Shall we walk?"

"I'd rather we went somewhere for a ruddy stiff drink," said Absalom, "but I suppose a walk will have to do."

The two men fell into step beside one another, strolling along the embankment in the near darkness, with only a glimmer of moonlight to guide their way.

As they walked, Rutherford tried to gather his thoughts—about Gabriel; the incident at the Fixer's house; the Russians, and the fact that someone *must* have tipped them off. It all spilled out in a long, not particularly eloquent, torrent.

When he'd finished, Absalom remained unnervingly quiet as they continued along the embankment for another hundred yards, then, with a sigh, he approached a wooden bench and dropped onto it. His whiskers twitched, as he appeared to consider his next move. He took another match from Rutherford's book—which he hadn't yet returned—and relit his pipe. Then, his eyes searching the water, he said, "Have I ever told you about Stephen Malhorn?"

Rutherford sat down on the bench beside him. "No. I don't believe you have."

"I'm not surprised. It's not an experience I care to relive very often," said Absalom.

"Was he an agent?"

"More than an agent," said Absalom. "He was a friend. Back when I was first recruited, fresh out of the navy." He chewed thoughtfully on the end of his pipe. "We saw things, he and I... things you wouldn't believe; things that no man should ever see. We fought them, too. Made a name for ourselves in the Service. We were young, and arrogant, and together with Angelchrist we went delving into things we shouldn't have."

"You're talking about the occult," said Rutherford. He'd heard stories about Professor Archibald Angelchrist, one of the founding members of the Secret Service, and his penchant for such matters. It was said that he'd operated a bureau of his own, a department within a department, chasing after spooks and ghouls and all the other monstrous things that lurked in the shadows. Given what Rutherford had seen himself during his short career in the Service, he considered it a darn good idea.

Absalom nodded. "We knew we had to put a stop to it, you see? All those fools who thought they knew better, who thought they could harness that power, control things that couldn't be controlled…" He trailed off, taking another draw on his pipe. "And then during the war, the enemy tried to turn them into weapons. They opened doors that should have remained shut, let things in…" He glanced at Rutherford. "Like the things you saw in New York."

"You mean they were conjuring those… *creatures* as weapons?" For a moment, Rutherford was back in New York, tumbling out of the sky while a massive, tentacled leviathan attacked a Ferris wheel at a fair on the docks.

"That and more. Out on the Eastern Front, we thought we were never going to be able to contain them; twisted, gangly things that came in the night, raiding the trenches, others that burrowed into your dreams. There was a secret war being fought, you see, a war in the shadows, using weapons of a different kind. And it's still going on today, only the combatants have changed."

"The Russians?" prompted Rutherford.

"Aye, the Russians. Once, they were our ace in the hole, the only thing that could stop the Prussian assault. They had a secret division, trained in the ways of the arcane. While we primed our machine guns and mumbled our prayers, they were engaging in rituals of a different kind. When the Prussians attacked, they were ready. They called on whatever dark arts they'd uncovered to banish those foul things back to the depths of hell. People say it was the Leviathan Land Crawler that won us the war, but it wasn't. It was *them*. The Koscheis."

"Koscheis?"

Absalom nodded. "Named after the figure from Slavic folklore, 'Koschei the Deathless'. They liked to put about the notion they were somehow immortal, impossible to kill; that they'd even mastered death itself. It wasn't true, of course—I saw plenty of them fall—but it added to their mystique. It worked, too; their reputation was fierce, and no one—not even the Russian soldiers—wanted anything to do with them. They just stood aside while the Koscheis dealt with the monsters, and then melted away again, using their strange magic to disappear into the night."

"Just like the attack last night," said Rutherford. "They seemed to be opening glowing portals in the air, transporting themselves through them."

"My understanding is that they can only travel short distances, and only then to locations they can see. Any further and they need a fixed network of some kind. There were tales of them ending up partially melded with walls, or trapped inside inescapable hollows, when they tried to push their luck too far. But this was a long time ago. The world is a different place. God knows what they're capable of now."

"What's it all got to do with Stephen Malhorn?" said Rutherford.

Absalom looked suddenly mournful. "After the war, we returned to our posts at the Service, more determined than ever to find a means to protect the nation from the things we'd seen. Angelchrist understood, of course—he always had. But no one else was willing to listen. The government had started to believe its own propaganda, and was funneling all its resources into developing new Land Crawlers, new guns, and new weapons of mass slaughter. They thought, if another war was coming, it would come from across the Atlantic, in fleets of airships and ironclads. The Americans were starting to get nervous by then, you see, and Alberta wouldn't stop going on about "the old colonials", and how we needed to reassert ourselves and reclaim the glory of the Empire."

He waved a hand, as if to indicate he considered all of this complete nonsense. "Whitehall allowed us to continue with our work, of course—a token compromise—but it wasn't enough. We all knew it. Only, Malhorn decided to do something about it. Unbeknownst to us, he went to the Russians, made some kind of pact. He would feed them information, and in return, they promised him protection, a schooling in the very arts we sought to oppose."

"He went rogue?"

"No. That's just it. He never saw himself as a traitor. He was doing what he thought was right. He was trying to protect the country. People had their suspicions, of course—the meetings he didn't log, the hours that went unaccounted for, but I didn't want to see it. I didn't want to believe my friend could undermine us like that, not after all those years."

Rutherford noticed Absalom's pipe had gone out again, but he hadn't seemed to notice. "What happened?"

"We were out on an operation. We'd received word of a coven in Bristol with a penchant for human sacrifice. When we arrived, though, they were waiting for us."

"The Koscheis?"

Absalom nodded. "They'd been using Malhorn all along. Of course they had. The fool should have realized it from the start. They'd mined him for all the useful information he had, and then they tossed him away like a used rag."

"They killed him?"

"They killed us both. At least, that's what they thought. I made it out of there wounded, but alive. Malhorn was branded a traitor, and for a while, my association with him nearly condemned me, too. If it hadn't been for Angelchrist... He stepped in, spoke up for me. He saved my reputation."

"So you think the Koscheis are back?"

"Perhaps," said Absalom. "But more importantly, I'm saying that you could be right—about there being a traitor in our midst. It worked for them before, and it's not beyond the realms of possibility that they could have turned someone's head. The promise of power... it's alluring. Last time I ignored it. I won't let the same thing happen again."

Rutherford reached for another cigarette. After a moment, Absalom passed over the matches. "So what next?"

Absalom shifted in his seat, fixing him with a hard stare. "You have a choice," he said.

"I do?"

"You've made yourself a target. They know you're on to them, and they know who you are. They're going to come after you."

Rutherford nodded slowly. None of this was news to him. "And...?"

"And we can either use that to our advantage, or we can get you the hell out of here and hole you up somewhere safe until this all blows over. But one thing's for certain—you're out in the cold. It's too dangerous to bring you in. Especially if there is someone working against us from within."

Rutherford took a long draw on his cigarette. There was

never any question of running away. "Alright. So I'm out in the cold. I'm going to need help, though. Resources."

"Your American friend," said Absalom. "Can he be trusted?"

"You read my report from New York," said Rutherford. "I trust him with my life."

"This is bigger than your life," said Absalom. "Or mine. Or any of ours. But I don't see that we have much choice." He looked distinctly uncomfortable. "Just play your cards close to your chest, and keep *him* even closer."

"What about Regina and Hargreaves?" said Rutherford.

"Leave them to me," said Absalom. He glanced around, and then reached into his coat pocket. When he withdrew his hand, he was holding a revolver. He passed it to Rutherford. "Here, take this."

The metal felt cold in Rutherford's grip. He weighed it for a moment, and then slipped it inside his jacket.

Absalom had taken out a scrap of paper and a pen, and was hastily scrawling an address. "This is the address of a safe house. It's off the books. You'll find ammunition, cash, and fresh clothes there. Spend the night, and then get out again. It's best if you keep moving."

"Thank you," said Rutherford.

"And one more thing. There's someone who might be able to help. Sir Maurice Newbury. He's an old colleague. I've written his address on the reverse. Tell him I sent you, and he'll do what he can."

TEN

Regina hefted the wrench, and not for the first time wished she'd managed to hold onto her gun. She'd considered going back for it, feeling her way through the eerie and, as she was now convinced, *unnatural* darkness, but it could have been anywhere in there, and she'd be wasting precious time trying to find it. If there was anyone else in the house, there was every chance they'd heard the shots that Hargreaves had fired, and the longer they waited, the more chance the enemy had of getting away, or readying an ambush.

She watched Hargreaves as he beckoned for her to move forward, edging open another door with the side of his boot. He disappeared through, and she followed after, glancing over her shoulder to ensure they weren't being observed from behind.

So far, the ground floor seemed abandoned. They'd emerged from the cellar beneath the staircase in the main hall, and having first secured the kitchen and back door, were now moving through the interconnected dining and sitting rooms.

The kitchen had shown evidence of recent occupation—food remnants in the bin, dirty plates heaped by the sink, a half-drunk mug of coffee on the worktop—but it was days old, and beginning to smell.

Similarly, the dining room had been used in the last few

days, as evidenced by the position in which the chairs had been abandoned and the three-day-old newspaper left in situ on the tabletop.

She moved further into the sitting room, while Hargreaves covered the door that led back into the hallway. The furnishing here was sparse and old—a cracked leather chesterfield, a writing bureau standing open and empty, an overturned side table. The once-vibrant wall cloths were faded too, save for three or four patches of bright green where pictures had once hung.

Regina was beginning to build a picture of what had happened here. It was clear that nobody had *lived* in the house for months. The Russians hadn't furnished the place, but had used it as a temporary base or meeting point, perhaps only in their dealings with Sabine Glogauer, or as a location for their attempted entrapment of Rutherford. She was beginning to think that Hargreaves was right—they'd cleared out the moment Rutherford's cover was blown, leaving the dog behind in the darkened cellar to deal with any subsequent intruders. It was looking increasingly likely that she and Hargreaves were going to leave the place empty-handed.

They moved out into the hallway. The light from the streetlamp outside was shining through the stained-glass panel above the door, forming bright pools of red and blue and yellow on the Minton tiles. A small heap of post lay on the mat—circulars, a newspaper, and something presumably addressed to the previous inhabitants or owners of the house. Nothing there that could help shed light on the Russians' activities.

She used the wrench to indicate the stairs to Hargreaves, who nodded his assent.

Hargreaves went first, still clutching his weapon in both

hands. As he climbed, Regina could see he was working his jaw back and forth, tense and alert, expecting danger at any moment.

Slowly, they ascended the stairs to the small landing at the top. Here, a door opened into a large bathroom—which was clean but empty—and another small flight of stairs doubled back, leading to a long, thin landing from which a series of doors led to what she assumed to be bedrooms. At the end of this landing, another set of stairs led on to the floor above.

Hargreaves approached the first door, but just as he was about to reach for the handle, cocked his head to one side, listening intently.

"What?" mouthed Regina.

Hargreaves touched the tip of his ear, indicating for her to listen. She paused, straining to make out what he'd heard. After a moment, she heard it too—a creak of floorboards from the landing directly above. Something—or some*one*—was moving up there.

Hargreaves stepped away from the door. He took a deep breath, and then met her gaze. By way of answer, she hefted the wrench, and nodded. He turned and strode purposefully toward the other end of the landing. Then, pausing only to glance back and ensure she was following, he turned and hurried up the stairs.

Regina broke into a run, taking them two at a time. If there was someone up there, they had him trapped—there was no other escape route from the third floor, and a leap from the window would either kill him, or shatter his legs. Perhaps this was the chance they'd been looking for; an opportunity to get some answers.

"Stop!"

She reached the top of the landing to see Hargreaves brandishing his gun at the back of a man in a hooded robe. He appeared to be dressed in identical fashion to the others they'd encountered during the ambush the previous night. He was standing at the far end of the landing with his back to them, facing a door.

"Stay exactly where you are, or I'll shoot." Hargreaves glanced at her, a cocky smile on his lips. The hooded man did as Hargreaves had commanded, and remained still, not even turning his head to look at his assailants.

"Now raise your hands."

The man did as ordered, raising both hands above his head. As he did so, however, the index finger of his right hand brushed the surface of the door, tracing a small circular pattern across the grain. Light flared, bright and obtrusive, as if the tip of his finger had somehow ignited the pattern in the wood. With a grunt of effort, he reached for the handle, trying to bundle himself through the door in one sudden, jerking movement.

Hargreaves was the quickest to react. His weapon bucked as he discharged a shot, and he launched himself forward, barreling after the hooded man, intent on bringing him down. Regina charged after him, gripping her borrowed wrench.

The shot had clearly struck home, and the man staggered, tumbling through the open door into the room beyond. Hargreaves reached the door seconds later and barreled through, kicking it aside as he rushed after the hooded man. It rebounded with a loud thud, swinging back at Regina just as she reached it. She threw her hand out, catching the edge of it, and used her momentum to shove it open again, bursting through into the small box room on the other side.

The room was empty.

Confused, Regina wheeled on the spot, the wrench still raised above her head like a primitive club. There was no sign of either Hargreaves or the Russian. The room was simply bare and unadorned—the scraps of an ancient maroon oilcloth on the floor, and yellowed paper on the walls that had once clearly been patterned with ostentatious peacock feathers.

"Hargreaves?"

No answer.

Had he succumbed to some kind of enchantment? Cautiously, Regina circled the room, testing the walls for a hidden panel or covered door. Nothing. There was no sign that anyone had ever been there. The two men had simply vanished into thin air.

She stepped back out onto the landing and pulled the door shut behind her. She studied the door for a moment. It certainly *looked* like an ordinary wooden door. Except… where the hooded man had described a circle of light with his finger, there was a rough groove cut into the wooden panel, as if someone had crudely scratched the design into the wood with a penknife. It was little more than a circle with three strange symbols inside of it, which looked to her like letters from a Slavic alphabet she'd never encountered before.

Slowly, she turned the handle and pushed the door open again. Still nothing. Just the same empty room beyond. She closed it again, tucking the wrench into the back of her trousers. What had she seen him do?

She reached up, mimicking the actions of the hooded man. Using the tip of her index finger, she followed the line of the circle on the door. As she did so, her finger seemed to leave a trail of fizzing, crackling light, as if live electricity was leaping from her body and imbuing the wood with energy. It tickled her skin, as if her body were somehow interacting with or reacting to the charge. She completed the circle, and started on the symbols. First one, then the second, watching them light up as she progressed… and then, without warning, the light seemed to sputter and fizz out. Within a moment there was nothing but a marked wooden door again.

Frustrated, she tried again, but the result was the same. Perhaps she was doing something wrong. She closed her eyes, trying to recall what the man had done. He'd definitely drawn the circle first, she was sure of that. But in what order had he marked the symbols? She couldn't be sure. She decided to try again, this time altering the order. When the light petered out again, she kicked at the door in frustration, sending a thunderous bang echoing through the empty house.

Taking a deep breath, she tried again, and then a fourth time, and on the fifth, she finally appeared to hit on the correct order, as the sigils continued to glow, even after she'd lifted her finger away from the design.

With a deep breath, she stood back, peered up at her handiwork, and then opened the door.

This time, when she stepped over the threshold, everything was chaos.

Hargreaves was on his knees before the prone body of the hooded man, on the floor of what appeared to be the kitchen of a Georgian farmhouse. Through the window she could see golden fields of wheat and barley, stretching away into the distance. Hargreaves was bellowing something at the hooded man, and his hands were pressing on the man's torso. They were covered in blood. She could smell it, rich and thick and tangy. The man was bleeding out from the gunshot wound.

"Hargreaves," she said, unsure what else there was to say. Her mind was reeling. Was she really here, in this farmhouse in the middle of nowhere? One minute they'd been in a terraced house in Belgravia, the next they were... *elsewhere.*

The door had clearly been some sort of portal, similar to the ones she'd seen the Russians conjure during their ambush—but she'd activated it herself. It seemed so surreal. And now this...

"Regina? Oh, thank God." Hargreaves looked up at her, the relief evident on his face. He glanced down at his blood-stained hands. "He won't talk."

Regina crossed the room and stooped over the body, placing two fingers to his throat. She felt for a pulse. The man's eyes were open and staring up at her, and there was a wry smile fixed on his lips. Blood dribbled from his mouth, matting his beard. She felt his body convulse, and he expelled a long, burbling wheeze. "He's gone."

"Shit. I only wanted to wing him."

"If it's any consolation, I don't think he would have talked."

She straightened up, wiping her fingers on her sleeve. Beside her, Hargreaves was also getting to his feet.

"Where the hell are we? What happened back there? One minute I was running along the landing of that house... the next I was wrestling him to the floor in *here.*" He crossed to the sink and turned the creaking tap on, rinsing his hands. Blood swirled around the porcelain basin, bright and obscene. She could see it was matted in the hair of his forearms, trapped beneath his fingernails. The thought turned her stomach, and she looked away.

Hargreaves turned the tap off and dried his hands on a rag.

He walked back to the door, opened it, and peered through. "It's a store cupboard," he said. "Filled with tinned food and grain. I just… I don't understand."

Regina walked over to join him. She peered over his shoulder for a moment, and then reached up and tapped her fingernail against the door. "Here. Look at this symbol. That's what he was doing when you shot him. The door is a portal. Trace your fingertip around it like this…" she ran her finger around the outer edge of the circle until it began to glow, "…and suddenly it points to somewhere else."

She stepped back, regarding Hargreaves. He was frowning, watching the fizzing light on the door as it slowly sputtered out. "How did you know how to do that?"

"I watched him do it, right before he went through the door. It took me a few goes to get it right, but that's how I was able to follow you," she said. A thought occurred to her, and she looked around the room. There were two further doors leading from the farmhouse kitchen. She walked over to one of them. Sure enough, there was a circle engraved here, too, but with a different configuration of symbols inside of it. "This one's the same, too." She began to trace the outline, watching it crackle to life. "They must have a whole network of them, leading them wherever they want to go."

"So this place is a sort of hub?"

Regina shrugged. "Perhaps. Or a safe house; somewhere to escape to if things get too hot. Somewhere they'd never be found."

"Well, we found it," said Hargreaves. He looked thoughtful. "Do you think more of them might come this way?"

"Hard to say, but we can't take any chances."

He nodded. "Help me hide the body, then."

With a grimace, she took the dead man by the arms and helped to lift him over to the store cupboard. His dead, staring eyes seemed to follow her every move. Hurriedly, they bundled him in and closed the door. It wasn't going to fool anyone for long, but it was something.

"We should get back to Absalom," said Hargreaves. "This is huge."

Regina nodded absently, as she returned to the other door. She opened it, peering into the small living room beyond. Then she closed the door again, and started tracing the Slavic symbols with her finger.

"What are you doing?"

"You're right. We need to tell Absalom. But what do we really know at the moment? That a house in Belgravia contains some kind of energy portal to a farmhouse in the middle of nowhere. But what if this door," she stood back as the sigils began to glow, "leads somewhere else? What if we can find out more about what they're up to? Where their *real* base is?"

"I'm not so sure, Regina. We might not be so lucky next time. What if we find ourselves trapped, or worse, stumble right into the middle of one of their weird pagan rituals."

"Then you'd better make sure you've still got that gun," she said. She reached out, opened the door, and stepped through.

ELEVEN

Ginny sat at the bar, sipping at her martini, reading the labels on the serried ranks of bottles behind the burly barman. She didn't recognize most of them. She'd had two already, just to steady her nerves. She'd have to pace herself.

Ginny had always had a liking for booze—a little *too* much—and she'd promised herself in the aftermath of the recent events in New York that she wouldn't allow herself to fall back into the comforting spiral. And yet… it was so enticing; to numb everything, to banish the little voice at the back of her mind that seemed intent on reminding her of the violation she had suffered, the uninvited presence that had taken possession of her body, the confusion she still felt now that she'd rid herself of its influence, yet understanding that, hidden away inside of her, a shard of it lived on. She could feel it from time to time, stirring, wanting to come out and reveal itself to the world. Since the battle with Amaury, however, she'd held it in check, burying it deep inside, afraid not that it might seize control of her again, but instead that she might grow to *like* it, just like the booze.

She heard footsteps behind her and turned around on her stool, to glimpse a rotund woman in a fur stole marching past, glowering at a meek-looking man who was propped against the wall across the other side of the room, partially obscured behind a veil of cigarette smoke. He blew more smoke from the corner of his mouth and looked away, as if hoping she hadn't seen him.

Ginny turned back to her drink. She wondered if the Glogauer woman was going to show. Rutherford had supposedly put word out in the right circles, circulating their concocted story: that a well-heeled but put-upon wife from Long Island was staying at the Hotel Cecil, and was looking for someone to help free her from her neglectful husband. More to the point, he'd been clear that she had plenty of money to spare.

She supposed it sounded plausible enough, as these things go—she'd met plenty of men and women back in the States thrown together after the war for fortune and security, and now feeling trapped and discontented with their lot. Many of them attended Gabriel's parties on a regular basis, searching for some sort of escape through booze and oblivion and meaningless sex.

She'd half been expecting a line of ne'er-do-wells to form behind her at the bar, but in truth she'd sat there undisturbed for over an hour, and was beginning to think that she was wasting her time. Perhaps Donovan had been right, and the logical place to start their investigation was the house in Belgravia, after all. Rutherford had seemed confident, however, insisting that his contacts would ensure that word reached the right ears, and that knowing Sabine's reputation, she'd find it impossible to resist.

Ginny drained the last of her martini and pushed the glass across the bar. "I'll take another," she said, catching the barman's attention. He cocked a crooked smile and set about mixing the drink. One more, and if there was still no sign of the woman, she'd call it a night and go and find Gabriel.

"Is that a New York accent?"

Ginny turned to see a slim, dark-haired woman sliding onto the stool beside her. The newcomer was wearing a loose, short-sleeved blue blouse, flowing black culottes and boots, but even still, Ginny could see she had a wiry, toned physique. The muscles of her upper arms were well defined, but not unladylike. She was smiling, but there was no warmth reflected in her sharp green eyes, which flitted back and forth, regarding Ginny with a cool, calculated look. When she spoke, she had a clipped, slightly Germanic accent.

"Long Island," said Ginny, with a smile. She accepted her drink from the barman, who peered inquisitively at the newcomer, anticipating an order. The woman waved him away.

"Now there's a thing. Someone else mentioned Long Island to me earlier this very day." She tapped out a nervous rhythm on the bar with her fingertips, drumming her nails against the polished lacquer.

"They did? Well I hope they were encouraging you to visit. It's a lovely place, particularly in the summer."

The woman cocked her head. "Ah, well, I suppose it depends on your perspective. I've heard it can be a lonely place, so far away from the bustle of the city."

"Oh, that's a bleak way of looking at it," said Ginny. "But then we all have our crosses to bear."

The woman laughed, and held out her hand. "Sabine," she said.

Ginny felt her heart skip a beat. "Ginny," she said, taking the woman's hand in her own. Sabine shook it firmly.

"What brings you to London?"

"A vacation. Look—can I get you a drink?"

Sabine shook her head. "No, thanks. I don't touch the stuff." She smiled, but again, Ginny noticed that the woman's eyes told a different story. She was sizing Ginny up, watching her every move.

Ginny swallowed, and then took another sip of her drink. Her mouth was dry.

"So, a vacation. Have you taken in the sights?"

Ginny shrugged, trying to keep things casual. "Not yet. We only arrived a couple of days ago, so we're just getting our bearings, really."

"We?"

"My husband." Ginny was careful to inject an inflection of venom into the word.

"Ah," said Sabine. "Is he here? I hope I haven't taken his seat?"

Ginny laughed. "Oh, no. To be honest, I have no idea where he is. He'd find all this a bit prosaic. He's probably off somewhere in town, making a fool of himself at some jazz club or other." She shrugged. "He gets about. I prefer the quiet life." She raised her glass and took a sip.

Sabine offered her a wry smile. "I understand. Men are all the same. They don't know how to appreciate what's under their noses."

"Ain't that the truth," said Ginny. "Are you married? You sound as if you speak from experience."

Sabine laughed. "Me? No. But let's just say that I know what men are like. It always begins with romance and devotion, but it ends with loneliness and despair."

Ginny swilled the liquid around in her glass. "You make it sound so fatalistic."

"It's in their nature. Men are like animals—cage them at your peril."

"In my case, it's not the man who's been caged," said Ginny. She allowed her shoulders to slump, as if she were suddenly letting her guard down. "You're right about Long Island. In many ways it's nothing but a beautiful prison. I mean, in many ways, I'm lucky. I want for nothing. Nothing at all. Except, perhaps, for the man I thought I married. But I don't suppose things will ever change."

Sabine leaned forward on her stool, until her face was only a few inches from Ginny's. Ginny could smell fresh mint on the woman's breath. "You know, I may be able to help you find your freedom, if that is what you're looking for?"

Ginny swallowed. She took another swig of her drink. This was it, the moment she'd been waiting for. It had taken only minutes to reel Sabine in, and she had to be careful not to blow it now. She had to seem interested, but not *too* enthusiastic. "Freedom? I'm not sure I know what you mean," she said, with a half smile.

Sabine grinned. "Perhaps we should take this conversation somewhere a little more private? Do you have a room here, at the hotel?"

Ginny nodded. "A suite."

"And your husband isn't expected back?"

"Not for some hours," said Ginny.

"Very well. Perhaps I can tell you a little more about the options available to you. I happen to be something of a specialist in this area."

Ginny nodded, and drained the last of her drink. She placed the glass on the bar. "Well, I don't suppose I've anything to lose by hearing you out," she said. She hopped down from the bar stool, beckoning for Sabine to follow her toward the elevators.

Sabine issued an impressed whistle as Ginny opened the door to her suite—which Gabriel had rented for the day—and beckoned her in. The plush surroundings were clearly having the desired effect, continuing to reel Sabine further into their little charade. Ginny could see from the look on Sabine's face that the woman thought she'd struck gold—that making a large amount of money out of the impending transaction was going to be a relatively easy matter.

"Are you sure I can't get you a drink?" said Ginny, closing the door behind them and strolling over to the drinks cabinet. She poured a large measure of neat vodka into a glass. The lights were off in the adjoining bedroom, and the door was closed.

Sabine crossed to the bedroom door, opened it, and peered in. "No, thanks," she said, apparently satisfied they were alone. "In my line of work it pays to keep a clear head."

"And what exactly *is* that line of work?" said Ginny.

Sabine beckoned to one of the divans in the center of room, and then sat when Ginny nodded her approval. "Come, now. Let's not be coy. I think you know."

"I want to hear you say it," said Ginny. She sipped at her drink, still standing by the drinks cabinet, watching Sabine with apparent interest. Her heart was thrumming. "This is all new to me."

"I'm a 'fixer'," said Sabine. "I fix things. People come to me with a problem, and I help to put it right."

"No matter the consequences?"

"I'm a professional," said Sabine. "There *are* no consequences. I do whatever is necessary and I leave no trail. But such a service costs…" She waved her hand at their surroundings. "Not that I expect that'll be a problem for a woman in your position."

"As I explained, I don't want for anything," said Ginny.

"Then I believe I'm in a position to help," said Sabine. "It would be a simple matter to engineer an 'accident'. Something quick and painless… unless, that is, you *want* him to suffer?"

Ginny had to fight down a rising tide of disgust. She couldn't believe how casually this woman was discussing the act of murder—the sly expression she was wearing, the playful confidence with which she presented herself. She wondered what had happened to this woman to lead her to this point in her life, to harden her so much that the thought of arranging the death—and potential torture—of an innocent man seemed so amusing. She realized she was frowning. "No… I…"

Sabine seemed to stiffen, as if spooked by Ginny's sudden hesitation. "Look, we can stop the conversation right here, and forget we ever met." She started to rise from the divan.

"No, no. It's just a lot to take in, that's all. For so long, I've thought about this day, and now that it comes to it… it's hard, that's all. I did love him, once. Perhaps I still do."

Sabine was standing, now. "Listen, perhaps I've made a mistake." Her eyes flicked toward the door.

"No, please, sit down," said Ginny.

Sabine paused. She looked uncertain, as if her instincts were telling her to go, but her greed was clinging on to the notion that she might be about to pass up a particularly lucrative job. Her instincts seemed to take over. She could tell something was wrong. She took a step toward the door.

"Sit down," said Ginny. "*Now.*"

Frowning, Sabine turned toward her, pivoting on the spot, raising her arms defensively, recognizing the sudden shift in Ginny's tone for the threat it represented.

A sudden gust stirred Sabine's hair, causing her to brace herself, gasping in shock, as Ginny raised her arms by her sides and began to rise slowly into the air.

The lights flickered, as the swirling winds caused the curtains to flutter uncontrollably, sending vases and teacups skittering to the floor, where they were dashed against the floorboards, shattering into a thousand tiny shards.

Ginny could feel the entity inside her stirring with pleasure. She embraced it, allowing it to flex, to flow out into her body and mind. She gasped, as its cold fingers spread into her limbs; felt its cool anger, its desire to obliterate the little human standing before her. She raised her hands, felt the ebb and flow of the energy swirling around her as she began to shape it, to give it form. She was floating now, her head only inches from the ceiling. She felt vital, *alive*, in control.

Below, Sabine was staring up at her in abject terror. Here was a woman who had seen horrors beyond belief—who had perpetrated horrendous crimes against her fellow humans—and yet, faced with this echo of Sekhmet, she seemed to shrink, to become nothing but an insect that deserved to be crushed. Ginny raised her hand, felt the power coursing through her body. All it would take was a single gesture, and she could rid the world of this foul stain. Surely that was righteous? Surely that was what was intended for her?

She heard a crash from the doorway, and looked down to see three men burst into the suite, all brandishing handguns.

"Thank God," said Sabine, shouting over the roaring of the ethereal wind. "Help me!"

One of the men approached her, raising his weapon. "I think *you're* the one who's going to be helping us," he said.

Ginny saw Sabine's shoulders sag, as she took in her situation. She seemed to recognize the man who had approached her.

"*You.*"

Ginny raised her hand. There was still time to end it. The woman didn't deserve to live. She could almost hear the snarl of Sekhmet's lions, ready to burst forth from the ether and consume her prey. If the men were killed too, then so be it — they were only humans, and could easily be replaced by other worshippers.

"Ginny?" the voice was coming from somewhere below. "*Ginny.*" She looked down to see a man by her feet, peering up at her, concern etched onto his face. "Ginny, it's *over.*"

She tried to focus on his face, on the meaning behind the sounds he was making. In her head, the goddess was whispering to her, urging her on, bidding her to smite her enemies. But there was something about the man below… something she had to remember.

With a sharp intake of breath, Ginny closed her eyes and reasserted her control. She felt warmth flooding back into her limbs, felt the fog clearing from her mind. The voice was gone, and all she could hear now was Gabriel, calling her name from below. She lowered her arms, felt the wind around her drop to a gentle breeze. For a moment she was falling, and blackness threatened to consume her. Then all was still, and she was standing once again, her feet firmly upon the floorboards.

She opened her eyes, overcome with a sudden wooziness, and then Gabriel was there beside her, sliding his arm around her shoulders, supporting her as she faltered. He led her over to a divan and lowered her onto it.

Rutherford was standing over Sabine, his gun leveled at his head. Donovan, also holding a pistol, stood by the door, blocking the exit in case she made a sudden bolt past Rutherford.

Sabine was openly staring at Ginny, slack-jawed with fear and incredulity. "What are you?" Her voice had lost it cocky, confident edge.

"You wouldn't understand," said Ginny. Her mouth was dry. She glanced toward the drinks cabinet, where her glass still sat upon the glossy wooden surface. Gabriel went to fetch it for her.

"And you're in league with *that*," said Sabine, glancing up at Rutherford.

"Whatever is necessary," said Rutherford. "Although *she* happens to be a friend."

"To be honest, I'm surprised you're still alive," said Sabine. "Those Russians were pretty pissed."

"Those Russians are why I'm here. You're going to tell us everything about them. Why they hired you. What they wanted."

Sabine smiled. "You know I can't do that."

Ginny leaned forward in her chair, fixing Sabine with a glower. "Oh, I think you will."

She watched Sabine swallow. "They'll kill me..."

"And yet I'm the one pointing a gun at your head," said Rutherford.

The fight seemed to go out of the woman. She pinched the

bridge of her nose between the thumb and forefinger of her left hand. "Alright. What do you want to know?"

"That's better," said Rutherford. "Start with the job. What did they hire you to do?"

Sabine smiled, despite the gravity of her situation. "It couldn't have been easier. They wanted me to obtain some blueprints for them. That was it."

"Blueprints of what?"

"Of the Underground system. Maps of the stations and tunnels. They were particularly interested in City Road, the disused station out by Islington."

"That's been closed for years," said Rutherford. "What use could they possibly have for an old Underground station?"

Sabine shrugged. "I don't ask questions. I do what I need to do, and then I get paid."

"What else did you see or hear, over in that house in Belgravia?"

"Bearded men in hoods, coming and going. That was it. Until you arrived, of course, and things went a bit 'hocus pocus'." She shot an accusing glance at Ginny.

"So you've no idea what they wanted with the Underground plans?" pressed Rutherford.

"I've already told you, I don't ask questions."

"Do you think they're looking to establish a base down there?" said Gabriel. The question was directed at Rutherford, rather than Sabine.

"I don't see why. They'd already got a stronghold in London, and it was only compromised because they failed to kill me." Rutherford turned to Sabine. "Alright, I think we've got what we need out of you. For now."

"You're not going to let her go?" said Donovan, from across the room. "She'll go straight to them. She can't be trusted."

"You really think I'd be that stupid," said Sabine. "If they find out I told you about the blueprints, they'll kill me on the spot."

"Bind her," said Rutherford, motioning with his gun for Gabriel to come forward. He did so, withdrawing a small coil of twine from his coat pocket.

"What are you doing?" snarled Sabine, twisting in her seat to stare up at Rutherford, who was keeping the muzzle of his gun pointed calmly at her forehead. "I told you what you wanted to know."

"It's for your own safety," said Rutherford. There was the faint hint of a smile at the corners of his mouth. "You said it yourself—they'll kill you if they get the chance. Consider this protective custody." He watched while Gabriel tightened the cord around her wrists, and then set about doing the same to her ankles.

"They'll kill you, you know, Rutherford. They'll kill all of you. They're not going to be scared off by a few conjuring tricks."

"Oh, I don't know," said Ginny. "It worked well enough on you."

Sabine looked panicked. "Rutherford, *please*. You know how it works. I won't be safe in custody. They'll have people on the inside. You haven't seen what they're capable of."

"Quite the contrary," he said. "And besides, I know some of my colleagues will be *very* anxious for a little word."

"Bastard," she spat. She struggled futilely against her bonds as Gabriel stepped away, and Rutherford finally lowered his gun.

"No need to get comfortable," said Rutherford. "Someone will be along shortly to pick you up."

He motioned to the others to follow him as he crossed to the door. Pausing only to down the last of her vodka, Ginny stood, smiled sweetly at Sabine, and then turned and left the room.

TWELVE

"Morning."

Donovan sat hunched over the breakfast table in the hotel restaurant, wreathed in a pall of cigarette smoke. There were two empty coffee cups on the table before him, and he nursed a third in his right hand. He looked up as Gabriel approached the table, and then used the side of his boot to push out one of the chairs by way of greeting.

Amused, Gabriel sat, reaching for the coffee pot. It was empty. He beckoned to the waiter. "Where's Flora?"

"She's eaten already. She's unhappy I decided to leave her out of last night's little encounter." Donovan gulped at his coffee as if it were medicinal.

"She's a capable woman, Felix."

Donovan leaned back in his chair. "I know that better than anyone. Of course I do. But that's not the point, is it? I mean— why put her in harm's way if I don't have to. Why risk it?"

"You make it sound as though it's your choice."

Donovan sighed. "She says I'm being selfish. The way I see it, I'm trying to protect her."

"Have you considered that she might feel the same?"

Donovan took another sip from his coffee cup, and then reached for his cigarette, which had been slowly burning down in the ashtray. "Maybe," he admitted, with some reluctance. He looked up as the waiter appeared at his elbow. The newcomer was a tall, lean man, impeccably dressed in a black suit. His upper lip looked as starched as his collar. Donovan took a draw on his cigarette.

"Good morning, gentlemen," said the waiter.

"Morning," said Gabriel. "Can I get some coffee? And some eggs. Scrambled, with Tabasco sauce."

The waiter raised an eyebrow, suggesting disapproval, but nodded curtly. "And for sir?"

"Just some more coffee," said Donovan.

"Very well." The waiter drifted away toward another table, at which a young family had just taken up residence. The mother was wrestling a menu from the hands of her youngest child, while the father sat looking in the other direction, as if embarrassed to be associated with them.

"Anyway," said Gabriel, returning his attention to Donovan. "You can make it up to her this morning."

"What do you mean?"

"Rutherford's got another lead. A man named Newbury, a former British agent with experience dealing with this sort of thing."

"You mean the Russians?"

Gabriel shrugged. He lowered his voice. "I'm not entirely sure, but Rutherford thinks he might be able to shed some light on what we saw during the ambush. That strange energy they were throwing around."

Donovan stared forlornly into his cup. "Maybe he'll know where to get a decent cup of coffee around here, too."

Gabriel laughed. He reached over and took a cigarette from

Donovan's crumpled packet. "Do you mind?"

"You know you don't have to ask."

Gabriel placed the filter between his lips and pulled the ignition tab. He allowed the smoke to flood his lungs. The taste reminded him of home.

"What did you mean, about making it up to her?" Felix pushed the remains of his coffee across the table in front of him, and twisted in his seat, looking for any sign of the waiter. The man had disappeared from view.

"Well, just that you can spend a little time with her this morning. Do something that she wants to do. Rutherford thought we should avoid descending on this Newbury guy mob-handed. That's all."

Donovan's lip curled in obvious disagreement. "You can't seriously expect me to go *sightseeing*, Gabriel, with all this going on?"

"Look, we're supposed to be on vacation. Think about Flora. You said yourself that you wanted to keep her out of it."

"Yes, but *I'm* a goddamned *policeman*. I can help." He paused to grind out the end of his cigarette. "And what about that Glogauer woman, and all that talk about the Underground stations? Don't you think we should be looking into *that*?"

"Look, don't get me wrong, Felix. You know there's no one I'd rather have by my side. But I think it's worth finding out what we're really up against before we go looking for them. We've no idea what we'll find down there, but judging by what we saw during that ambush, it can't be anything good." Gabriel nodded to indicate the waiter was returning with their coffee.

Donovan practically seized it from the man's hands. He splashed some into Gabriel's cup.

"If we don't act quickly, there's every chance we'll miss our window of opportunity. You know how this works. The moment they find out the woman talked, they'll be gone. It'll be as if they were never there."

"We have to trust Rutherford to handle it."

Donovan shrugged. "Look, this is Rutherford's business. I'm here to help, just like you. And I'm telling you, it's a mistake to wait."

"Alright. He'll be here soon, so you can tell him yourself."

Donovan grunted something non-committal, and then lit another cigarette. Gabriel sighed, leaned back in his chair, and willed his eggs to arrive more quickly.

Donovan's exchange with Rutherford had, in the end, been brief and to the point. Rutherford maintained that the priority was to find out all they could about their enemies before making their play, and while Donovan protested, Rutherford wasn't about to be swayed. Like Gabriel, he'd seen first-hand what this faction of Russian occultists—which he'd taken to calling "Koscheis"—was capable of, and he was intent on finding a means to comprehensively defeat them. If, he argued, they were establishing some sort of presence on the Underground, then they'd work together to flush them out—just as soon as they understood what they were contending with.

As a result, Donovan—who'd remained adamant throughout—had taken Flora out for the morning, having agreed to rendezvous with the others back at the hotel after lunch.

Now, Gabriel, Ginny and Rutherford were across town in Chelsea, searching for the address that Rutherford's commanding

GHOSTS OF EMPIRE

officer had provided him with. They were standing in the correct
street, as far as Gabriel could tell, but Rutherford appeared
somewhat less certain. Gabriel watched him turn the scrap of
paper over in his hand and examine the scrawled address for a
second time. He looked up at the house, then back at the paper,
as if finding it somehow difficult to correlate the two.

"Not what you were expecting?" said Ginny.

"Well... no," said Rutherford. "It's just that... well, Sir Maurice
Newbury has a certain *reputation*. I don't really know what I
was expecting. Something a little less *traditional*, I suppose."

Gabriel looked the place up and down. It was traditional in a
way only British houses could be—a smart, terraced property,
probably built sometime toward the end of the previous century,
with large bay windows, a pillar-box red front door, and a small
rose garden enclosed by a low wall, which was capped by a
row of ornamental iron railings. It looked homely—if a little
conservative, and small, for Gabriel's taste.

"Well, are you going to knock on the door?" urged Ginny.

"Yes, sorry," said Rutherford. He walked up the path to the
house. The others hung back. Rutherford smoothed the front
of his jacket, and then lifted the knocker and rapped loudly,
three times.

Moments later the door swung open, and a short, thin
woman appeared in the opening. Her hair had once been
midnight black, but was now shot through with streaks of gray,
and she was wearing wiry spectacles, pushed right up to the
bridge of her nose. She was wearing a red cardigan and black
skirt, with a lace-edged apron tied around her waist. "Hello?"
she said, her voice cracking slightly with age. Gabriel guessed
she must have been in her sixties, if not older.

"Ah, yes, hello," said Rutherford. Gabriel could tell from his bumbling manner that he was nervous about the impending meeting. He seemed to be treating the whole matter with the sort of reverence usually reserved for movie stars or retired politicians of great standing. "My name is Rutherford, and these are my associates, Mr. Cross and Ms. Gray. We were hoping to speak with Sir Maurice, if he's at home?"

The woman smiled. "Secret Service?"

Rutherford frowned. "Well, I'm not—"

"It's always been easy to spot them."

The woman eyed him through her spectacles, and then nodded, as if coming to a decision. She opened the door a little wider and stood to one side. "Come in. He's in the drawing room."

Rutherford thanked her, and led the way into the house.

"I suppose you'll be wanting tea," said the woman, whom Gabriel took to be the housekeeper. "We're not interested in that American nonsense here, I'm afraid."

"You mean coffee?" said Gabriel, with a smile.

"That's the stuff." The woman pulled a face. "Never understood the attraction. Sir Maurice, on the other hand, prefers a pot of Earl Grey. Now that's an afternoon tea, by tradition, but we all have to make compromises sometimes."

"Blythe, leave the visitors alone!"

The voice echoed from a room down the hall. The housekeeper rolled her eyes. "Sounds like you'd better hurry along." She ushered them down the hallway with her hands at their backs, until they were standing before the door in question. Rutherford knocked, and then pushed it aside, stepping into the room beyond. Gabriel and Ginny followed, while the housekeeper tottered off toward the kitchen.

The drawing room was not at all what Gabriel had expected. Where the exterior of the property had appeared orderly and well maintained, here, inside, it was a triumph of chaos and disorder. Crooked bookcases with bowing shelves lined the far wall, overstuffed with peeling spines, fat paper files and bizarre trinkets. Further books were heaped in tottering piles in the middle of the floor, forming a barely navigable island of dusty paper and board. A yellowing cat skull sat on the mantelpiece above the fireplace, which was black with soot and ash. A sideboard groaned beneath the weight of a bizarre mechanical contraption, for which Gabriel could discern no obvious purpose, and a thick fug of cigarette smoke hung in the air, swirling in the shafts of light from the window. Gabriel thought he could detect the faint aroma of something sweet and pungent beneath the nicotine musk, too.

Two wingback armchairs were placed before the fire, and a soft divan was almost hidden beneath the piled cushions and blankets. A small, mechanical owl was perched atop one of the chairs, and it turned to regard them as they entered, cogs whirring.

Newbury himself was sitting in another armchair by the window, his head turned away from them. Smoke from a cigarette wreathed his head. He was wearing a rather dapper brown suit, and appeared wiry and fit despite his advancing years. His hair was silver-gray, and he had a square, clean-shaven jaw. Despite the sea of chaos around him, he looked peaceful and serene.

Rutherford cleared his throat. "Sir Maurice?"

Slowly, Newbury turned to take in the interlopers. He raised a single eyebrow, as he looked Gabriel up and down. "You're a long way from home, Mr. Cross."

Gabriel grinned, immediately disarmed. "Quite. I must

admit—it's not exactly the vacation I had planned."

Newbury grinned. "Let's hope someone's keeping an eye on matters back in New York while the Ghost is abroad in London, eh?"

So Newbury knew exactly who he was. He must have read Rutherford's report, following the matter with the *Goliath* and the attempt to unleash a doomsday weapon on London. Either that, or he was uncannily perceptive and up to date with foreign affairs.

Gabriel noticed Ginny was staring at him. He fired her a reassuring smile. "I'm sure they can make do for a couple of weeks. And besides, if things get out of hand, it'll give me something to do when I get home."

Newbury laughed. "Indeed. And a delight to meet your companion, Ms…?"

"Gray, Ginny Gray."

He turned to Rutherford. "And you, Mr. Rutherford. I understand you're making quite a name for yourself in the Service."

Rutherford looked flustered. "It's a pleasure to meet you, Sir Maurice." He walked forward, his hand extended, and Newbury shook it with an amused grin.

"Well, as you can see, I don't get many visitors these days," he gestured to the state of the room, "but then, even when I did, it looked much the same. If you can find somewhere to sit, you're welcome to it."

Gabriel felt himself warming to the man immediately. He crossed to one of the armchairs by the fire. Embers were still crackling in the grate—the remnants of a fire from the previous evening. Ginny perched on the edge of the divan, and Rutherford remained standing, close to where Newbury was sitting.

"I'm sure Blythe will be along with the tea shortly—along with a scattering of acerbic words. In the meantime, I presume your visit has something to do with your visit to the Fixer the night before last, and the ensuing conflict with a number of hooded characters in the street?"

"You remain incredibly well informed," said Rutherford. There was no hint of suspicion in his voice—clearly, Newbury was still very much connected to the Service, even if he was no longer an active agent himself. Rutherford had explained a little of his reputation on the drive over, explaining how Newbury had once served Queen Victoria herself as an agent of the Crown, but had later defected to the Secret Service to work against the Queen, after it became clear that she no longer had the best interests of the nation at heart. His exploits were legendary, Rutherford had claimed, and he continued to be held in very high regard. Gabriel could see why.

"It pays to stay abreast of the news, Mr. Rutherford."

"We're hoping you might be able to shed some light on the nature of the men we encountered. They were Russians, presumably part of some clandestine order. They were somehow able to harness a type of 'light energy', using it to open portals, or control the very air around us. Major Absalom referred to them as 'Koscheis', and said that he'd encountered something akin to them during the war."

Newbury sucked thoughtfully on his cigarette, resting his head against the back of his chair. "From what I know of them, the Koscheis were an elite fighting force created during the war, schooled in the ways of the arcane, and taught how to turn themselves into weapons. They had no need for machine guns or artillery—it was said they could conjure demons from the abyss itself, and bend reality to their whims." He plumed smoke from the corner of his mouth. "That was the propaganda, anyway, although I gather it wasn't very far from the truth. There's some disagreement about whether the creatures they pressed into service were really 'demonic', but that's just a matter of semantics."

"Major Absalom said that he encountered some of them back here, after the war, working out of a house in Bristol," said Rutherford. "He implied that they'd escaped. Do you think they could be back?"

"It's quite possible," said Newbury. "These days, the Empire is not what it was. Queen Alberta's rule is faltering. While her attention has been overseas," he flicked a glance at Gabriel, "her domestic policies have left her open, and there are those even within the Empire itself who would see it crumble. Our enemies take advantage of our weakened state. It wouldn't surprise me if the Russians—or at least the followers of this particular imperial cult—were seeking to further destabilize the nation."

"Alright, so what more can you tell us about these Koscheis?" said Gabriel.

Newbury placed his cigarette between his lips, and stood, straightening his back. "That'll have to wait a moment, I'm afraid. Here comes Blythe with the tea."

Almost on cue, the door opened and Newbury's housekeeper walked in carrying a tea tray adorned with an array of mismatched crockery and teapots. Unsteadily, she crossed the room and placed the tray upon the top of the sideboard.

After she'd shut the door behind her, Newbury turned to the others. "Anyone for tea?"

Five minutes later they had all returned to their seats brandishing steaming cups of tea. Rutherford was still standing by the window. "You were saying, Sir Maurice?"

"The Koscheis, yes. As I understand it, they originated as a secret order created by the self-proclaimed 'mystic' Grigori Rasputin, who at the time was a favored member of the Tsar's inner circle. Rasputin claimed to have mastered a form of elemental magic, drawing upon ancient pagan texts recovered from the vaults of monasteries he visited during his many pilgrimages around Russia. He plundered these texts for references to ancient rites, and spent years deciphering them, slowly discerning how to recreate them. It's thought that hundreds of people died during those early experiments, as he lost control of the things he had created, but that, over time, he was eventually able to master them.

"Following his arrival at St. Petersburg, he performed demonstrations of his hard-won powers, and soon came to the notice of the Tsar himself, who took him under his patronage ostensibly as an advisor and a 'healer'. But secretly, the Tsar charged Rasputin with assembling an inner circle of 'black monks'—an order of magicians trained in the use of elemental magic, as a means of protecting the realm. These were the Koscheis."

"Elemental magic?" said Rutherford.

"Yes, in that it draws upon the fundamental energies of the universe. The Koscheis made use of light and air, time and gravity, life and death. It is a distinct and esoteric discipline, most distinct from my own particular field of interest, which tends toward the more spiritual." Newbury sipped his tea.

"So how do we stop them?" said Gabriel. "We took some of

them down with brute force, but there are clearly greater forces at play."

"Indeed," said Newbury. "Although I fear my own expertise in this area is severely lacking. I've never had the misfortune to be on the receiving end of such an attack, although it must be quite fascinating to witness. As I understand it, the solution lies in deploying opposing elemental forces to combat the conjured elements of the Koscheis—countering death with life, and so forth. But I fear my most useful role in this matter may be in pointing you in the direction of another. There is an old acquaintance of mine, a man named Roland Horwood, who may be able to assist you. He is far better versed in such matters, and I suspect, if the Koscheis are, as you fear, in London, then Roland might well know of it already."

"Thank you," said Rutherford. "Your help in this matter is much appreciated, Sir Maurice."

"Thank me when the matter is closed," said Newbury. "Now, pass me that notepaper and pen, would you, and I'll give you Horwood's address. I'll telephone ahead to warn him I've sent you."

Rutherford placed his teacup and saucer on a small side table, and passed Newbury the notepad and pen for which he'd gestured.

Newbury wrote the address with a brief flourish, tore the page from the pad, and handed it to Rutherford. "I trust you can decipher my scrawl."

Rutherford grinned. "Quite so."

"Then I bid you good day, and good luck. The gentlemen in the room, at least, are likely to need it."

Ginny narrowed her eyes. She looked as if she was about

to say something, but the amused expression on Newbury's face told them everything they needed to know. Not only had he correctly identified Gabriel, but he knew precisely who Ginny was, too—and more, had implied he was aware of her particular... *circumstances*. Gabriel got to his feet, and took Ginny by the hand. "It's been a pleasure, Sir Maurice," he said. "I hope we'll meet again."

THIRTEEN

"It's not that I don't appreciate what he's trying to do for us. He paid for us to come all the way out here, to give us time together, away from all that business back home." Donovan chewed on the end of his cigarette. He was feeling agitated. It was cold out, and the streets were slick with the aftermath of a sudden downpour. He was beginning to get a sense that the weather here—like his mood—was eminently changeable.

He knew he wasn't being fair to Flora, dragging her all the way out here. But what else was he supposed to do? He couldn't stand by and allow Rutherford to lead Gabriel and Ginny on a wild goose chase around London, while the men who had tried to kill them made good on their escape.

"I think I know what's coming next, Felix," said Flora, from beside him. She sounded more amused than concerned. "You're going to say 'but I'm a cop, and I should be out there helping them, and they're making a mistake'. Or something along those lines, anyway."

Donovan turned to look at her, and couldn't help but grin. She hit him playfully on the upper arm. "You know me too well," he said.

"I know that the man I married wouldn't sit by while his friends put themselves in danger. No matter what *they* thought about it. I've told you before, Felix, you don't have to make allowances for me. I wouldn't have married you if I hadn't known what I was getting into."

"I know," said Donovan. "It's just… it's Rutherford's case. And if he doesn't want to listen…" He flicked the butt of his cigarette into the gutter. Close by, cars and omnibuses streamed past in a seemingly endless parade, stirring puddles of surface water and belching thick black smoke in their wake.

"You've never let that stop you before."

"No, but it's always been on my own turf. That's the difference. What if I'm wrong? If there's something I'm not seeing?"

"And what if you're *not*?" said Flora. "Look, this isn't getting us anywhere. Trust your gut, Felix. Do what you think is best."

Donovan had reached the street corner, and paused outside a tall, pentagonal brick tower, which looked like to him like the bizarre offspring of a neo-classical temple and a local shop. It had clearly been boarded up for some time—white paint was flaking off the brickwork, the hoardings were damp and partially rotten, and trash was collecting in the grounds. Dead leaves from the surrounding trees were slowly turning to mulch. He could smell the mold from the street.

"That's exactly what I *am* doing." He put a hand on her arm. "I'm just going to be a few minutes, alright? Then we can go and get some lunch, wait for the others back at the hotel."

"Why, what is this place?" She looked up at the tumbledown building in confusion.

"This is City Road Underground station," said Donovan. "The concierge at the hotel told me how to find it. It's been closed for years."

"So there's a whole abandoned subway station down there?" She jerked her thumb at the building.

"Yes. And that woman we interviewed last night said the Russians who attacked Rutherford were particularly interested in it. They were trying to get blueprints of the whole Underground system."

Flora laughed. "I *knew* it! I knew you were up to something. There's me trying to give you a bloody pep talk, and all the while, you've been bringing us out here so you can go snooping around regardless! I knew you wouldn't be able to sit it out."

Donovan shrugged. "I owe him, Flora. Not just for the flights and hotels. For everything. I can't let him go headlong into this without me."

Flora smiled, sincerely this time. "I love you, Felix Donovan." She looked down at her dress. "I just wish you'd warned me about this little excursion before I went and put on a nice dress."

"Oh, no. Hold on a minute. You can't come in there with me."

"To hell I can't! You try to stop me."

"Flora…" She shot him a warning look so severe that he almost took a step backwards. He held up his hands. "Look, if these Russians are down there…"

"Then we face them together, or not at all."

"I don't like this, Flora, not one bit."

"And you think I do? Every day you put on that suit and go out to work, and I'm left wondering if you're going to come home that night, or if you're going to get shot at, or stabbed, or sacrificed to some damn pagan god from the dawn of time. Well I'm telling you, Felix, I've had enough of sitting around too. If there's something I can be doing to help, then I'm going to do it."

Donovan grinned. There she was, standing before him, chest heaving as she fought to catch her breath, just as beautiful as she'd been the day he met her, all those years ago. And just as strong and single-minded, too. He took her hand. "I'm sorry. I'm sorry for all the times I haven't listened. It's not because I don't trust you. It's because I'm so scared about what life would be like without you."

"I'd rather we *lived* it together than tried to keep each other wrapped in cotton wool," she said.

"Alright. I'll take you with me. But you're right about one thing?"

"What's that?"

"You're going to regret wearing that dress."

Still holding her hand, he led her around the rear of the old station building. Here, the hoardings had partially collapsed, and within minutes they'd clambered through to reach the boarded-over door that had once, he presumed, served as a staff or engineering entrance.

Sheltered from view behind the remains of a hoarding, it was a relatively simple matter to jimmy the board away from the door, and while Flora kept watch, he used the corner of an old brick to smash open the rusted padlock behind. Within five minutes, the door hung open, revealing a gloomy, dust-ridden ticket hall beyond.

"Come on," he called, beckoning Flora over. "We're in." He'd brought a flashlight with him from the hotel—another helpful concierge had helped him to procure that—and he withdrew it from his jacket pocket and passed it to Flora as she came over to join him, wrinkling her nose at the foul stench emanating from the abandoned station.

"What *is* that?" she said.

"A flashlight. I know we're in England, but I wouldn't have thought they're *that* different."

"Alright, smart alec. I meant the smell. It's… *disgusting*."

"It's been abandoned for years," he said. "God knows what people have left down there to rot." He stepped over the threshold, drawing the gun that Rutherford had provided him with the previous night. Flora came in behind him, waving the beam of the flashlight back and forth so they could get their bearings.

It was a small station, tiled in the same manner as many of the others he'd seen since his arrival here. A small window in the left-hand wall had once served as a ticket booth, and on the right, a flight of stairs led down to the platforms below. Dust, animal droppings and broken tiles littered the floor, and as the beam of the flashlight stabbed into the corners, he could see no evidence that anyone had passed this way for years.

He moved slowly across the ticket hall, Flora just behind him. Their footsteps stirred plumes of dust, which swirled and danced with their passing, picked out by the beam of the torch.

"Are we going down to the platforms?" whispered Flora.

Donovan nodded, leading the way toward the steps. Down below was a sea of inky blackness, and the stench here was even worse. It was a thick, cloying odor that seemed to lodge in the back of his throat, threatening to make him retch. It reminded him of nothing so much as the stink of rotting vegetation—but surely here, deep underground, where there was no light and no water, nothing could be growing in the tunnels? He considered turning back, feeling suddenly overcome by uncertainty. Was he doing the right thing, ignoring the others, coming down here with Flora? He tried to shake the feeling, knowing that he had to press on. He was here now, and he was seeing it through.

Cautiously they crept forward, steadily making their way down the steps toward the gloom below. The beam of Flora's flashlight picked out signs warning them to "keep left", or listing the stations accessible from each of the two platforms.

"Which way?"

"Left," said Donovan, following his gut. That was where the worst of the stench seemed to be coming from, and every fiber of his being was crying out to him that there was something *wrong* about that smell.

They reached the bottom of the steps and took a left, passing under a low archway and out onto the platform. Here, the gloom seemed even more eerie and oppressive. The tunnel wall loomed over them, disappearing into yawning chasms at either end of the short platform. Below, mice skittered about beneath the tracks, anxious to get out of the sudden, piercing light.

Donovan glanced at Flora, but all he could discern in the reflected torchlight was her silhouette, and her bright, shining eyes. "I'm going down there," he said, indicating one of the tunnel mouths.

"Are you sure it's safe?" said Flora.

"There are no trains, if that's what you mean. Haven't been for years. But there has to be some reason the Russians are interested in this place." He jumped down in-between the tracks, landing with a thud.

"Alright. Help me down," said Flora. She placed the flashlight on the edge of the platform and extended both arms, so that he could take her hands. She jumped down, narrowly avoiding catching her ankle on one of the rails.

"Careful!" he hissed.

She ignored him, reaching for the flashlight. Donovan knew that the thought of rodents scuttling around her boots would be absolute anathema to her, but he had to give her credit—she seemed to be taking it all in her stride. Clearly it'd been unfair of him to be so protective of her over the years. Not that he was about to start letting her battle mobsters, automatons and all the other weird stuff that he and Gabriel found themselves battling in New York. But perhaps he'd start teaching her how to defend herself. With the Reaper waiting to cash in his debt when they returned, he'd certainly feel a lot safer if Flora knew how to handle herself.

"What do we do if we find something down here?" she said.

"We either put a stop to it, or we get the hell out of here and come back with reinforcements."

Flora made a noncommittal sound, and waved the flashlight beam back and forth across the tunnel mouth. "There's something there, on the ceiling."

"Hold the torch beam still. I can't see where you're looking."

She pointed the beam up at the ceiling, holding it steady. There, just above them, the tunnel roof was clad in a thick, vegetative mass. It looked like a kind of algae or slick moss, oozing with a clear, viscous fluid, which dripped ponderously in bulbous droplets, spattering on the tracks below. Clearly, this was the source of the sickening stench.

"Oh, God," said Flora. "What is it?"

"I don't know," said Donovan. "But whatever it is, I don't think it's natural." As he watched, the substance seemed to quiver and move, sliding slowly to consume another few inches of the tunnel walls. "Come on. We'd better go a little further."

They trudged along the tunnel, careful to avoid the glistening puddles on the ground. As they worked their way deeper, the effect—and the stink—became increasingly pronounced. Here, the strange substance had spread to cover the walls as well as the ceiling, coating the entire tunnel. Up ahead, it was beginning to creep onto the tracks. The smell was starting to make Donovan feel dizzy.

"Alright, that's enough. We should turn back. We don't know what this stuff is doing to our lungs. We should find the others. Whatever the Russians are doing down here, it can't be good."

Something sounded in the tunnel behind him—the crackle of an electrical discharge—and he turned, expecting to see some of the fluid had dripped onto an exposed cable and caused it to spark.

Instead, however, the sight of four floating circles of light greeted him, spitting and fizzing as they formed in the air, as if traced by an invisible finger.

"Umm, Felix…" said Flora, edging closer, the beam of the flashlight now trailing uselessly across the floor.

"Get behind me," he said, "And if you get chance to run, then take it."

As he watched, smaller symbols began to form inside the circles, forming what looked like symbols or pictograms. And then the light started to bend, as if reality itself were warping, and five hooded figures were standing before them in the tunnel, strange blue light crackling at their fingertips.

"Goddammit," said Donovan, and he pulled the trigger on his gun.

FOURTEEN

"Shhh."

Regina shot Hargreaves an exasperated look. If he didn't stop moving, he was going to give them away. A single scuff of his boot and he risked drawing the attention of the gathered crowd.

In response, he frowned, shifted his weight from one foot to the other, and returned to peering down through a gap in the wooden railing at the scene unfolding below.

She, too, was growing stiff, and she rubbed at her aching back where the metal wrench had been pressing uncomfortably for the last hour, tucked into the waistband of her culottes. Absently, she hoped she hadn't got bloodstains on her blouse.

After leaving the cottage, they'd emerged into the drawing room of a country estate, still furnished in the trappings of the previous century, but left to molder and decay. The once-plush sofas were now infested with rodents, their white stuffing scatted over the dusty floorboards like so much dirty snow. They'd passed through a library that smelled of festering damp and into a dining room, the table of which was still set for a dinner that had never happened, a ghostly imprint of a time now lost, a path that had never been trodden.

Here, they'd encountered not only a choice of two marked

doors through which to continue their bizarre journey, but a hooded Russian, who had recognized them immediately as trespassers and set about raising the alarm. Regina was the quickest off the mark, battering him across the side of the head with the wrench, resulting in a harrowing crack of splintering bone and a sudden gush of vivid red blood. He'd gone down instantly, his jaw still working soundlessly as she'd stood over him and put him out of his misery with a second determined blow.

Hargreaves had watched with a mixture of admiration and abject horror as she'd wiped the weapon on the dead man's robes, before telling him to hurry up and select which door to open as the next portal.

She knew that, when all of this was over and she was once again sitting alone in her living room, she'd be haunted by the expression on that young man's face: the appalled realization that it was already too late, the pleading look in his eyes as he'd searched her face for the slightest hint of mercy. A death like that—it was brutal and personal. You had to look your victim in the eye. She'd killed people before—more than she cared to remember—but it had always been at one remove, with a gun; the sudden punch of the recoil, the jerk of the victim, and then go. That was how she'd been trained to do it. Quick and efficient, then move on before you were seen—or before you had time to think about what you'd just done. This, though… she was going to remember this.

Hargreaves had chosen the door on the left, and with fingers still oily with spilled blood, she'd traced the runic symbols and caused the circle to ignite.

The door had exited onto a cobbled lane, slick with rainwater, somewhere—she'd been certain—in the outskirts of London.

Here, the sky had been a brooding canopy of gray, smudged clouds divesting themselves upon the rooftops of the city. Hargreaves had suggested they quit while they were ahead—to make a run for it, find their way back to Absalom and report in. Regina, on the other hand, had argued that they had to press on, to keep opening doors until they found some answers.

They hadn't yet established the purpose of the network of doors, or been able to find out anything more about the Russians' plans in London. These men had evidently been moving unseen throughout London—and farther afield—for some time, co-opting abandoned properties, and establishing a series of temporary bases. Yet only now had they had shown their hand, brazenly attacking the van the previous night, demonstrating their considerable power, and perhaps even more telling, allowing survivors to flee the scene. That suggested their plans were in motion, and perhaps even close to completion— and so Regina had convinced Hargreaves to continue.

They'd found another marked door in the alleyway, ostensibly the rear entrance to a baker's shop, and had passed through, finding themselves here, in a small chapel in what looked, to Regina, to be somewhere deep in the remote Scottish highlands.

Now, they were crouched upon a small balcony above the main vestry, peering down at an assembly of men—and, to a lesser extent, women—in hooded robes. Regina had counted eighteen of them, standing in a circle around a large table, which was covered in an array of technical documents and blueprints. As far as she'd been able to ascertain from her slightly dubious vantage point, they all appeared to relate to the London Underground system. There were maps of the tunnels and schematics of the stations, and they looked as if they'd been heavily annotated in a scrawl that was illegible from this distance. Although she suspected that, even with a pair of binoculars, she wouldn't have been able to make much sense of the documents—neither engineering nor the Russian language had ever been particular strong points for her.

Hargreaves was shifting again, trying to discern the faces of the people below. They'd clearly stumbled upon a meeting of the Russian coven, and below, a bearded man appeared to be in the process of disseminating his plan to his followers. She'd been able to understand little save for the occasional word, but she was certain that whatever they had in mind, it involved some sort of takeover of the Underground, using the tunnels and stations for a malign purpose which was, as yet, not entirely clear.

Not for the first time, she wondered if these people were state sanctioned. Could the Tsarina really be plotting to move against the Queen? It seemed unconscionable that two such mighty nations would risk all-out war, but then the British Empire was not what it once was under Victoria, and Alberta had a habit of making enemies abroad. Perhaps the Tsarina had seen her opportunity and sent these agents in to attempt to weaken the Queen's position, in advance of an all-out assault.

Or perhaps it was simply another cult, armed with esoteric rites and arcane knowledge, come to destroy the world in order to give rise to their new order. She'd dealt with plenty of those in her time, too. The one thing they'd all had in common, however, is that they were small, and disorganized, and too reliant on their faith. This, on the other hand, appeared to be something else entirely. This was organized, efficient, and dangerous.

The Underground was the heart of London's transport system, a warren of deep tunnels beneath the city that served as arteries connecting all the major hubs, right across the city. If the Russians were planning to bring it to a standstill, there'd be pandemonium. Worse, if they were planning to somehow sabotage the tunnel system itself—a distinct possibility, given the extensive blueprints they'd acquired—then there was a chance they could endanger the lives of hundreds of thousands of people, causing the tunnel system to collapse, and bringing much of London down on top of it.

She considered their options. They had one handgun and a wrench. There was no way they could take down eighteen men and women, even if they weren't highly trained and capable of performing unnatural feats. Additionally, there was no way of knowing if the people below represented just one cell of the wider Russian operation—a situation she considered likely, given the size and scale of their network, and the sheer number of combatants they'd faced the previous night. Worse, there was every chance that one of them would get away, disappearing through a marked door or conjuring up one of their iridescent portals, in order to warn the others. If she and Hargreaves were to make a move now, they risked hastening the Russians' plans. Not to mention the fact they'd most likely end up dead.

No, the better option was to move on, find a way back to London and warn Absalom. Now that they had something to go on, the Service could deploy agents to all of the Underground stations, make preparations against a suspected attack, and begin raiding the Russian safe houses she and Hargreaves had already uncovered.

She beckoned to Hargreaves, indicating the stairwell at the

end of the balcony. They'd come this way earlier, and knew that it led to a small antechamber off the main hall. From here, they could find another of the marked doors and make good their escape.

Hargreaves nodded his assent, and together, inching painfully slowly on their hands and knees, the two of them crossed to the mouth of the stairwell. Below, a Russian voice continued to drone on in deep baritone, punctuated only by the occasional murmur of consensus from his audience.

Regina got to her feet, drew the wrench from the back of her culottes and slowly descended the spiral steps, keeping her back to the wall as she did so. Hargreaves followed behind, weapon still drawn.

The chamber at the bottom was empty, but they were now only a few yards away from the proceedings they'd been observing from above. She could see the hooded figures from where she was standing. If any one of them turned around now…

She edged a little further along the wall toward the door.

Directly opposite was another chamber of similar size and shape. The door was hanging open, and inside she could see two other doors on the far wall, both of them marked with the symbols that would allow her to open another portal.

The only problem was that they'd have to cross in the open to get to it. It was only about three steps, but all it would take was one of the hooded figures to spot them, and the game would be up. She glanced at Hargreaves, and she could see from the uncertain expression on his face that he'd come to the same realization. They had no choice. They had to make a break for it.

Her heart was hammering in her chest. She could feel sweat beading on her brow. She swallowed, took one final glance at

Hargreaves, and then lurched out into the open.

One step.

She tried to remain focused on the goal. She didn't turn her head, didn't even look at the Russians only a few feet away from her.

Two steps.

She was in the shadow of the doorway now. If only she could make the next step…

Three steps.

She ducked inside the chamber and fell back against the wall in relief, gasping for air. No one had raised the alarm. She hadn't been seen.

She caught her breath. Now it was Hargreaves's turn.

She peered across at him. He was standing just inside the doorway, gun raised, looking flustered. He was watching the Russians, waiting for his window of opportunity.

She risked a glance. The meeting appeared to be coming to an end. The leader had finished speaking, and now the others were beginning to mill about, conversing. They had only moments before they were discovered, and Hargreaves still had to make it across unseen.

She glanced back, and he met her eye. A bead of sweat trickled down his forehead. Was he considering something drastic? He had a determined look in his eye. Surely he wasn't going to open fire? He seemed to be tightening his grip on his gun.

Time was running out. She could hear the Russians laughing and joking. It was now or never.

"Now," she mouthed, waving for him to make a run for it. All he had to do was make it across. Even if they saw him, there was every chance she could open the portal in time for them to escape.

Hargreaves worked his jaw. She saw him swallow. And then suddenly he was running, charging toward her, head down.

The seconds seemed to stretch as he lurched toward her. She expected the cry of alarm at any moment.

And then he was in the room with her, panting for breath, red-faced and anxious.

Out in the hall, the Russians were still laughing. She allowed herself a brief sigh of relief.

While Hargreaves covered the doorway she approached the marked door on the right, tracing the now familiar pattern with the tip of her index finger. As before, the sigils began to crackle with power, fizzing and sparking with unnatural light.

She opened the door and stepped forward, right into the path of a hooded figure bearing a flame gun.

For a moment, the man simply stared at her, eyes wide with shock. He was lean and wiry beneath his robes, with a pale face and startling red beard. He frowned, and then blinked, and fumbled with his weapon. It was just like the one she'd encountered during the ambush, and she knew instantly if he managed to arm it, she'd be disintegrated by the strange, rippling flame.

She moved, her instincts taking over. With a sudden guttural roar, she dived at the man, lurching forward and catching him by the shoulders, throwing her whole weight into him, so that—caught off-balance—he went over backwards, crashing to the ground. She went down on top of him, slamming her elbow against the floor and feeling the muzzle of his weapon jab her hard beneath her ribs. The wind went out of her lungs, and she rolled, gasping for breath. She had no sense of where they were, or what might be happening around them. All she knew was that she had to stop the man from powering up his gun.

He was fumbling now, trying to untangle himself from beneath her, hands straying for the whorls and symbols on the barrel of the weapon. He mumbled something in Russian that sounded like a curse.

Suddenly, she was breathing again. She dragged the air into her lungs. She'd lost her wrench in the fall, and she could see it now, about three feet away across the other side of the room. She cast around, but there was nothing she could use as a weapon. Nothing but her fists.

The Russian had managed to get one of the whorls on his gun glowing, and was dragging himself away from her, using his heels to push himself across the carpeted floor while he traced his finger around a second set of symbols.

Regina wasn't about to let it end like this. With a gargantuan effort, she threw herself at the man, trying to grab him by the head. He squirmed, unwilling to release his grip on the weapon, as she caught hold of his beard in her left fist, while bringing the right around in a roundhouse blow that caught him hard in the left temple.

He groaned, trying to shake her off, jabbing the muzzle of the gun at her like a baton. She absorbed the blow to her gut, gripping harder, forcing his head down by yanking on his beard. She came at him with another blow, and then a third, hammering as hard as she could across the side of his head.

He rocked, groggily, and his hood slipped back, revealing a young man in his early twenties. His cheeks were scarred with crude circular patterns that echoed those on the doors and the barrel of his gun — the strange language of his order.

He was determined, though, still trying desperately to

activate his weapon, clutching it as if it were a sort of talisman; the only thing that might protect him against this terrible, relentless onslaught.

As she pulled back for another blow, his fingers slipped across the barrel, completing the orbit of the second whorl. Arcane light fizzed, and, emboldened, he swung out his elbow, catching her hard in the chest.

He rocked, trying to bring the gun around to bear, but she grabbed for the barrel, forcing it up and away from her, so that the muzzle was pointing to the ceiling. The Russian grunted as he fought against her, one hand on the trigger, the other on the top of the barrel, trying to force it back down. He met her gaze, his eyes filled with hatred and fury.

She knew then that he was never going to give in. Pure, unadulterated hatred was driving him, lending him strength. And her muscles were already starting to burn with the strain. Unless she could think of something, she had only moments left to live.

Behind her, through the still-open door, she could hear the barking report of gunshots being fired. Hargreaves wasn't coming to save her.

She fixed the man with a glare, gritting her teeth. And then, without warning, she stopped pushing.

The man, caught off guard by the sudden lack of resistance, rocked forward, dipping the muzzle of the gun. She saw his eyes widen in realization—the gun was pointing directly at her belly—and his finger began to tighten on the trigger.

The moment seemed to stretch. Regina knew she was playing a dangerous gambit. As the trigger slowly depressed, she threw all of her strength into pushing the gun back up again, away from her, and toward him.

This time, the man wasn't expecting it, and his arms were forced up and back with the sudden violence of her action, until the muzzle was pointing directly at his face.

He screamed, but it was too late.

Crackling, silvery flame burst from the end of the gun in a brilliant stream of twisting, liquid light, fizzing and popping with ethereal energy. All she could hear was the whoosh of the escaping energy, the burbling end of his scream, and the vague notion of whispering voices somewhere far off in the distance.

The stream caught the man directly beneath his chin, and as Regina held on desperately to the gun, she watched with horror as his face began to *dissolve* before her. His flesh seemed to wither and crumble, decaying before her eyes; first the skin and muscles of his cheeks bubbled away from the skull, billowing away like so much dust, and then his eyes, too, putrefied and sloughed away. Within seconds his jaw had utterly disintegrated, and then even the uppermost half of the skull began to cave in and collapse, until all that was left was a horrific, ragged stump of flesh and bone where his head had once been.

The body twitched, and the finger released the trigger. The stream from the gun ceased, and the room was plunged into an awful, deafening silence. Slowly, the remains of the man toppled backwards, thudding to the floor, dust spilling from the headless stump across the pale blue carpet.

Regina was still holding the gun. She wanted to scream, to somehow exorcise the horrific thing she had just witnessed—that she had just *done*—but her body was running on pure adrenaline now, her training taking over, and she lurched to her feet, finally taking in her surroundings.

She was standing in a small, rectangular room, in what appeared to be another house. There were no furnishings, aside from drapes at the window. A further, unmarked door led out into what she assumed would be a hallway.

Behind her, through the open portal, she could still hear shouting and the rapid report of gunshots. That meant Hargreaves was still alive.

She hefted the gun warily. It was like no weapon she'd ever seen. There was no fuel tank or ammunition housing; no moving parts at all, aside from the trigger. Just a long, fluted barrel engraved with swirling patterns and symbols, and a stubby handle, still slick with the sweat of the previous owner.

Cautiously, she ran the tip of her finger around the sigils, just as she had with the doors. As expected, the symbols sprang to vivid life, imbued with the same twisting, fizzing energy. She could feel the weapon humming in her grip, demanding to be fired.

She had two options: make a run for it and try to get word to Rutherford and Absalom, or step back through the portal to assist Hargreaves. Protocol demanded the former, but today, she was done with protocol. Besides, no one would believe her story if she didn't have Hargreaves to back her up.

Steeling herself, she hurried through the door.

The scene on the other side was utter carnage. Hargreaves was crouched behind the door in the small chamber, hurriedly attempting to reload his gun. Four hooded figures were slumped dead in the doorway, and as she ran for cover on the other side of the door, she glimpsed at least two more in the hallway outside, bleeding out onto the flagstones.

The air crackled with the discharge of the Russian's bizarre magic. Gouts of translucent flame, in the form of small, swooping birds, dived through the opening, splashing across the stone floor like puddles of burning oil.

She slammed her back against the wall. Hargreaves shot her a look.

"I guess they saw you, then," she said.

"Where have you *been*?"

"Busy," she said.

He slammed his pistol shut, now fully reloaded.

"So…?"

"So cover me," she said.

Hargreaves gave a brief nod, braced himself, and then ducked into the mouth of the opening, his gun spitting round after round into the gathered crowd of Russians. As he strafed across the opening, the elemental bombardment temporarily ceased, as the enemy either ducked for cover, or collapsed to the flagstones, clutching their wounds.

Regina saw her opportunity, and took it. She lurched out of Hargreaves's way, coming around behind him to stand fully in the opening, facing the surviving Russians. She didn't have time to count them—didn't want to know how many of them were still standing—as she squeezed the trigger of the flame gun, unleashing a cone of broiling death into their midst.

Her ears filled with the roar of chattering voices—not, she realized, from the dying Russians, but from someplace else; somewhere unseen, and unknowable.

The Russians caught in the blast began to wither and crumble, aged obscenely to dust, while those unaffected dived for cover, rolling behind the altar, or the font, or a wooden pew. She adjusted the angle of her attack, searching them out, wracked with nausea as she watched them crumble to nothing, caught in the searing light of their own diabolical weapon. She couldn't allow any of them to survive. Their bodies—or what remained of them—would be discovered soon enough, of course, but Regina hoped that would give her and Hargreaves time to get away, to spread word of what they were planning.

She sensed Hargreaves by her side.

"They're all dead now," he called. It took a moment for his words to register. "Regina? I said, they're *all dead*. You can stop now."

She released the trigger, allowing the stream of death to peter out to nothing.

Where there had once been a heap of bodies, there was now nothing but swirling dust, stirred by the air currents to spiral through the air, picked out in the light streaming in through the church windows. All that remained of eighteen men and women. She felt sick.

"Where did you get that thing?" said Hargreaves. He was leaning against the wall, breathing heavily. There was a burn across his left temple, and blood was trickling down his lower lip.

"Through there," she said, indicating the still-open portal with a nod of her head.

"Well, thanks for coming back for me." He was grinning, happy to be alive. She supposed she might feel the same, later, but for now, she didn't feel very much like celebrating. "We make a good team."

She nodded. "Come on. There's another house through there. Maybe we can find a way out."

On the other side of the door, the corpse of the young Russian was just where she'd left it, decayed skull spread like fine powder across the carpet where it had fallen.

She glanced quickly through the window, down at the street below. They were on the first floor of a large house, and the street outside looked vaguely familiar. "We're in London," she said. "Close to St. Paul's. We need to find a way out of here."

"You won't hear any argument from me," said Hargreaves. He crossed to the unmarked door, opened it a fraction—wincing as the hinges squealed—and peered out. "I think we're clear."

"Let's go. Straight onto the landing, down the stairs, and out the front door," she said. "Then we split up, in case they come after us. You go to Absalom, I'll find Rutherford."

Hargreaves frowned. "How are you going to do that?"

"Start with the American," she said.

"Alright." He opened the door a little wider, ready to step through.

"And if you see anyone," she said, "shoot them and keep moving. We have to get word out about what they're planning, and the location of this and any other buildings linked to their network."

Hargreaves nodded, and slipped out. Cautiously, she followed behind.

The landing was nondescript—just like the upper hallway of any number of high-end residential properties in London with a series of bedroom doors, all unmarked, stemming off from it. There was no one else in evidence.

They hurried to the top of the stairs. Here, too, it was mercifully quiet, and together they crept down to the entrance hall, Hargreaves covering the front, Regina the rear.

"Regina," said Hargreaves, just as he reached the bottom few steps. "Have you *seen* this?"

She turned on the spot, half expecting to see an array of

hooded figures awaiting them, but instead, she found herself utterly surrounded by doors.

She blinked, disorientated, trying to take it all in. It was almost as if her eyes were having difficulty focusing. They were standing in a large, open hallway, roughly square, of the relative size and shape she'd expect to find in a large terraced property in this area of London.

The walls, however, were covered in doors.

Doors where there should never have been any doors, regimented lines of them, covering every available inch of wall, defying all sense of geometry. Just looking at them left her feeling giddy. Even more bizarre was the fact that many of them also appeared to be freestanding; doorways into nothingness, hanging suspended in thin air. It was as if she could have wound her way between them all, circling them each in turn. There must have been fifty or more, each of them marked with the now-familiar sigils. Every single one of them was a portal.

All save for one: directly across the hall from them was the main entrance to the house, and beyond that, the relative safety of London.

"It's some kind of central hub," she said, hurrying down the last few stairs. "This must be the heart of their network."

"Can we destroy it?" said Hargreaves. "If we can disrupt their network, we might be able to prevent them from carrying out their plans. Maybe there's a way."

Regina shook her head. "Not alone. *Look* at this place. Think about the power needed to sustain it. And besides, we know they have designs on the Underground. We have to go for help."

"Okay, you're right," said Hargreaves. "Come on."

They crossed the hall, wary of any emergent threat from the doors. Thankfully, though, none was forthcoming.

Hargreaves turned the latch on the door, and suddenly they were standing outside in the fading afternoon light. Around them, London bustled as it always had—as if everything they'd seen, everything they'd done, was simply some bizarre dream from which they'd now woken. But Hargreaves still wore the scorch across his face, and Regina's ribs still ached from the battering she'd taken during the fight with the young Russian. It had all been terrifyingly real.

She tucked the flame gun into the back of her culottes—now filthy with grime and dust—and pulled the door shut behind them. "You'll go directly to Absalom, right? Tell him everything."

Hargreaves nodded. "Of course. I'll tell him to get word to the police, have them man all the Underground stations."

"Good."

"And you're still going after Rutherford and the American?"

"Yes. He needs to know what we've found. We can compare notes; try to figure out a plan to stop them. He's been working this case for months. He knows it better than any of us."

Hargreaves put a hand on her shoulder. "Just make sure you look after yourself," he said.

"And you."

She watched as he turned away and hurried off down the street. Then, deciding the Savoy was as good a place as any to make a start in her search for the American, she set off at a run, keen to put as much distance between herself and the Russians as possible.

FIFTEEN

Roland Harwood sat bolt upright on his bed, startled by the sudden thudding sound from below. The bed sheets were in disarray, the back of his head damp with perspiration.

He swallowed. His mouth was thick and dry, filled with the stale aftertaste of cheap wine.

There. The thudding sounded again, like someone trying to break out from the inside of his skull with a mallet. His thoughts stirred slowly, questions blooming. Was there something wrong? What was the noise all about? What had happened?

He wondered for a moment if there was something wrong with the avatar. Had it broken loose again? Was it banging on the window like it had the other night?

He swung his legs over the side of the bed and rubbed his cupped hands over his face. He felt dreadful. He'd drunk too much again, and passed out on his bed. What time was it? He glanced at the wall clock. It was approaching four in the afternoon.

He'd been asleep for hours. It hadn't been restful—he'd been plagued by the same recurrent nightmares again: images of searing lights describing whorls and geometric patterns in the air; an endless cycle of them, dancing through his dreams. No matter what he tried to banish them—booze, pills or rituals—they kept on coming back, haunting him, even in his waking hours. It was as if someone had etched them on the inside of his eyelids, as if they wouldn't leave him alone. The worst thing was, he had no real notion of what they meant.

Unsteadily, he got to his feet, stretching his weary limbs.

There it was again. The banging, even more insistent this time. He decided he'd better go and check. He was halfway down the stairs before he realized what it was: someone was banging on the door.

He reached the bottom step and stumbled into the porch, reaching for the door handle. Who could be visiting him now? He so rarely had visitors that he'd forgotten the last time someone called. It had probably been Newbury, bringing another little problem to his door. In fact, it was most likely Newbury now…

He opened the door and peered out blearily into the waning afternoon sunlight.

There were three people standing in the driveway, a woman and two men. He blinked at them warily. The woman was pretty—short, blonde and slim, with a heart-shaped face and full lips.

The man on the left was tall and dapper, despite the rather crumpled appearance of his suit. He wore a tie, although his top button had been loosened, and had a neat parting of short, sand-colored hair, falling in a loose comma across his forehead. The bulge of an underarm holster was visible in the line of his jacket.

The second man was a little shorter, with a square jaw and startling blue eyes. He had a muscular build with a broad chest, but looked as if he'd recently been in a brawl, due to a long scratch on his left cheek and a slight hint of bruising around the orbit of his right eye.

He didn't recognize any of them.

"Roland Horwood?" said the first man. He had an English accent of the sort that could only be achieved through years of boarding school education. Horwood let the moment stretch. The man coughed.

"Look, we're here to see a man named Roland Horwood," said the second man. This one was American, with an East Coast drawl. "Is he here?"

Horwood looked from one of them to the other. "Yes," he said. "I'm Horwood." He ran a hand through his hair. It was still damp. He hadn't had time to wash or change, and he was still wearing the clothes he'd slept in. He smoothed down the front of his shirt. "And you are?"

He could see the American man was beginning to grow impatient.

"Peter Rutherford, from the British Secret Service," said the first man, "and my colleagues, Mr. Gabriel Cross and Ms. Ginny Gray. An associate of yours, Sir Maurice Newbury, gave us your address. He thought you might be able to assist us with a rather pressing matter."

Horwood appraised the man with new eyes. *The Secret Service*. And visiting on Newbury's recommendation, no less. He supposed he'd better hear them out. He stood back, beckoning them in. "Well, Mr. Rutherford, you'd better come in, then."

He ushered them through to the living room, cringing at the state of the place. He'd have been more embarrassed if he hadn't felt quite so unwell. He supposed there was only one thing for it. "Drink?" he said, as the three of them looked for somewhere to sit. He hurried over to move a pile of books from an armchair so that the woman could sit down. She smiled graciously. He decided there was much to like about her.

"No, thank you," said Rutherford. The others echoed the sentiment.

"What, none of you? Well, no doubt it's terribly rude of me, but I'm going to have one anyway." He grabbed a half-empty bottle of red from the top of the bureau and sloshed it into a glass, which he found on the coffee table amongst some abandoned teacups and newspapers. He drank it down thirstily, willing it to do its work. Then, realizing that his guests had taken all of the available seats, he pulled out a small footstool from beneath one of the other chairs and perched on that, meaning he was sitting a full head and shoulders lower than the others. "So, Newbury sent you, did he?"

Rutherford looked at him slightly askew. "Yes. He said you were something of an expert in elemental magic."

Horwood couldn't help but beam at the compliment. "He did? That's very kind of him." He met Ginny's eye, and then looked away, embarrassed. "How can I be of assistance?"

Rutherford took a moment to fill him in on everything they'd learned so far about the Russians, their unusual powers, and their interest in the London Underground.

Horwood sat in silence throughout it all, listening intently. He didn't know if it was the wine, or the sudden realization that these people held the key to helping him understand what had been going on with the avatar—why it had seemed so restless of late, and who had attacked it the other night—but he was starting to feel a lot better.

"The Koscheis haven't been seen since the war," he said, drumming his fingers upon his knees. He was feeling agitated, excited. "But it was always believed that the order survived, slowly rebuilding. The rituals they perform, the power they harness—it's primal, raw, *fundamental*. It's not to be messed with."

"Oh, we have no intention of messing with it," said the American. "We just need your help to know how to stop it."

"To *stop* it…" Horwood leaned forward on his stool, elbows on his knees. It wasn't particularly comfortable. "There's very little you can do to stop it. There are wards I can show you, patterns you can mark on your skin to help disperse the elemental energy if it strikes you, but the only way to stop it is to fight fire with fire, so to speak. Or rather, fire with water."

"Sir Maurice explained a little of this," said Rutherford. "He said it was possible to fight back by harnessing the opposing elemental force."

Horwood nodded enthusiastically. "Yin and Yang. Fire and Water. Life and Death. Yes, that's correct. But it takes someone of great ability to wield such power. The Koscheis have trained for years, and these rituals are all but forgotten in the West. I can think of no single person with the capacity to do what you're suggesting. And there are what—five, six of them?"

"At the very least," said the American. "Probably more."

"Then I can see no means by which you can oppose them. Protect yourselves, yes, but go against them head to head? You're lucky to have survived the encounter."

"We were rather hoping you might volunteer your services," said Rutherford.

Horwood gave a nervous laugh, which he immediately regretted for fear of revealing his cowardice. "I'll help in any way I can, Mr. Rutherford, but please understand—whilst I've studied the esoteric arts, I'm no practitioner. As I explained,

I can help provide you with protective wards, to understand the nature of what you're up against, but I fear I'd be of little use to you in the field." In truth, he was both intrigued and appalled by the notion of facing living, breathing Koscheis. The order was legendary—if morally questionable—but to see them wield such power would be magnificent.

Still, there were other things he might do to help. Now that he had a fuller understanding of the threat facing London and the Empire, the reason for the avatar's return, he might work to guide it, to help it root out the festering corruption in their midst.

"Then what do you propose we do about these Koscheis?" said the American, interrupting his train of thought. It was an impertinent question—who was Horwood to tell the Secret Service how to go about their business? Nevertheless, he bit his tongue.

"Look to their plans. Find out what they're doing, and run interference. That's the most effective way to combat an enemy such as this. Their rituals depend on accuracy. Get in their way, prevent them from seeing through whatever it is they're plotting. Oh, and don't allow yourselves to be killed in the meantime."

"Can you think of anything else that might prove useful to us?" said Rutherford.

"There is one thing," said Horwood. "A legend from Anglo-Saxon times. A pagan tale of the days when the beings of the otherworld walked amongst men, and all cowered in their wake."

"Go on," said Rutherford.

"In the early days of the seventh century, long after the Romans had abandoned London, the Anglo-Saxons founded a new settlement, close to the walls of the ruined metropolis, in an area that now encompasses much of what we know as Central London. They called this new town Lundenwic, and it soon became the center of trade and commerce in the region. As such, it became a target, too, a prize sought by many who would claim its treasures as their own.

"So it was that an Anglo-Saxon *dry*, by the name of Aldwyn, raised an entity to defend the borders of Lundenwic against a Danish raid; an avatar of the ancient land, birthed from the soil of the town itself. This entity took the form of a great warrior, its living shell formed from twisted vines and branches, its spirit imbued by the will of the people it was sworn to protect—those of Lundenwic, who would see the Danes repelled." Horwood moistened his lips. He had their attention now; they were all hanging on his every word.

"It worked. The entity joined battle, fighting alongside the brave warriors of Lundenwic, and the Danes were unsuccessful, losing half their number before fleeing back to their boats. Aldwyn was heralded a hero. With the battle over, however, the entity returned to the soil: its shell withering, its spirit dispersing.

"And yet it is said that the entity lived on, and lives on still. It returned again and again during the years that followed, defending Lundenwic against persistent attempts by the Danes to breach its walls. Indeed, throughout all of London's history there are stories of its return; glimpses of the 'Albion' entity, which rises whenever it is needed to defend the people of Lundenwic, given form by the land itself, wild and elemental."

"And you believe this legend to be true?" asked the American. Surprisingly, there was not a hint of scorn in his tone.

"I…" Horwood paused, unsure how far to go. He didn't

know these people, after all, despite Newbury's apparent assurances. "It's hard to say. I don't completely discount the notion, as others might. But if this entity, this 'Albion', were to rise, surely it would be at a time like this, when the nation is threatened by enemies from afar?"

"I'd give my eye teeth for it to be true," said Rutherford. "We could use all the help we can get." He sighed. "Now, about those 'wards' you mentioned?"

Horwood got to his feet, feeling awkward and gangly. At least his headache had abated somewhat—although another glass of wine would probably help. He crossed to the writing bureau. "You'll have to give me a few minutes to copy them down," he said, taking out a sheaf of paper. "Any small error, and they lose their potency. As I explained, it's all about accuracy. Remember that when you make your own facsimiles later."

"Of course," said Ginny. "Take your time. We appreciate all of your help."

Horwood walked over to the bookcase, and began searching the cracked spines adorning the third shelf. He knew it was there somewhere...

After a moment he put a hand on the correct tome—the one he'd long ago annotated with drawings of counter runes and protections, filling the margins with scratchy illustrations gleaned from other precious manuscripts he'd been fortunate enough to examine. These books represented his life's work—the sum of his research into the esoteric—but now, he couldn't help but wonder if his greatest triumph was still to come. The avatar of Albion, the bestial thing growing in his garden—now he understood why it was here, why it had come to him. And soon he would set it free.

Horwood carried the book over to the coffee table, swiping

away a pile of old, well-thumbed story papers with his forearm. They crumpled in a heap to the floor, and when Ginny started forward to assist him, he raised a hand to protest. He'd deal with them later. They weren't important now.

He propped the book open on the table and spread the notepaper out before him, and then, having selected the correct symbols, began copying them down with a pencil. The others watched in silence as he carefully drew a triad of strange markings, before sitting back, holding the paper up to the light, and then finally nodding in satisfaction.

"There," he said. "Three protective wards. Copy them onto your chests and backs. These should help if you run into any more Koscheis. They won't save your life, but they will lessen the potency of the Koscheis' attacks. Just be careful they don't rub off." He handed the paper to Ginny, who folded it carefully away inside her jacket.

"Now, if you'll excuse me, I have rather a lot to attend to," said Horwood, getting to his feet. In truth, he was anxious for them to leave, now that he'd heard everything of use.

"If you think of anything else that might be of use to us," said Rutherford, "ask for Gabriel Cross at the Clarington Hotel. Tell them the 'Ghost' sent you." He handed Horwood a small white card, with a Central London address printed on it.

"Yes, yes, of course," he said, shaking Rutherford by the hand. "Anything at all, and I'll be in touch."

"Thank you for your help," said Ginny. She, too, took his hand for a brisk shake, before turning to leave.

"Until next time," said the American, with a desultory wave of his hand as he strolled out of the door. Horwood grimaced, but didn't reply.

He watched through the open door as they trudged down the gravel path toward the road, from where they'd most likely catch a cab back to the city. He hoped he'd done enough to at least keep them alive while they waited for Albion to rise.

He shut the door, turned back to the living room, and reached for the rest of the wine in the near-empty bottle.

After they'd gone, he sat for a while on the sofa, wondering if he'd done the right thing. How did he know he could trust these people? They'd come with Newbury's recommendation, of course, but even that wasn't really worth what it used to be. Newbury was old, now, and while he still kept his wits about him, he was no longer active in the field—at least not if it could be avoided. Could he really know enough about these Americans to be certain of their allegiance?

Then there was the matter of Albion, and the avatar growing in his garden. He'd reserved that information for himself, at least for now. Not even Newbury was aware of *that*. And Horwood wished to keep it that way. This way, he could control it; keep it safe. This way, no one would interfere.

He swilled the last of the wine around his mouth, and then prised himself up off the sofa with a groan. His limbs were aching, and he was dog-tired. The sudden vibrancy he'd felt earlier, while they'd been reciting their tale, had now diminished, and now he was overcome with lethargy once again, as if it were a kind of malady from which he had not been able to fully recover.

He arched his back, trying to stretch away the aches. It was time for a stroll in the garden. He walked around to the kitchen, and out through the back door into the side passage. The afternoon had grown cold, and pale sunlight slanted through the clouds in thin spears, like the fingers of gods bestowing gifts upon the faithful. Yet there was a sharp, biting wind coming in from the east, a reminder of ill omens, of the storm still to come. He knew, now, of the threat that awaited them. The Koscheis had inveigled their way into London, bringing with them a dark elemental magic from abroad. No wonder Albion had stirred, fresh shoots poking through the soil like questing fingers, searching for life.

He rounded the corner and entered the garden proper. Here, the lawn was like a crisp, emerald blanket, and the surrounding vegetation flourished with a rare vitality, encouraged, no doubt, by the presence of the avatar. He breathed in the scent of the wild plants he'd allowed to take hold here, rich with heady pollen.

He crossed the lawn, ducking beneath an overgrown stone archway and down the short flight of steps to the lower level at the rear of the garden. Here, an oval-shaped bed of wild flowers had taken root, blooming in starbursts of color—roses, violets, poppies and chrysanthemums—all irrespective of the season and the weather. These plants were imbued with something more than natural, something ancient and primal. It had long been said that the rise of Albion heralded a period of rebirth and renewal; for Horwood, it symbolized hope, too—survival against the odds. Whatever the Koscheis had brought to their shores, Albion would rise to the challenge to defend them.

The avatar was resting in its hollow, having returned to its natural, vegetative state. Its arms had intertwined with the branches of the trees around it, and it had extruded roots, burrowing into the soft loam in search of vital nutrients. Its consciousness lay dormant, awaiting the call to wake. It had almost healed, now—its broken limbs reformed, the holes in its chest knitted shut. Its head lolled gently to one side, inanimate, at rest. It looked peaceful, like a child. Could he really wake it again so soon?

He supposed he had little choice. The Koscheis were here, and there were none but Albion who could defeat them. It had to rise once more, to defend the people of London. Without Albion, the Koscheis would surely claim dominion over the city, and from there, the entirety of the United Kingdom.

Horwood stepped into the hollow, standing in the shadow of the great avatar. It was seven feet tall—taller, if its thorny antlers were taken into consideration. Its face resembled an approximation of a human being, yet androgynous, with a soft, elfin-like quality. Thorns and thickets, fungus and shoots sprouted from the back of its head, tumbling down its back like a mane. Its limbs were like branches; bundles of sinewy willow shoots plated in ancient bark. Deep inside its chest, its heart, visible amongst the tangle of brambles that served as its ribcage, was a single red rose, its petals furled into a tight, inanimate bud. This was what Horwood had come for. It was time to kick -start the creature's heart.

He leaned closer, nostrils filled with the rich, heady scents of damp earth and fresh leaves. He peered between the brambles. With any luck, he should be able to reach inside.

He sought out an appropriate thorn—one that was jutting from the avatar's elbow—and steeling himself, jabbed his right index finger against it, hissing at the sharp pain. He glanced at the tip of his finger, to see bright blood welling at the wound.

He shifted his weight nervously from one foot to the other. He'd never done this before — the first and only time the avatar had awoken, it had been unexpected, spontaneous. This time, he was forcing it from its healing slumber.

Carefully, he wormed his hand between the brambles, pushing his hand deeper into the avatar's chest cavity, until his hand hovered above the rose. Then, wincing as more thorns bit into his wrist with every movement, he rotated his hand so that his pricked finger was poised above the bloom. He used his thumb and middle finger to squeeze the tip of his index finger, coaxing droplets of blood from the small wound. It beaded to the surface, glossy and bright. He watched the beads gather, form one larger droplet, that, carried by its own weight, rolled slowly down the side of his finger, before dripping onto the uppermost petals of the rose.

Swiftly, Horwood withdrew his arm and stepped back, waiting to see what would happen. For a moment, it seemed as if nothing would occur — as if he'd done something wrong — but then the rosebud began to slowly unfurl, petals easing themselves apart as he watched. Like an opening fist, the rose expanded, and then, just before it reached its full extent, it went into reverse, folding back on itself, petals curling in until they had once again formed a tight bud.

Horwood smiled. He'd done it right, after all. As he watched, the petals unfurled once more, before retracting again. It repeated this process a number of times, gathering speed as it went, until it was opening and closing at a steady, regular rhythm, just like a beating heart.

Horwood backed away slowly until he was outside of the hollow, looking in. The avatar had begun to stir, turning its head, snapping the roots that bound it, untwining itself from the supporting branches. Its eyes had begun to glow with a deep red light, like embedded rubies, glinting in the gloaming.

And then suddenly the avatar was free, and Albion once again walked before him. It stooped to retrieve its blade: an enormous, two-handed sword inscribed with indecipherable symbols, that Horwood had spent years tracing, his research finally leading him to a sealed well shaft into which it had been cast in the Middle Ages—the last recorded time that Albion had walked the land.

It stalked forward, and the trees around the edges of its hollow parted in a wave, leaves shimmering as the branches folded back to enable the avatar to pass. It stood for a moment in the brisk evening night, resplendent, a demigod raised from the ashes of history, and then it turned to look directly at Horwood, and he knew that something was terribly wrong.

The creature's eyes no longer glowed with hope, but with cold, bleak menace. Spots of mold had begun to form upon its arms, and chest, and face, and its expression was dark and malign. It opened its mouth, and out spewed a stream of crackling black energy, like pooling oil that formed around its feet; an absence of light, the essence of midnight.

Around them, the flowers began to wither and die, wilting on their stems and desiccating, as if the avatar were somehow drawing all of the life from the surrounding flora.

It waved its arm in Horwood's direction, and curling vines shot from the soil, swimming up around his legs, gripping hold of him with a ferocity that caused him to whimper in pain.

What had he done? What had he unleashed? Surely it shouldn't be like this? Something had corrupted it. It had to be the Koscheis, the ones who had engaged in battle with it the other night. They'd poisoned it, somehow, infecting it with their malignancy.

"No," he called. "I can put this right."

But it was too late. The avatar was already striding off into the night, leaving an accursed trail of black in its wake—and Horwood, pinned to the ground by squirming vines, could do nothing at all to prevent it.

SIXTEEN

"Oh, thank God you're back."

Flora's expression was ashen, and Gabriel could tell immediately that something was very wrong.

He, Ginny and Rutherford had arrived back at the hotel just a few moments earlier, taking the elevator to their floor— only to discover Flora pacing the corridor outside their room, flustered, disheveled and distraught. Her mascara had run with her tears, streaking her cheeks with black tributaries, markers of her anxiety and frustration. The hem of her dress, along with both of her knees, was thick with what looked like silt or sludge.

"What is it?" said Ginny, rushing to her side. "What's happened?"

Flora fixed her with an alarmed stare. She was trembling, and Gabriel realized she must have been suffering from shock. "It's Felix," she said, her voice cracking with barely contained emotion. "They *took* him."

"What? Who took him?" pressed Ginny.

"Those Russians," said Flora. "The ones you were talking about, with the robes."

Gabriel and Rutherford exchanged glances.

"Where?"

Flora chewed her lip. "The tunnels."

"The *tunnels*?" said Gabriel. "You mean the Underground?" Flora didn't answer, but he could see from her expression that she did.

"Alright," said Ginny. "Let's get you inside, and you can tell us everything. Don't worry. We'll get him back. I promise you." She fished the key from her pocket and unlocked the door, ushering Flora inside.

Rutherford put a hand on Gabriel's shoulder, holding him back for a moment. He waited until the door had swung shut before he spoke. "Look, I'm sorry to say this, Gabriel, but if the Koscheis have got him..." He trailed off, silently making his point.

"No," said Gabriel. "I refuse to believe that. We're going to find out exactly what's gone on, and then we're going after him. And God help any of those damn cultists if they've laid a finger on him."

Rutherford nodded, but it was clear he remained unconvinced.

Inside Gabriel and Ginny's suite, Ginny was administering a large brandy to Flora, who was perched on the edge of one of the armchairs, hugging herself. She looked up as Gabriel entered the room. "It was my fault," she said. "If I hadn't encouraged him..."

"You and I both know that Felix doesn't need any encouragement," he said. "He does what he believes is right, and damn the consequences—that's what makes him the man he is." Flora gave the briefest of smiles. "Now tell us *everything*."

Slowly, she outlined everything that had happened that morning—how Donovan had led them to the abandoned City Road Underground station and forced their way in, how she'd insisted on going along with him down into those hellish tunnels, the strange growths they'd discovered, and how the Koscheis had come for them, folding out of the darkness through their glowing wheels of light.

"He told me to run," she said. "To get to safety. He said he'd be right behind me, that he'd meet me back here. But he hasn't come back. There's been no word. No calls. Nothing. So I waited here for you."

"How did you get away?" said Rutherford.

"Felix still had that gun you'd given him, and I saw him shoot one of them in the chest. He drew their attention as I ran. He covered my escape, put himself in harm's way so I could get away. I didn't stop running until I was all the way back here. I didn't look back. I thought he was right behind me..." She'd curled her fists into balls on her lap. "I should have stayed with him. I should have helped him *fight*."

"You did the right thing," said Ginny. "He'd want you to be safe. There was nothing you could have done against those men."

Flora looked her straight in the eye. "Do you think he's dead?"

"No," said Gabriel. He crossed to the wardrobe, flung open the doors and dragged out a battered leather case from inside. He carried it over to the bed, popped the latches, and threw the lid back. Inside was a black leather trench coat, a hat, a pair of red goggles, twin rocket canisters, and his flechette gun.

He sensed Ginny at his side. "I thought you left those in New York!"

Gabriel shrugged. "He's a part of my life, Ginny. Wherever I go, he goes too."

She put her hand on his arm. "Well, I suspect we're all

pleased about that." She looked over at Flora and Rutherford. "So, what's the plan? I presume we're going after him."

"Damn right," said Gabriel. "Peter—I'll understand if you can't. You've got plenty to worry about already. But I'm not leaving my friend down there alone."

"Oh, I'm coming with you," said Rutherford. "Don't you worry about that."

"Flora?" said Ginny. "Are you up to showing us where it happened?"

Flora stood, wiping her eyes on her sleeve. "I'll damn well show you, alright. And I want a gun, too. I'm going to put a bullet in some of those bastards if it's the last thing I do."

Gabriel nodded, impressed by the steely tone and the bravery of the woman. She wasn't a fighter, and she hadn't chosen this life—but she was determined to get her husband back, whatever the cost. Gabriel could understand that. He'd felt the same way about Ginny, after what happened in Egypt. He understood that ire, that burning need for revenge, the need to cling on to the people you love and do anything in your power to keep them safe. "Ginny—those wards that Horwood gave you—do you think you could copy them?"

"Yes, I think so."

He reached for his hat. "Alright. Ten minutes. Be ready."

The door to the Underground station was still hanging open, just as Flora had left it. Everything seemed still and silent within; a deep, empty chasm, a wound in the heart of the city. The air emanating from inside smelled foetid and stale, causing the Ghost to hack and splutter as he stood in the doorway.

There was something wretched about this place. He could feel it, standing there on the threshold. Something that caused his hackles to rise; something that wanted to repel him. Perhaps that was why he'd seen no sign of birds or rodents as he'd scanned the ticket hall. Instinctively, they wanted nothing to do with the place.

Behind him, Rutherford turned on his flashlight, sweeping beams into the darkness beyond. To the Ghost, wearing his night-vision goggles, they were like a weapon, cutting through the abyssal canvas to bleed light and color into the world.

He turned and gave Rutherford the signal. The Ghost was to go ahead, sneaking alone into the tunnels below, scouting ahead with his night vision while the others followed behind at a reasonable distance. That way, the Ghost would be able to alert them to any impending danger, or perhaps even deal with it himself. Assuming, that was, that he didn't become embroiled in an ambush himself.

He waded forward into the inky black, his trench coat billowing out around him as he walked. It felt good to feel the heft of his flechette gun down the length of his forearm once again, to know that the cord for his rocket thrusters was just inside his jacket. More, though, it felt *right*. For the first time since he'd arrived in London, he felt like himself again. Although he'd taken steps in recent months to reconcile the two, distinct aspects of his personality—the hardened combatant of the Ghost with the carefully constructed playboy image of "Gabriel Cross"—it was true that he never felt more himself than when he was wearing his costume, taking control of his own life and destiny, making a *difference*. And now, here he was on the other side of the Atlantic, delving into the velvet darkness of a long abandoned train station in search of his dearest friend and the men who had taken him. Rarely had he felt more alive.

He crossed the ticket hall to the top of the stairs. Here, the darkness seemed to solidify, becoming ever more portentous. What was he going to find down here? The stench presumably originated with the strange growths on the tunnel walls that Flora had described. As yet, he'd seen no sign of them up here. But what about Donovan? Would he still be alive? He'd felt so certain earlier, back at the hotel, but realized now that it was all bluster, words of denial. He'd insisted Donovan would be alive because he *wanted* him to be.

He took the steps two at a time, silent, save for the gentle tap of his boots. Above, he saw the beam of Rutherford's flashlight stabbing through the darkness as the others followed behind, and it reminded him of New York, and the view of the police blimps, searchlights rolling across the rooftops like a series of miniature dawns.

He reached the platform and turned left, following the path described to him by Flora. There was another reason he'd volunteered to go ahead of the others—there was every chance Donovan was being held as a lure. It had occurred to him that the Koscheis might have anticipated they'd come looking for their colleague, and were lying in wait a little further into the complex, ready to spring a trap. Flora had exhibited impressive resourcefulness in getting away from them, but he couldn't help wondering if, in part, the Koscheis had *allowed* her to go, to get word out to him, Rutherford and the others, to bring them down here into the tunnel network before they were truly ready. If so, the Ghost wanted to be first on the scene. If they came for *him*, they wouldn't be expecting Rutherford and the others hitting them as a second wave.

He leapt down from the platform edge, landing amongst the rails with a loud *clang*. He waited until the reverberations had ceased before he moved on.

Slowly, he entered the tunnel mouth. Even through the filter of his goggles he could see the iridescent colors of the mulch covering the tunnel walls and ceiling. It was almost as if he could see it breathing, as it oozed across the concrete and tiles like a living, thinking entity. It was deeply unnatural, and his every instinct told him to turn back, now, to get the others out of there as quickly as he could. It was as if the mulch was asserting some sort of malign influence, urging him back, leaving him feeling despondent, uncertain.

Instead, though, he forced himself to go on, edging ever further into the grimy tunnel. What had Donovan thought he was doing, coming down here without backup? He was lucky Flora was as resourceful as she was, otherwise they wouldn't even know he'd been taken. The Ghost supposed he could understand Donovan's impatience; as he'd said to the others back at the apartment, he was a man who always insisted on doing what he felt was right, and that morning, he'd been worried about the trail going cold, about losing sight of their prey.

There were just too many moving pieces, and none of it was quite making sense yet. It was clear the Koscheis were working to somehow undermine things in London—but what wasn't yet clear was *how*, and whether they really did have help inside Rutherford's organization. And what did the Underground have to do with it?

Even if Horwood was right—that the Koscheis were simply

using their powers to create disruption, to further undermine the position of the Queen and her government—that didn't explain the strange growths on the tunnel walls. He was certain the Koscheis were behind it, but to what purpose he had yet to fathom.

Up ahead, the tunnel swung to the right in a sweeping curve. Here, the walls were completely covered in the dripping mulch, and it had begun to grow over the disused tracks, too. He tried to avoid stepping in it as he wound his way deeper underground.

As he entered the straight on the other side of the bend, he noticed a series of large, bulbous growths attached to the left -hand wall, a little further down along the tunnel. They looked like nothing so much as giant chrysalises, webbed against the wall by strands of glistening mulch. The stench here was worse than ever, threatening to overpower him, and he reached for a handkerchief, tying it around his mouth and nose to offer at least a modicum of respite.

There were no lights in the tunnel, and no sign of any Koscheis. He decided to take a closer look at the chrysalises. He crept down the tunnel, sweeping the barrel of his flechette gun back and forth, half expecting glowing lights to form in the air at any moment.

He approached the first chrysalis. It was man-sized, at least as tall as the Ghost himself, and formed from the same weird vegetation as the growths on the walls. In fact, it seemed to the Ghost as if the mulch had simply shifted to accommodate something already on the wall, slithering over some obstruction, obliterating it entirely as it went.

He moved on. The second chrysalis was of similar size, but

here, it became immediately apparent what the contents of the bulbous shell had originally been: a human woman. The Ghost fell back, grimacing at the grisly sight. He felt his stomach lurch.

What remained of the woman had been almost completely consumed by the mulch. Her head was jutting from the sticky membrane, half decayed, so that the flesh of the left side of her face had melded with the mulch. Even the bone beneath had become nothing but food for the vile substance, warping and twisting out of shape as it was slowly eroded. The right side of her face was largely unblemished, which, to the Ghost's eye, made for an even more horrific sight. The skin was white and smooth, the eye open—although now glazed with a milky sheen—and the mouth open in a silent scream. Stark red hair erupted from what was left of her scalp.

He stepped back, looking the corpse up and down. The mulch had covered much of her body, now, with just her left hand still erupting through the glutinous layers, fingers clutching uselessly at the air.

Is this what had become of Donovan? The thought turned his stomach, and he hurried over to the third chrysalis. It contained the body of a man—thankfully not Donovan. The victim had been short, and fair-haired, with a full beard. Much of him was still intact, save for his stomach, which had burst open as the mulch had invaded, spilling its contents down the tunnel wall, where it had pooled on the floor in a festering puddle. Even now, the mulch was feeding on it, creeping down the wall to lap at the edges of the foul liquid.

He wondered what these people were doing here. He supposed the abandoned tunnel was as good a place as any for the Russians to dispose of the evidence of their operations;

until recently they'd been keeping their presence in London low key, and whatever the disgusting mulch was, it was doing an admirable job of consuming the corpses. Presumably, the victims were all people who'd somehow got in their way, or discovered too much information for their own good.

The Ghost hacked, clearing his throat, unable to maintain his silence any longer.

"Gabriel?" The voice from behind him was weak, but familiar. He twisted on the spot, turning toward the opposing tunnel wall.

There, wrapped in a glistening web of mulch, was Donovan. He'd been pinned to the wall, spread-eagled, and despite the fact he seemed to have worked his left arm partially free, the mulch had already begun to slither over him, almost completely covering his right leg, and swallowing his foot up to the ankle on the left. It was climbing up the side of his neck, too, threatening to engulf his face. He was straining, trying to turn his head away from it.

"Felix!" He hurried over, trying to ascertain the best way to break the other man free.

"You took your damn time," mumbled Donovan. He sounded relieved, if weary.

"You can thank me later. Are you hurt?"

"No. But I'm dying for a cigarette."

The Ghost grinned. "Hold on and I'll get you out of there."

"Gabriel?"

"Yes?"

"About Flora... she was okay? She got away?"

"You did good, Felix. She got away, and came straight to find us. She's fine. Scared, but fine. She's been worried about you."

Donovan heaved a sigh of relief. "She's not the only one," he said. "Have you seen what this stuff can do to a person?"

"Yes. Now hold still. I'm going to try to cut you down." The Ghost unsheathed a blade from a leather sheath attached to his belt.

"I knew it," said Donovan. "I knew you wouldn't be able to resist bringing all of that with you."

"All of what?" said the Ghost, with mock innocence. He raised the blade, trying to work out where to start cutting. Perhaps he'd do well to finish working Donovan's left arm free first of all, so that Donovan could help to free himself more swiftly, too.

There was a crackle from behind him, just a short way along the tunnel. He knew immediately what it meant—exactly what he'd feared. The Koscheis had been expecting him.

"Gabriel…" Donovan said, his voice low.

The Ghost gave a minute incline of his head, to indicate that he understood what was happening. He shifted his weight to his left foot, placed the tip of the blade against the wall beneath Donovan's left arm, and hung there for a moment, waiting.

Another crackle. The Ghost turned, pivoting on his left foot and flicking his wrist in the direction of the crackling sound.

The knife shot through the air like a loosed missile, striking one of the emerging Koscheis in the chest, directly below the cup of his throat. It buried itself to the hilt, and the man fell forwards and sideways, his fingers dragging a trail of light behind them from where he'd been engaged in casting another symbol. He gurgled, blood bubbling from his lips.

The Ghost yanked the cord inside his jacket, igniting the rocket packs strapped to his calves. With a roar that seemed to echo the entire length of the tunnel, he shot up, riding twin plumes of light, pressing his hands against the tunnel ceiling.

There were five Koscheis below, and a sixth still emerging from a portal, not counting the dead one already crumpled on the steel tracks at their feet.

The Ghost rolled beneath the arch of the tunnel roof as a bolt of electrical light burst from below, striking the brickwork only inches from his head. Where it struck, the mulch seemed to boil and burst, retreating from the site of the impact like an animal skittering away from danger.

He didn't have time to consider it now, though, as he dived, spinning through the air toward another of the Koscheis, who frantically began to spin wheels of light before him in the air, raising what the Ghost took to be defensive shields or barriers. He twisted right at the last moment, turning his dive into a fly-by, skimming the top of one of the fizzing shields and unleashing a hail of flechettes. They thudded into the back and shoulders of the Koschei, causing him to arch his back in spasmodic pain, before dropping to his knees and pitching forward into the tracks.

Two down, four to go.

He shot upwards, throwing his hands out and using the tunnel mouth to pivot and change direction, his gloved fingers pulling away clumps of the foul-smelling vegetation.

He fell into another dive, as the remaining four Koscheis formed a circle, back to back, attempting to cover themselves from all angles. He showered them with a further blast of flechettes, but this time, the tiny silver blades rebounded from their shields, as they swung their arms, directing the motion of the swirling wheels of light to protect themselves.

Too late, he realized he wasn't going to have time to pull up, so he rolled to the right, colliding with one of the runic shields. It might as well have been a wall, as he rebounded painfully, his crossed forearms protecting his face as he went into a spiral, wheeling around unsteadily, the jets at his ankles scorching the top of a Koschei's head and causing him to howl in pain.

He fought for balance as he thundered along the tunnel, first striking the left wall, then the right, and finally steadying himself against the ceiling, before launching himself back into the fray.

This time they were ready for him, and lightning crackled as they flung their brutal elemental magic like javelins, attempting to spear him as he harried them from above. He twisted and ducked, easily avoiding their attacks and returning fire with his flechette gun—until he realized their attacks had been nothing but a distraction, an attempt to keep him busy while one of their number completed a more complex ritual.

Without warning, the air around him grew suddenly thin. He twisted, trying to break through whatever atmospheric pocket they'd created around him, but it was no use—the spike of flame from his rocket boosters was beginning to peter out and die. They'd snuffed the air supply to his canisters, causing the flames to sputter out.

The Ghost's flight stuttered in mid-air, before he dropped like a lead weight toward the ground, slamming down, hard, against the rails below. He howled as one of the rails bashed against his shin. He shook his head, sucking air down into his lungs before rolling onto his back and unleashing a hail of flechettes at the oncoming Koscheis.

They deflected them easily, battering them away with their

airborne shields of light.

One of them said something in Russian—a short, barked command—and the others responded immediately, summoning balls of sparking blue energy into their palms. They hurled them like grenades, which exploded over the Ghost's torso, rippling like waves of electrical current, causing his body to twitch and shudder as he writhed in pain. He could feel the wards that Ginny had drawn on his back and shoulders begin to absorb the energy as it coursed over him, glowing hot and painful. Keeping him alive.

He gritted his teeth as he waited for the energy to burn itself out. He could see the Koscheis were peering down at him in confusion. Clearly, they expected him to be dead.

One of them—the one the Ghost had taken to be their leader—raised his hands, both of them working in time to describe a new, complex symbol in the air before him. He was grinning, his hooded face under-lit by the spectral light of his spell. Clearly, he intended to fell the killing blow.

The Ghost could hear Donovan calling to him, but the words were lost beneath the ringing in his ears and the crackle of the charging light, hovering in the air above him.

And then the Koschei was toppling forward, a wet red hole in the middle of his forehead, blood and bone fragments dribbling down his face. One knee buckled, and the corpse went down awkwardly, falling heavily across the Ghost's lower legs.

The other three Koscheis turned, glancing down the tunnel to where Rutherford stood, weapon still trained on them. His gun spat, and the Koscheis flung their shields forward, deflecting the bullets so that they careened wildly around the tunnel, thudding into the sludge-covered walls.

Still on his back, chest burning with every breath, the Ghost raised his right arm and sent a stream of flechettes into the lower back of one of the Koscheis, shredding his internal organs. He dropped to his knees, fingers tracing the outline of a portal as he fell, so that his corpse tumbled forward into nothingness, enveloped by the shimmering light as he went.

The Ghost kicked his legs free from beneath the other body and scrambled to his feet. A quick glance told him that Flora was hurriedly shredding the mulch that still pinned Donovan to the wall, tearing it off in great gobbets to get him free.

Rutherford was hurriedly reloading his gun, and Ginny was nowhere to be seen. Surely she hadn't hung back from the conflict?

The answer came in the form of a swirling wind, blowing through the tunnel, whipping up the lapels of his long coat. "Oh, no," he mumbled.

He backed away, edging down the tunnel, away from the remaining two Koscheis, who were wordlessly summoning further shields of swirling light. He wondered if they knew they were already doomed.

A new source of light appeared at the other end of the tunnel, beyond Rutherford. At first it seemed small, but it grew in size and presence as it drifted closer, resolving into the form of Ginny, hanging in the air above the tracks, her arms outstretched by her sides, her legs together, feet pointed toward the ground. She was surrounded by a halo of soft yellow light, and her eyes were ablaze with a cold white glow. Ethereal wind whipped around her, stirring her clothes and whipping her hair back from her face. She looked utterly captivating, imbued with unearthly power.

The Ghost realized he was holding his breath; he let it out, utterly in awe of this woman.

She rotated her wrists, and beneath her cupped hands swirling clouds began to gather, slowly coalescing into the form of two enormous, spectral lions.

One of the Koscheis began hurling handfuls of sparking electrical energy at her, but they burst ineffectively off her torso, fizzing to nothing, like droplets of water boiled away in a hot pan. She drew closer, and then stopped about fifty yards from the Koscheis.

"Your souls are forfeit," she said, her voice underscored by a cavernous echo. "Sekhmet hungers." She closed her fists, and the ghostly lions surged forward, unleashed for the hunt. They thundered down the tunnel toward the Koscheis, who were given no time to react.

The lions leapt into the air, synchronized in their attacks. They fell upon the Koscheis, utterly ignoring their shields, roaring as they burst through the men's chests, before dissipating into clouds of smoke that simply whorled away on the same ethereal wind that had formed them.

There was no blood, no wounds—no outward sign that the two Russians had been harmed in any way—but nevertheless, their legs buckled and they tumbled lifelessly to the ground, their hearts stopped, their souls devoured.

The Ghost ran forward, his chest burning, the wards on his back still aglow with the sharp heat of the energy they'd absorbed. Above him, Ginny hovered in the air, imperious. "It's over, Ginny," he said.

She looked down at him, and for a moment he saw

nothing behind her strange, glowing eyes—no flicker of acknowledgement or recognition. But then she threw her head back, and breathed in, and the howling wind around them ceased. Slowly, she lowered herself to the ground, and collapsed into the Ghost's arms, utterly spent.

The Ghost brushed her hair from her eyes. "Thank you," he said. It didn't seem enough.

Ginny smiled up at him. "It was nothing," she said, laughing. Her eyes widened. "What about Felix?"

"Oh, it takes a lot more than a light show to impress me," said Donovan. He had one arm around Flora's shoulders, as she helped him along.

Ginny beamed. "It's good to see you, Felix."

"Right—it's time we were getting out of here," said Rutherford. "There'll be more of them coming. I can guarantee it. Once they find that body…"

The Ghost cursed. He should never have allowed the dying Koschei to summon a portal and escape. There was no way he could have survived, but his body would be enough to allow the others to discern what had happened.

"What about all this?" said Flora, indicating the mulch.

"We'll have to deal with it later," said Gabriel. "We need to get back to the hotel, to regroup and deal with our injuries." Not for the first time, he wished he understood how the Koscheis could warp space around them to create portals. A shortcut to his hotel room would be most welcome about now.

"Agreed," said Rutherford. "Come on, this way."

They set off down the tunnel, back in the direction from which they'd come.

With every step the Ghost expected to hear the crackle of

opening portals, to find themselves overwhelmed by a small army of Koscheis, but as they drew closer to the platform at City Road, he allowed himself to feel a faint sliver of relief. Donovan was still alive, they'd defeated the Koscheis in another encounter, and Horwood's protective wards had proved effective, despite the fact his back and shoulders still felt as if they were on fire. It was hardly the breakthrough they'd been looking for, but it was something.

The Ghost boosted himself up onto the platform—his rocket canisters now restored—and then helped the others up one at a time, heaving them up off the tracks. The mulch had made inroads here, even during the short duration they'd been in the tunnel. It was seeping from the tunnel mouth, edging onto the platform, a relentless wave that was slowly washing out from the tunnel in both directions. Left unhindered, it would soon spread deeper into the Underground network.

He found he was growing used to the stench now, able to breathe normally—but it was clear that whatever the Russians were doing down here, it involved some sort of disease or corruption. That much was evident from the extent of the mulch and the manner in which it had consumed those other corpses. Although the Ghost didn't like to consider the fact that those people had probably been alive when the mulch began to do its work.

He guessed the Koscheis must have been cultivating it in the abandoned station, with the intent of spreading it through the rest of the London Underground system, disseminating it amongst the population. To what end—other than a series of slow and painful deaths—he had no idea.

They mounted the steps to the ticket hall, slowed by

Donovan and Ginny, both in desperate need of time to recover from their ordeals. They'd have time back at the hotel, where he, too, could tend his bruises. And fix himself a stiff drink. It was turning into quite some vacation.

They emerged into the London night a few moments later, the cool breeze a welcome restorative. Nearby, cars hissed by on damp asphalt, and people streamed along the street, chattering and laughing, enjoying the cool city night.

"I'll find us a cab," said Rutherford. He glanced at the Ghost. "You'd better make your own way."

The Ghost nodded. The last thing he needed was people talking about sightings of a New York vigilante in London, just when Gabriel Cross was on vacation in town. He'd take to the rooftops; find a less direct way back to the hotel.

He watched the others limp toward the sidewalk.

Around him, the trees creaked in the breeze. A crow cawed. He reached inside his coat, feeling for the ignition cord for his boosters, but something—some instinct, some unrecognizable sound captured by his unconscious mind—caused him to turn.

There, looming over him, was a creature that looked as if it had stepped out of a children's fairy tale. It was a man—or at least, it had the basic shape and form of a man—about eight feet tall, with massive antlers erupting from the top of its head. Its eyes burned a deep and violent ruby red, and its body was formed from sinewy branches, plated with thick, ragged bark. Vicious-looking thorns jutted from its forearms, and it was carrying a double-handed sword in its right fist. A murder of crows rested upon its head and shoulders, hopping excitedly between its antlers. Shadows seemed to swirl around its feet, withering the grass and fallen leaves.

"Ah, I guess hello is in order?" said the Ghost.

The creature made a sound like distant thunder; a deep, bass rumble. It raised its right hand, the tip of its sword hovering over the Ghost's chest.

"Or perhaps not."

"Gabriel!" He heard Ginny call from behind him, but he didn't dare avert his view from the creature.

"Rutherford—stick to the plan. Get them to safety. Now!"

"No!"

"Ginny—go!" He peered up at the creature's face. Its expression was near unreadable, but it was clear it didn't have his best interests in mind.

His hand was still inside his coat, his fingers brushing the ignition cord. Slowly, almost imperceptibly, he closed them around it. And then he yanked it down, hard, and he was shooting up in the sky as the creature, frustrated, lurched forward, moving with a speed belied by its size and form, attempting to spear him through the chest with its sword.

The Ghost twisted, diving low over its shoulder, the flames from his boosters brushing the bark and searing the leaves that ran in a tumbling wave over its back. It screeched—a harrowing sound, like rending wood—twisting around and sending the crows squawking into the air. Terrified, they swarmed in front of the Ghost, blinding him with a fluttering mass of beaks and leaves, and sending him careening off path, ducking out of the way of the sudden obstruction.

The creature, seizing its opportunity, grabbed for him with its free hand, catching hold of one of his legs and swinging him around like a doll, before slamming him down onto the concrete. He groaned, spitting blood, as the creature released him, pulling back its hand, palm blackened and smoking from the flame of his boosters. He slid across the ground, still propelled by his boosters, uncoordinated and flailing. He crashed into the rear wall of the Underground station, jarring his shoulder, and then hauled himself up, clutching at the brickwork for purchase.

He righted himself and shot up, just as the creature's sword clanged off the wall where he'd been standing, scoring a clean line through bricks. The Ghost gawped at the deep scar in the wall with horror.

What *was* this thing? Another creature manifested by the Koscheis? Is that why they hadn't sent reinforcements— because this thing was already waiting for them outside the station? Or was it the Albion entity that Horwood had spoken of? If so, it was hardly helping to protect them.

He twisted through the air, risking a glance after the others. They were nowhere in sight. Rutherford had done as directed, getting them as far away from the creature as possible.

He turned, hovering for a moment, while he trained his flechette gun at the creature's head. Then, falling into a dive, he let rip, tiny blades thudding into its face, burying themselves in the thick bark. The creature waved its left arm before it, as if irritated by an insect, forcing him to twist away.

It thrashed out again, this time catching him with the back of its hand, sending him careening toward the road on the other side of the station building. A red omnibus was trundling down the road, full of passengers. He was heading directly for it.

The Ghost threw his weight to the left, roaring with the effort, as he forced his legs around, altering his trajectory. He soared over the top of the omnibus on his back, only inches from colliding with it, spinning up into the night sky on a glowing plume.

The creature was still in the grounds of the old station building, searching the skyline for him. There was no way he was going to beat it alone. His only hope was to get away, to reconvene with the others and formulate a plan. But first he had to lose it, to prevent it from following him.

Perhaps if he could gain enough momentum he could knock it from its feet. He couldn't think of any better idea, other than setting the thing on fire. His rocket canisters had so far only managed to scorch it—and he could see nothing nearby that might serve as a flammable fuel source, particularly without putting too many civilians at risk.

Knowing he had little other choice, he turned, falling into a steep dive, aiming directly for the station grounds. Firing at it was no good—at this speed, he risked flying through a cloud of his own flechettes. He'd just have to take his chances and hope he could catch it off guard.

Nearly there…

He could see the creature looking up at him, raising its sword, ready to skewer him on its razor-sharp tip as he came at it.

Three seconds…

He had to hold his nerve. Make it think it had him.

Two seconds…

The tip of the blade glinted in the moonlight.

One second…

He jerked his body, screaming in pain as he pulled up at the last minute, feeling the blade score his left leg even through the protective fabric of his suit.

Gritting his teeth, he grabbed for the creature's antlers and hung on, as his momentum dragged the creature off the ground.

The Ghost's arms burned with the exertion of holding on, his shoulders straining. He turned, still propelled at an immense speed, and holding his arms out wide, swung the creature bodily into the side of the station building.

It struck the wall with a loud *crack*, its sword tumbling from its fist. The Ghost's onward momentum meant that he couldn't stop, and he spiralled, spinning out of control, coming down hard on his shoulder just a few feet from where the creature lay slumped and unmoving. His rocket canisters sputtered out, their fuel spent.

Drawing ragged breaths, bleeding and battered, the Ghost clambered to his feet. The creature lay still, its tame crows now returning to their perch amongst its antlers. He knew it wasn't dead—if a thing like that could die—but it was the chance he needed to get away.

Wincing, he staggered toward the road. If he kept to the shadows, he could find a route to the hotel through the back streets.

He needed that drink more than ever.

SEVENTEEN

For the second time in as many days, Gabriel staggered into the lobby of the Clarington Hotel looking beat up and bedraggled. It was late, and there was only a handful of guests still sitting in the foyer bar, sipping cocktails and making idle chitchat.

He'd removed his hat and goggles, and fastened the front of his trench coat to conceal the rest of his outfit—and the worst of his wounds—and yet still he drew their unwanted attention as he hurriedly crossed the lobby. An overweight man, sitting at the bar sipping gin and wearing a suit that was at least a size too small, gawped at him with open disdain. He glowered back, and the man raised an eyebrow, before turning away, shaking his head. Sometimes, Gabriel had to wonder why he spent so much time trying to save these people.

He hurried across to the elevator, his heart sinking as he saw that, standing just inside the open doors, was the same attendant who had helped him the previous day.

"Sixth floor?" said the young man, with a cocky smile.

"If you don't mind," said Gabriel, stepping into the elevator. The doors closed.

"Excuse me for speaking up, sir, but I think you should know that there's been a few folk around the hotel asking about you today."

Inwardly, Gabriel groaned. "Well, how does the saying go? 'It's better to be talked about…'"

The attendant coughed politely into his fist. "That's not quite what I mean, sir, although now you mention it, there have been a few guests who've been a little perturbed by your… choice of attire. But I was referring to the fact there's been a few folk come to the hotel to enquire as to whether you're staying here today."

"Ah," said Gabriel. He felt the elevator shudder as it began its ponderous journey to the sixth floor.

"Yes, sir. I thought it might be of interest."

"And did you enlighten them?" said Gabriel.

"Oh, no, sir. It's hotel policy that we don't give away that sort of information. We're used to having guests of a certain caliber here, sir. We tend to employ discretion in these circumstances."

"Well, thank you," said Gabriel. "Much obliged."

So, there'd been people asking about him at the hotel. He wondered if that had anything to do with Rutherford, and the potential traitor operating in the Secret Service. Or maybe it had been Horwood, following up on their meeting yesterday. He supposed he should ask for descriptions, but all he could concern himself with at the moment was getting safely back to his suite.

"Not at all, sir. Just part of the service. Although if you don't mind me asking, sir—is there anything we should be worried about? Only, I get the sense that's something's afoot. You know, word on the street and all that. And you look to me like a man who knows about that sort of business."

"I do, do I?" said Gabriel, grinning. He fished around in his pocket for a handful of coins. "Put it this way. You might want to think about taking a short break in the country. Just a couple of days. I'm sure if there's anything to worry about, it'll all have blown over by then."

The young man turned and smiled at him. "Thank you, sir. I've been meaning to pay a visit to my old uncle down in Sussex. Keeps bees."

"Very wise," said Gabriel. The elevator chimed, and ground to a halt. The doors opened. Gabriel handed the attendant his pocketful of change. "Bring me back some honey."

"I'll do that, sir."

The doors slid shut, and Gabriel hobbled down the corridor to his suite. His leg was in serious need of attention. He'd only checked it briefly, but the creature's sword had opened a four-inch wound in his thigh. He was going to have to stitch it.

He practically fell against the door, which swung open a moment later to reveal Rutherford. He grinned when he saw Gabriel, and helped him in, turning the key in the lock behind him.

Ginny was asleep on the bed.

"Felix and Flora are back in their own room," said Rutherford. "I checked him over. He's got a few scratches, and some irritation from whatever that slime is, but he's going to be fine. You, on the other hand..." He eased Gabriel down onto the sofa.

"My leg," said Gabriel. "I need to stitch it. There should be bandages and needle and thread in the cupboard over there."

Rutherford nodded. "I'll fetch some water and towels, too."

"Thank you."

"It's really the least I can do. After everything you've done for me. You came here for a rest, and now look at you."

Gabriel laughed. "I was bored, anyway. At least this way I'll have something to talk about when I get home."

Rutherford laughed. "Cigarette? It's American... I haven't been able to stand an English one since New York."

Gabriel took the proffered cigarette, pulled the ignition tab, and sank back into the sofa. "You'll stay the night on the chaise longue? I think it's best we remain together until this is all over."

"Agreed," said Rutherford. He disappeared into the bathroom, and Gabriel heard him running the tap.

He closed his eyes for a moment, and then the room spun, and oblivion took hold.

"Look, he told me to ask for him here. Couldn't you just tell me his room number and I'll be on my way?"

Horwood was beginning to feel exasperated. The man on the reception desk wouldn't even confirm that Gabriel Cross was staying here, despite the fact that Horwood had shown him the card.

He'd spent a fitful night at home, waking every few minutes to check if the avatar had returned. After cutting himself free of the snaking vines—his grandfather taught him every good gardener carries a penknife at all times—he'd returned to the house and swiftly downed a bottle of wine, just to settle his nerves. He'd half expected a repeat of the avatar's previous outing, to find it had returned, injured, in the middle of the night—but he knew deep down that there was something fundamentally wrong this time. Somehow, something had corrupted the incorruptible— Albion had been poisoned. It wasn't coming back.

Worse, if the Koscheis had the power to infect Albion itself, then whatever they were planning had grave consequences indeed. Albion was the only thing that could properly counter their ancient rites—and now it, too, was lost.

When the dawn light came streaming through the window, Horwood had washed and changed, and then, with a heavy heart, set out to find Peter Rutherford and his associates. He had to get the warning out. London was doomed.

And now, here he was, the weight of the world bearing down on him, and the silly little man on the reception desk of the hotel was refusing to listen to him.

"It's vital that I speak to him," said Horwood. "It's of national significance."

The receptionist raised his eyebrows and hid his smile behind his hand. "*National* importance, sir?"

"Yes!"

"Look, I don't understand what's taking so long. He told me himself I could find him here." There'd been something else, too. Something Rutherford had said, but Horwood had only been half listening at the time. Something about a specter… He clicked his fingers. That was it! "He told me to say a ghost had sent me."

The receptionist smiled. "Ah, well, if only you'd said, sir." He opened a folder and ran a finger along a list of names. "You'll find Mr. Cross in room six-zero-zero-four."

"Thank you," said Horwood, heaving a sigh of relief. He turned away from the desk and took a step toward the elevators. A woman was coming toward him. He looked her up and down—a black jacket over a white blouse, black culottes, calf-high boots, and a figure to die for. He went left, making way for her, but she followed him, stepping out directly in front of him to block his path.

"Um, sorry," he said. He took another step to the left, and she did the same, this time catching him by the arm.

"Room six-zero-zero-four, is it?" she said. "I think you should come with me."

"What? Who are you?"

"That doesn't matter," she said, leading him toward the elevators. "Now smile nicely for the attendant."

Horwood beamed at the young man in uniform standing by the bank of buttons.

"Sixth floor, please," said the woman.

"Yes, miss," replied the attendant, before hitting the button.

The elevator doors shut, and Horwood swallowed. The woman was still gripping his arm.

Gabriel woke to the sound of someone taking a shower in the other room. He sat up, bleary-eyed, feeling the wound in his leg pull sharply, testing the strength of the stitches. Rutherford had done a good job with the needle and thread, after cleaning the wound with a bottle of rather good vodka, much to Gabriel's annoyance.

He glanced over at Ginny's side of the bed, only to realize it must have been her in the shower. Sure enough, Rutherford was still asleep on the chaise longue across the other side of the room. He swung his legs over the side of the bed and stood, testing his movement. He was sore, but he could still fight. He'd put his body through worse.

He pulled on a shirt and pants, and looked out the menu for

room service. He was about to call down with an order when there was a sharp rap at the door. He guessed that Ginny must have called them already, before taking her shower.

He crossed to the door and peered out through the eyehole. Then, having seen who was waiting on the other side, he yanked the door open and bundled the two visitors inside.

"Rutherford," he called. "We've got visitors."

"Hello again," said Regina. "I found this one making a fuss at reception. I think he must be yours?"

Horwood shrugged sheepishly. "Can I have my arm back now, please?"

After gathering the others—waking Donovan and Flora in the adjoining suite—the seven of them assembled for a conference in Gabriel's suite, to compare notes on everything they had learned.

Regina spoke first, outlining what had happened after she and Hargreaves had followed up Rutherford's lead in Belgravia, finding the marked doors, learning how to operate them, and everything that had followed, including the meeting of Koscheis they'd witnessed at the old church, the extensive maps of the Underground system they'd been discussing, and the ensuing battle for survival.

"Where's Hargreaves now?" said Rutherford. There was no hint of suspicion in his voice, but Gabriel knew he was thinking it. Was Hargreaves the one who'd betrayed him in the first place?

"We split up," said Regina. "After we found the house near St. Paul's. I told him to report back to Absalom, while I tried to find you. I figured we needed to compare notes."

Rutherford nodded. "Any word from Absalom?"

"Not yet," said Regina. "But then I've not called in. You're a difficult man to find, Peter."

"When I want to be," he said.

"How did you find us?" said Gabriel. He was standing by the window, smoking another of Rutherford's cigarettes. Donovan, meanwhile, was listening intently from the comfort of a nearby armchair, while Ginny had taken her now customary perch of the edge of the bed. Rutherford was pacing, and Horwood was standing over by the drinks cabinet, looking longingly at the brandy.

"A relatively simple matter, really," said Regina. "I started at the Savoy, and worked my way around all of the expensive hotels in London, until I hit upon the Clarington. Your friend here was making quite a fuss at reception, demanding to see you, and so I loitered until I overheard your room number, and the rest..."

Gabriel's eyes flicked to Horwood, who'd finally given in and poured himself a large brandy. He gulped it down as Gabriel watched, as if he were a parched man in the desert who'd just happened upon an oasis. "You're right about the Underground," he said, returning his attention to Regina. "We've been down there. We found the Glogauer woman, got her to answer a few questions. She pointed us to an abandoned station called City Road."

"I know it," said Regina. "It's been disused for years."

"Well, the Koscheis have got a use for it now," said Donovan. "They're growing something down there. Something unnatural, covering the walls. And it's spreading, too. Soon it'll have infected any connected stations through the tunnel system."

"That's *it*!" exclaimed Horwood, excited. He hopped from foot to foot, almost sloshing his drink out of his glass. "That's what they're up to."

"What do you mean?" said Ginny.

"The Koscheis. They're infecting the Underground."

"Well, yes, we'd established that," said Rutherford.

"No, no, no! But you don't understand *why*."

"Then you'd better tell us," said Gabriel.

"Oh, it's clever," said Horwood. "Very, very clever. Don't you see, that tunnel system, it runs beneath much of Central London, and more specifically, the site of the old Anglo-Saxon town of Lundenwic. Covent Garden, Charing Cross, the Embankment… the sheer amount of people, the density of the population… it's the perfect delivery system for an attack such as this."

"Go on," said Rutherford.

"City Road is just the origin point, the site of the initial infection. They're planning to infect all of Central London, to weaken us and leave us defenseless, ready for attack."

"I'm not sure I follow," said Donovan. "You think if this stuff spreads throughout the Underground, it'll bring the transport system to a halt?"

"No, it's not about the transport system," said Horwood. He was getting animated now. He took another slug of brandy. "It's about people's hearts and minds. The Underground is just a convenient means by which they're deploying their magic. Whatever that stuff you found in the tunnels is, it's not a *literal* poison, but an *elemental* one. It's there to corrupt people's souls, to erode their spirits, to turn their thoughts against each other. It's like they've introduced a drug into the system, one that affects people's minds, sapping their will."

"You've lost me," said Donovan.

"No, I think I get it," said Gabriel. He'd always had a sense of New York as a living city. The people flowing through its streets were its lifeblood, the thrumming of the traffic its pulse. When he stood upon the rooftops in the quiet hours before dawn and truly *listened*, he could hear its heartbeat, pounding in his ears. It wasn't about the fabric of the place. It was more *elemental* that that, more profound.

More, though, he'd felt that malign influence himself in the tunnel—the way the mulch had affected his mood, leaving him momentarily uncertain and heavy-hearted when he'd first entered the station. He'd fought the feeling off, but he could see now what Horwood was driving at. Prolonged exposure to such an influence would certainly have a devastating effect.

"They're targeting Lundenwic. They must know about the Albion avatar, and they're trying to manipulate it. Remember what I said—that the avatar draws its strength, its direction, from the will of the people of Lundenwic. But what if the will of those people was corrupted? If their faith in one another was undermined, their sense of community lost. That stuff in the tunnels must already be altering people's moods, their perception. And it's already affecting Albion, too. That's why I'm here, you see?" Horwood gasped for breath. "I woke Albion. The avatar, I brought it to life, just like I promised. But something was wrong. Something had corrupted it, poisoned its spirit. It's out there, somewhere, the only thing that can help us, but somehow, the Koscheis have turned it against us."

"Let me guess," said Gabriel. "This avatar—it's about eight

feet tall, made of wood, carries a big sword…"

"Yes!" said Horwood. "Have you *seen* it?"

"Let's just say that it *definitely* isn't batting for our team," said Gabriel.

"It's the sickness," said Horwood. "It's affecting it. It's affecting *everything*."

"Well, this is all well and good," said Regina, "but what the hell are we going to do about it?"

Horwood had starting pacing the room, tapping his fingernail against the side of his glass. "We have to clear the tunnels. Kill the infection, and we free the avatar. It's the only thing that can help us defeat the Koscheis."

"And how do we do that?" said Rutherford. "I've seen that stuff. It's virtually indestructible. And it's *everywhere* down there."

Gabriel had finished his cigarette. He crushed the end of it between his fingertips and tossed it out of the window. "There *is* a way," he said. "When the Koscheis were firing that blue energy at us yesterday, I saw a stray bolt hit the wall. The mulch *recoiled*, like a living thing. Where the energy touched it, it blistered and boiled away. If we could find a way to harness some of their power, we could do it."

"Ah, now that's where I think I might be able to help," said Regina, reaching around and pulling a strange-looking weapon from her waistband. She laid it on the table before her. It was shaped like a large handgun, with an oversized barrel, engraved with symbols that resembled those used by the Koscheis. "I took this off one of them yesterday. It fires a kind of blue flame, if you know how to trigger those symbols."

"And do you?" said Donovan.

Regina grinned. "I learned from an expert," she said.

"Then we have a plan," said Gabriel. "We rest up and prepare, and then this evening, we return to City Road to cleanse the tunnels of the infection. And hope we don't meet your friend while we're at it," he added, glancing at Horwood.

"And the Koscheis?" said Rutherford.

"We know we can beat them," said Gabriel. "In small numbers, at least."

"And there's more of us now," said Flora. "We can do this."

Regina looked to Rutherford. "What about Hargreaves, and Absalom?"

"We can't risk it," said Rutherford. "Someone at the Service has been feeding information to the Koscheis. If they find out we're coming…"

"I don't like it," said Regina. "Absalom could send backup."

"And so could the Koscheis. I'm sorry, Regina. I can't countenance it. Absalom is fully aware. He authorized this. I'm out in the cold."

"Absalom *knows*?"

"And now so do you. So what will it be?"

She met his gaze. "I'm with you. Of course. But we end this tonight. All of it. We burn that shit out of the tunnel, and then we go for the rest of them, too. We take down that house near St. Paul's, and we break open their entire network."

"Alright," said Rutherford. "If we're all agreed?"

"Agreed," said Gabriel.

"Agreed," echoed the others.

EIGHTEEN

The stench emanating from City Road Underground station was now so pungent that it was noticeable from the street. Pedestrians had taken to crossing the road to avoid it, eyeing it warily, and the Ghost wondered how long it would be before some unwary public health inspector found himself descending into the stinking bowels of the tunnel system, only to find himself caught up in the mulch like the other poor innocents he'd found bound to the walls down there, slowly being consumed and forgotten.

As he hopped down from the rear of the van, he scanned the immediate area for any sign of the Albion avatar. Mercifully, it appeared to have moved on. The only evidence of its passing was the deep furrow in the brickwork it had made with the tip of its sword, and a scattering of dead leaves, dislodged when the Ghost had slammed it against the side of the building. He stooped to pick one up, wincing at the sudden pain in his leg.

Despite Rutherford's ministrations, his wounds were still causing him difficulties. Realistically, he knew he was in no fit shape for another encounter with the Koscheis, but he had little choice. He'd just have to put it out of mind and hope that his enemies didn't use it to their advantage.

He'd taken time to repair his suit as best he could, stitching up the slashed leg, reinforcing the padding around his torso. He'd also reloaded his rocket boosters and refilled his flechette cartridge, as well as packing a small handgun in the top of his boot, just in case it might prove necessary.

While Ginny had spent much of the afternoon ensuring everyone in the small group had been marked with Horwood's protective wards, Donovan had rested, and Regina and Rutherford had paid a visit to Absalom's unrecorded safe house to stock up on weapons and supplies. Additionally, they'd called in some favors to organize the use of the van. It was a battered old thing, spouting coils of black smoke from its coal-powered engine, but it had sufficed to get them all here without drawing too much unwanted attention.

Now, as they gathered around the station's rear door, the Ghost couldn't help but think that they looked like a motley bunch, hardly in a fit state to take on an army of Russian occultists. But then he'd always been an underdog. Perhaps he was attracted to the challenge—the need to look danger in the eye. Or perhaps he just had a death wish, and somehow, he'd unwittingly lured all of these people into his bizarre crusade. He looked at each of them in turn, seeing the steely determination, and the fear, in their eyes. Whatever the case, they believed in their cause—and who was he to stand in the way of that?

"Alright," he said. "We're going in. We know what we have to do—protect Regina while she deploys the weapon. We get finished down there as quickly as possible, and then we're back out again. If we get split up, we rendezvous at the hotel. Any questions?"

There was a murmur of agreement from the others. They'd discussed this at length back at the hotel, and then again in the van as they'd rumbled through the London streets, outlining each of their roles if the Koscheis attacked. They were as ready as they were ever going to be.

"Straight across the ticket hall, down the stairs, and onto the platform," said the Ghost. "We start there, working our way down the tunnel until we've cleared it all." He hoped Regina's stolen weapon would work—otherwise they'd put themselves in extreme danger for nothing. There was no alternative plan.

He braced himself against the stench, and then darted in, running straight for the stairs. He heard the footsteps of the others behind him. He took the stairs two at a time, hitting the platform a few seconds ahead of the others, sweeping the barrel of his flechette gun across the tunnel entrance. "Clear," he called, as Regina emerged behind him, the barrel of the Koschei weapon already aglow with elemental energy.

"Over there," said Donovan, pointing to the mulch that had now seeped fully out of the tunnel mouth, completely coating the far end of the platform and working its way along the tracks.

Regina nodded, raising the weapon. "Stand back," she said, as she squeezed the trigger and unleashed a bizarre, nightmarish stream of pale light, which seemed to crackle, fizz and spit as it gushed out of the muzzle of the gun, striking the edge of the platform. Reality itself seemed to stutter as the light flickered, causing a strobe effect, deepening the shadows all around them.

Regina held the stream steady, and as it struck the mulch, it appeared to have a similar effect to the Koscheis' lightning, causing the vegetation to boil and hiss, bubbling away into nothingness. Within seconds, she'd cleared a large patch of the platform, and was moving onto the tracks.

"It's working," said Ginny, triumphantly.

Regina jumped down from the platform onto the tracks, and the others clambered down after her, forming a protective semicircle around her as she strode forward, blasting the walls, floor and ceiling of the tunnel as she went.

The mulch had begun to retreat, inching away from the edge of the blast radius, but it was too slow, and soon the air was filled with the cloying odor of burning vegetation. They marched on, deeper into the tunnel, meeting no resistance as they went.

"It's too quiet," said Donovan from beside the Ghost, as they backed along the tunnel, keeping watch behind them. "Something's wrong."

"Maybe they abandoned the place after last time," said Flora. She was gripping her gun with both hands, arms raised, walking in step with Donovan, eyes scanning the murky darkness behind them. "They know we're onto them now. They could have fled."

"I think that's unlikely," said Donovan. "It's more plausible they've already achieved what they wanted to down here, and have moved on to the next stage of their plan."

There was a thud from further down the tunnel, coming from the platform area they'd just cleared.

The Ghost narrowed his eyes, trying to see what was coming. "Either that," he said, "or they're not worried about having to defend it anymore, because something else is…"

A second thud, followed by a third, echoing through the tunnel like the rumble of thunder.

"What is that?" said Rutherford. "It sounds like a train is coming."

Nearby, a crow squawked, fluttering out of the shadows toward them. Rutherford, spooked by the sudden movement, snapped off a shot, and the bird wheeled, feathers erupting from its ravaged corpse, before tumbling out of the sky, thudding to the tracks below.

"Not a train," said the Ghost. "More like a demigod."

Crows burst from the tunnel mouth, swarming at them in the hundreds. They seemed to fill the entire width of the tunnel, an oncoming wave of disorienting feathers, talons, and snapping beaks. Rutherford opened fire again, dropping a handful of them, but it wasn't enough, and they were forced to take cover, burying their faces in the crooks of their elbows as the birds swarmed around them, scoring the tops of their heads with their claws.

Horwood called out in terror as one of the birds took a chunk out of his ear with its beak, until Flora battered it away with the grip of her gun, wielding it like a cosh to keep the screeching creatures at bay.

Behind him, the Ghost could still hear the crackle of the Koschei weapon as Regina continued to scour the walls of the foul mulch, inching ever forward, protected by the others.

Within seconds, the swarm of crows had dissipated, fluttering away into the dank depths of the tunnel system, leaving them bleeding, frustrated, and confused.

And that was when the avatar of Albion thundered into the tunnel, eyes blazing with rage.

"Oh, God," muttered Horwood, still clutching his maimed ear. Blood was trickling down the side of his face.

The avatar ran straight at them, taking long, lolloping strides, its antlers brushing the ceiling of the tunnel, sparking where the ivory scratched against the concrete. Its blade hung low and ready by its side.

"Go!" said the Ghost. "We'll cover you. Stick to the plan."

He planted his feet, readying his flechette gun—for all the good it would do. Beside him, Donovan and Rutherford stood their ground, while the others closed in around Regina, urging her on into the tunnel.

Donovan opened fire, snapping off a series of shots that pinged harmlessly off the avatar's bark-encrusted face, sending up clouds of fine splinters where they struck.

It raised its arm, swinging its sword, ready to cleave their paltry barricade in two.

"Now, Gabriel!" bellowed Rutherford, diving left, as Donovan dived right.

The Ghost tugged on the ignition cord for his boosters and propelled himself into the air, colliding head-on with the avatar's face, just as the creature's sword arm came down where he'd been standing.

The avatar twisted, but the Ghost scrabbled for a grip, catching hold of its antlers, clutching tight as it swung its head from side to side, trying desperately to shake him off. He clung on, obscuring its view, as it raged, thrashing out with its blade, striking the tunnel walls as it marched forward.

"Hurry up!" he called. "I can't hold on for long."

The avatar roared—a deep, guttural screech of anger that reverberated through the Ghost's belly. It was primal and terrifying. He felt his grip slipping on the antlers. "Come on!"

Down below, Rutherford was pressed against the tunnel wall, fumbling with a length of cord. He ducked as the avatar took another blind swing, gasping as the blade scored the wall only inches from the top of his head. Finally, the knot uncoiled, and he tossed the loose end of the cord to Donovan, across the other side of the tunnel.

Their eyes met. And then they pulled the cord taut, and ran at the avatar's legs.

Above, the Ghost was struggling to maintain his grip, as the avatar had begun scrabbling at him with its free hand, catching hold of his trench coat and trying to yank him free. His left hand slipped, losing purchase on the antler, and he swung wildly, maintaining his grip through his right hand alone. If it managed to prise him free before the others were done, it would dash him off the tunnel walls in a matter of moments.

And then the avatar was suddenly falling, toppling forward as Rutherford and Donovan wrapped the cord around its legs, causing it to stumble as it tried to take a step, losing its balance and pitching over.

The Ghost released his grip, using the force of his rocket boosters to propel him out of the way as the beast went down, thudding to the ground, scrabbling at the tunnel walls for purchase.

The Ghost went high, and then dipped again, before cutting power to his boosters and coming in to land, behind the avatar, where Rutherford and Donovan were hurriedly finishing off knotting the cord that now bound its legs.

The avatar screeched again, dragging itself along the tracks with its hands, still trying to reach Regina and the others, who were distant now, much further along the tunnel, and visible only by the sparking light of the stolen weapon. In their wake, the mulch had been almost entirely obliterated, leaving nothing but steaming ash and blackened walls as evidence of their passing.

The avatar twisted, trying to turn itself over in the tunnel, but it was too large to easily maneuver down here, its antlers catching on the steel rails.

The Ghost picked his way over the rails, stepping over the creature's legs, until he located its sword, laying abandoned on the tracks. He stooped and collected it, hefting it, his muscles burning under the sheer weight of the thing. He turned the blade over, resting it on his palm. It was exquisite, decorated with an intricate knotwork pattern of what he presumed to be ancient origin. The hilt was gold, inlaid with rings of polished jet.

Slowly, he carried it up onto the avatar's back, and stood upon its shoulders, holding the blade with both hands, its tip poised over the avatar's neck. A single blow would remove its head. He raised the sword.

"No!"

Horwood's voice echoed along the tunnel, from somewhere up ahead. He was running toward them, gasping for breath. He hove into view, the left side of his face now covered in blood from his wounded ear. "Please, don't hurt it."

"What are you talking about, man?" said Donovan. "Your plan isn't working. It's still trying to kill us. We have no choice."

"Regina's almost finished clearing out the tunnel ahead. At least wait until she's done. If Albion's spirit can be restored, it can help us against the Russians. *Trust me.*"

The Ghost hesitated, blade tip still poised over the back of the thing's neck. "Are you sure?"

"No, I'm not *sure*," said Horwood, "but it's a risk we've got to take. It's the only thing that can stop the Koscheis."

"Alright," said the Ghost, lowering the blade. "But just until—"

He was cut off abruptly as the avatar twisted, jerking its

shoulder so that the Ghost lost his footing, lurching to one side, going down on one knee. He dropped the sword, scrabbling for a handhold, but the avatar was too fast, and its thorny fingers snagged him, puncturing his damaged leg and whipping him forward, over its shoulder, slamming him down across the tracks.

"Gabriel!" Donovan was running forward, across the avatar's back, firing shots into the back of its head, but the creature just seemed to shrug them off, bullets thudding into the outer layer of bark.

Its hand tightened around the Ghost's leg, dragging him closer, his back scraping painfully across the wood and gravel between the tracks. It snarled, its eyes shining with malign intent.

It was looming over him now, still on its front but supported on its elbow, one hand pinning him down, the other extruding what appeared to be a long, thin thorn. It grew as the Ghost watched, its needle-like tip closing in on his left eye.

He struggled, trying to force his way free, to snap the branch-like fingers, to worm his way out, but the creature's grip was fast, and no matter what Donovan tried, he couldn't even wound it enough to distract it.

"The sword," yelled the Ghost. "Get the sword!"

He realized that Rutherford must have already been trying to wrest it free, but a quick glance told him it was no use — the avatar had uncoiled a snaking vine from its flank, which had encircled the weapon, drawing it in, out of the reach of the British agent.

The thorn was only inches from his eye. It would burst through his goggles any moment, piercing his eye, first blinding him, and then killing him as it skewered his brain.

He could hear Horwood calling to the avatar from

somewhere behind him, telling it to stand down, to fight against the corruption, to free itself from the Koscheis' control, but it was no use—the thorn continued to grow, and the expression on the avatar's face told him everything he needed to know.

The tip of the thorn clinked against the glass lens of his goggles. Not long now. He wished he'd been able to speak with Ginny before it was over. "Felix?"

"Yes?"

"Tell her... tell her..." He trailed off. Something subtle had altered in the avatar's demeanor. It was peering down at him, more inquisitive than malign.

"Yes!" called Horwood. "Yes, that's it! *Remember.*"

The avatar shifted, lifting its hand away as the thorn seemed to withdraw inside of its arm once again, sliding away from view.

Its grip on the Ghost's leg loosened, and he pulled himself away, sliding backwards along the tracks. Blood was weeping from several puncture wounds in his leg... but he was alive.

He heard voices calling from the far end of the tunnel, and turned. The others were returning—Ginny, Flora and Regina.

"Gabriel?" Ginny came running when she saw he was down on the tracks.

"I'm... fine," said the Ghost, not quite sure whether to believe it himself.

Horwood was clambering over the avatar's legs, already working on the knots that bound its legs.

The Ghost took Ginny's proffered hands, pulling himself up. "You did it," he said, turning to Regina.

She nodded. "The tunnel is clear of that filth. But that still leaves the Koscheis to deal with."

The Ghost nodded. "No time like the present." He groaned,

stretching his sore muscles. "You'd better show us where this house is."

Behind him, the avatar was climbing to its feet, with a sound like a forest being stirred by a gale. It reached for its sword, the vines on its leg unraveling to free the weapon. It peered at the Ghost, and then turned and marched back down the tunnel, in the direction of the platform and the exit.

"It looks as if he already knows where *he's* going," said Rutherford. "I vote we follow him."

They emerged from the exit a few minutes later, still jubilant from their apparent victory. The night had turned frigid, a cold wind stirring up from the east. The Ghost turned up the collar of his trench coat, wrapping his arm around Ginny's shoulders.

The avatar of Albion was standing by the rear of the station building, staring up into the clear night sky. Out on the main road, a passerby called out in alarm, and then ran off into the night, shouting something about a tree-man. It mattered little— no one would believe his testimony, and Albion would be long gone before anyone returned to investigate.

"I get why you do this, you know," said Ginny, as they strolled toward the van.

"Oh, and why's that?" said the Ghost.

"Because of moments like this," she said. "The rush of victory. Knowing you've saved people's lives. It feels good."

The Ghost laughed. "I suppose it does. But it's not over yet."

"Well, as good as," said Ginny. "We've foiled their plan. Do you really think they're going to stick around now, after this?"

"I don't know," said the Ghost. "But I don't get the sense

they're the type of people who'll give up easily." He glanced at the avatar. It was still staring up at the sky, as if it were expecting something. He followed its gaze, trying to discern what it was watching. There was nothing there. Nothing but a few scattered clouds, and a clear, inky night, speckled with the lights of distant stars.

"Hold on, what's that?" said Regina. The Ghost glanced over to see that she, too, was looking up to the stars. She was pointing at something—a tiny pinprick of light.

"It's just a beacon," said Flora. "Probably an airship, heading off for some distant shore."

"No," said the Ghost. "Look, it's getting bigger." He watched with a dawning sense of horror as the light in the sky began to take shape, tracing an immense circle high above the rooftops of the city. Lines appeared inside it, forming the outline of a pentagram. Sparking symbols appeared like circlets, tracing a bizarre pattern around the orbit of the immense portal.

"Look, there's another," said Horwood, pointing out a second portal, still forming, close to the first. Lightning cracked the sky, high above the dome of St. Paul's, lighting up the underside of the clouds.

"I don't like the look of this at all…" said Donovan.

The first portal shimmered, and reality seemed to crack inside of it, swirling with vivid colors, like a rainbow had been smeared, warped out of recognizable shape and form. Something was coming through. Something large and rotund, with a silvery skin, emblazoned with the same glowing symbols.

An airship.

The Ghost glanced at the second portal to see that it, too, was birthing an airship in matching livery. The first of them was almost through, and even as it emerged, biplanes began to detach from its flanks, buzzing like hornets over the rooftops of the city. As they watched, the aeroplanes loosed streams of tracer fire upon the city streets below, causing buildings to erupt in flame, billowing black smoke on the horizon.

The avatar stirred, turning toward the site of the opening bombardment. Without another glance at the Ghost and his assembled party, it marched off into the street, brandishing its sword.

"It looks as if the Koscheis had a plan B," said Donovan.

NINETEEN

The van hurtled through the streets, swerving to avoid the oncoming rush of terrified pedestrians as they fled for their lives, desperately evacuating their homes, trying to get as far from the carnage as possible.

Ahead, the avatar was running, feet rupturing the asphalt with every step, causing Regina to have to steer around the newly formed potholes as she tried to keep up.

Overhead, at least a dozen biplanes were swooping low over the city now, bringing flaming death with every dive, machine guns chattering, engines howling. The Ghost wanted to be up there, ducking and weaving amongst them, blasting them out of the sky—but he knew he was needed elsewhere. Regina was right—they'd have to rely on Albion and the armed forces to defend the city, while they infiltrated the Koscheis' main base of operations. If they could take that down, there was a chance they could put a stop to the entire invasion.

Someone there had to be pulling the strings. That was their target.

The biplanes were concentrating their fire in the area immediately around St Paul's. Clearly, the Koscheis were attempting to gain a foothold here, and as the van screeched around another bend, it became apparent that they'd already achieved as much. There were scores of them in the streets, energy flickering around them as they blasted buildings—and civilians—with their unnatural light.

Regina slammed her foot on the brakes, and the van mounted the curb, screeching to a halt. The Ghost didn't wait for the others, but flung open the rear door and leapt out, flechettes streaming from his gun.

Two Koscheis fell, tiny metal blades catching them unexpectedly, shredding their throats.

The avatar was wading amongst them, swinging its sword in a wide arc before it, cutting through the Koscheis in a swathe. They turned their fire on it in response, electricity crackling over the avatar's torso, cracking flakes of bark from its chest, but failing to stop its advance.

Overhead, a biplane swooped low, the roar of its engines splitting the sky, and the avatar looked up, raising its free hand and sending thick vines shooting into the air. They snared the tail of the nearest biplane, and the avatar whipped its arm, dragging the machine out of the sky, bringing it crashing down amongst the Koscheis like a wrecking ball. It burst into flames, engine oil and munitions going up like fireworks. All around, Koscheis burned in the aftermath, hooded robes becoming cloaks of roaring flame.

Around the Ghost his friends had formed a line, weapons barking as they attempted to keep the Koscheis at bay. Regina had broken from the formation, wading deep into the fight, her stolen weapon spitting death to all in her way.

The rat-a-tat of machine gun fire from overhead caused the Ghost to dive, and the pavement where he'd been standing erupted in a slew of dust and chippings. Vines burst from the broken ground, curling up to grab at a Koschei's ankles, yanking him to the ground and dashing his head against the concrete.

All around them branches were twisting out of the soil, grasping for the enemy—a forest of deadly thickets and thorns, brought to life through the elemental control of Albion. The avatar of Lundenwic had risen, and it was *angry*.

"We need to get to the house," called Donovan, from close by.

The Ghost nodded. "Regina!"

She turned to glance at him, just as a Koschei raised his hand, targeting her with a crackling blast of energy. She fell, the Koschei weapon tumbling from her grasp as she writhed on the ground, screaming with pain.

The Ghost leapt toward her, his flechette gun spitting death, but the Koschei flicked his wrists, deflecting the deadly blades with his glowing shields. The Ghost strafed left, and the Koschei flung another bolt, scorching the trailing edge of his trench coat. On the ground, Regina was still fighting against the crackling energy, mouth open in a silent scream, electricity arcing between her teeth. He hoped the wards on her back would be enough to save her.

The Ghost circled, keeping step with the Koschei. He was an older man, in his fifties, with a bald pate and thick beard. Tattoos adorned every inch of his exposed flesh, and his eyes seemed manic and darting. He was grinning insanely, baring his yellowed teeth.

The Ghost squeezed off another flurry of flechettes, but once again, the Koschei easily deflected them.

He risked a glance at the ground, searching for any sign of Regina's lost weapon, but it was nowhere to be seen, kicked away in the chaos. The distraction, though, was the opening the Koschei had been waiting for, and he lurched at the Ghost, pushing on the air to create a wave like a brick wall, which slammed into the Ghost, sending him toppling backwards. He tried to roll, but the Koschei stood over him, fingers splayed, manipulating the air currents around the Ghost, preventing his every move.

The Koschei said something in Russian, but the Ghost couldn't hear it—couldn't hear anything—over the rush of wind that was pummeling him, coming at him from all directions at once. He gasped for breath, but felt the wind being drawn from his lungs, and he clutched at his throat as the world started to swim into darkness around him.

And then suddenly he was free again, and the Koschei was on the ground, a vine wrapped around his leg, pinning him down. He scrabbled at the wiry root, trying to pull himself free.

The Ghost sucked at the air, relief flooding his body. He glanced around to see the avatar looming to his right, skewering another Koschei with its blade, even as more of its vines grappled with another biplane, yanking the pilot out of the machine and crushing the life out of him in the process.

It glanced at the Ghost, catching his eye, and the avatar held out its hand, extruding a long, fat thorn from its palm. It nodded to the Ghost, and he reached for it, pulling it free from its socket. He weighed it in his hand like a sword.

At his feet, the Koschei was screaming, his leg now severed above the knee by the tightening vine. He raised his hands, trying to conjure a portal, but the Ghost put an end to him with the thorn, burying it deep in the man's chest. He gurgled something incomprehensible, before falling still.

The Ghost yanked the thorn free, tucking it inside his trench coat, and then turned to help Regina to her feet. She looked pale, but alive. Nearby, he could hear the wail of sirens, and the report of machine gun fire. The armed forces were beginning to respond, joining the fray. Soon, the Air Force would engage the biplanes and airships, too.

He pulled his spare handgun from his boot and tossed it to Regina. "Show me the way to the house."

"There's too many of them," she said. "We'll never get through them that way. But I know another route."

The Ghost nodded. He still didn't know how much he could trust this woman, but he supposed he had little choice. He started after her as she made for the van.

Donovan and Rutherford were using the vehicle for cover, taking turns to cover each other as they blasted away at the Koscheis. They'd already managed to take down three of them, and as the Ghost ducked toward the van, he saw another bullet hit home, catching a Koschei in the side of the head and dropping him where he stood.

"Into the van!" he called across to them. "We're going after the house."

Donovan frowned. "What about Flora?"

The Ghost glanced back, to see swarms of uniformed soldiers flooding into the street, machine guns chattering. Flora was nearby, crouched behind a postbox, taking potshots at the Koscheis. Vines had broken through the pavement around her, creating a barricade. A little further down the street, Ginny floated three feet off the ground, ethereal wind rippling her hair as she summoned her immaterial lions to feast on the souls of the Russians. Horwood was nowhere to be seen. "I think Flora will be fine," he said, smirking.

Donovan nodded, although he didn't look particularly reassured.

Regina hauled herself up into the driver's seat, and the Ghost, Donovan and Rutherford crammed in behind her.

"Where to?" said Rutherford, taking another shot out of the window, and winging a Koschei in the leg.

"Belgravia," said Regina, as she stamped on the accelerator.

TWENTY

London had erupted into chaos.

Every turn they took, the roads were blocked by swarms of fleeing pedestrians, or lines of honking cars, as people tried to evacuate the capital. They were fleeing for the bridges, trying to cross the river, blocking every route that Regina knew to get them closer to Belgravia.

"I hope this works," said Donovan. "I can't quite fathom why we're heading *away* from the fight—where we've left Flora and Ginny, I might add—when the house we're trying to reach is right there, near St. Paul's."

"They're defending it," said Regina. "There're scores of them in the streets. But this is a back way in, one they won't think we'll try."

Rutherford nodded. "It makes sense. If we can use their network against them, hopefully we can get close to the heart of the enemy operation. Take that out, and we may just be able to win the day."

"Exactly," said the Ghost.

Regina hit the brakes, stopping the van in the middle of the road, where a taxi had apparently been abandoned, its doors hanging open. "This is as close as we're going to get. We're going to have to make a run for it."

They jumped down from the van and followed her as she ran through the streets, going against the tide of civilians.

"This is it," said Rutherford, as they rounded a bend into a large square, where large, sweeping terraces surrounded a meticulous park. It was clearly an affluent area—the most pristine that the Ghost had seen since arriving in London—but now, it seemed disturbingly quiet, its people gone, fearful of being caught in the fallout of the Russian invasion.

Regina ran up the steps to the front door of one of the terraced houses and tried the handle. It was locked. She took a step back, raised her gun, and fired twice at the wood around the lock. Then, with a sharp kick, she opened the door with a splintering bang.

"Come on, it's upstairs." She led the way, up onto the landing, and then along to a small, rather nondescript door at the far end. "It's still here," she said, with some relief. She reached up and traced her fingertip around the edge of a barely perceptible mark in the paintwork. As she did, the symbol began to glow, fizzing with the same unnatural light as the Koscheis' portals.

"How did you find out how to do this again?" said Rutherford. He sounded both impressed and a little wary.

"Desperation," said Regina. "I copied one of them, after Hargreaves fell through the portal and it shut behind him. This one leads to a farmhouse..." She completed tracing the sigil, and opened the door, stepping through.

With a shrug, the Ghost followed. Sure enough, he found himself standing in a farmhouse kitchen, just as Regina had explained. Bemused, he crossed to the window, peering out at the grassy wilderness beyond.

"My God," said Donovan. "It's incredible."

"It's dangerous," said Rutherford. "Come on, we can't hang around. Stick to the plan."

Regina crossed to another door, and repeated the action, hurrying them through. This time they emerged in the drawing room of an old country manor house. She led them on to the dining room. Here, there was evidence of a scuffle, and the remains of a dead Koschei, now moldering on the floor.

"I see you were busy last time you were here," said Rutherford.

"Not through choice," said Regina, her voice level.

More doors led them through a cobbled lane, an old church—where a scene of intense carnage had taken place—and finally onto a box room in another terraced house, this one also occupied by a body.

The young Koschei had had his head caved in, or something to that effect—the top half of his skull was entirely missing, and the flesh around the wound was blistered and black. "The former owner of the weapon I was carrying," said Regina, her voice barely above a whisper. "This is the place. The house near St. Paul's, with all the doors."

The Ghost nodded. "Downstairs?"

"Yes. In the hallway. There's about fifty of them."

He crossed to the window, careful not to show himself as he peered out. Russian biplanes were still tearing through the sky, showering the streets with tracer fire, but now other fighters had engaged with them, too, ducking and weaving in a deadly, balletic dance. He could hear voices in the street below, too, and risked a quick glance, before stepping away from the window. "There's at least ten of them in the street below."

"That could mean there's more in the house," said Donovan.

Rutherford nodded. "Where do we go when we get down there?"

Regina shrugged. "I don't know. Hargreaves and I got out of here the first chance we could. I don't know where any of those portals lead."

"Then we'll just have to take our chances," said Rutherford. "Come on." He raised his pistol and walked to the other door, peering out onto the landing. He glanced back, indicating it was safe to proceed. They followed him out.

There were no voices down in the hallway. The Ghost took point, creeping down the steps one at a time, his flechette gun trained first at the bottom of the stairs, and then, as he made his way further down, into the hallway, sweeping his arm back and forth over the banister.

He could see immediately that Regina had been telling the truth—the view here was utterly disorientating, as if geometry itself had somehow broken down, allowing the walls to accommodate more doors than they should naturally be able to. Not only that, but there were rows of freestanding doors, too, just hovering in the air, supported by nothing. It hurt his eyes to look at them, causing him to feel dizzy and nauseous.

"What is this place?" Donovan whispered beneath his breath, as he came down the stairs behind the Ghost, trying to take it all in.

"A hub. A base. The place we have to find a way to destroy," he said. He'd reached the bottom of the stairs.

"No," said Rutherford. "A hub, certainly, but I'd wager one of these doors leads to the place we're looking for. This isn't where they do their planning."

Someone coughed.

The Ghost spun, searching for the person responsible. There was no one there. The room was empty. He waved the others silent, walking slowly forward into the center of the hallway. Here, he could almost lose any sense of which way was left and which way was right. All he could see was the doors, swimming in the periphery of his vision.

Another cough, followed by a stream of words in Russian. He turned again, disoriented, thinking it had come from behind him. But again, there was no one there.

What was going on? Where had the voice originated?

He turned back, just in time to see two hooded figures emerge from one of the portals in the rear wall. They looked up, surprised, raising their hands defensively, just as two rounds snapped from the stairs, and both men dropped, blood spattering across the tiles behind them.

The Ghost looked over to see Regina and Donovan, weapons smoking with the recent discharge.

"We need to get out of here, now!" said Rutherford, hurrying down the stairs. "Those gunshots will bring them in from the street."

"Which door?" said the Ghost.

"The one those men just stepped through seems as good as any," said Rutherford.

They hurried to the portal. The symbol on the door was still glowing. "Well, here goes nothing," said Rutherford, before stepping through.

With a quick glance at Donovan, the Ghost leapt through behind him.

TWENTY-ONE

They emerged from the portal into a cold chamber of frost-limned stone.

Here, the walls appeared to have been constructed from huge blocks of chiseled granite, polished smooth to form glistening walls, engraved with pictograms that resembled the hieroglyphs in an Ancient Egyptian tomb, but sharper, more angular, and surrounded by circlets of flowing symbols. Ice had encrusted much of the wall on the left, obscuring many of the pictograms from view.

Icicles dripped from the ceiling, sparkling in the light of three torches, which had been placed around the edges of the chamber in metal brackets, and burned with the same foul light as the weapon Regina had used to purge the Underground of the Koscheis' blight.

The floor, too, was rimed with frost, which crunched underfoot as they entered the room. The Ghost noticed his breath was fogging. His extremities were already beginning to react to the deep chill, growing painfully numb, as if icicles were attempting to form inside his fingers and toes.

The room was divided by a short flight of stone steps, leading to a raised platform against the opposite wall. Here, there were two apparent exits—a banded door of polished ebony in the far wall, and an open archway in the stonework to the right. There were no windows, and little in the way of furnishings, just a faded tapestry hanging to one side of the ebony door, depicting a shirtless man wrestling a polar bear—and a small table, upon which a series of three wooden bowls rested.

"Well, this wasn't quite what I was expecting," said Donovan, stamping his feet to ward off the chill. "Where do you think we are?"

"Inside a temple," said the Ghost. "All those pictograms on the walls—they look religious to me, as if they're setting out some kind of parable. It's difficult to make out, what with all the frost…" He crossed to the wall on the left, rubbing away some of the ice with his gloved hand, revealing a series of images that appeared to represent a Koschei, opening a portal before him.

"Actually, it's more of a tomb," said a voice from the archway. "But I'll let you have that one, Mr. Cross."

The voice was English, and seemed familiar, although he couldn't quite place it. Footsteps followed. The Ghost raised his weapon, and the others followed suit, training their guns on the shadowy recess and the outline of the figure within.

"Oh, put your guns away. I'm quite equipped with the means to deal with such paltry toys." The figure that emerged from the archway wore the same hooded robes as the others of his order, but carried himself with a confidence that set him apart from his brethren. Perhaps more disturbing, he seemed to know exactly who the Ghost really was.

He entered the room with his head bowed, his hands clasped before him as if in silent prayer. Behind him, two others followed in single file, both of them sitting astride hulking polar bears, whose sheer bulk seemed impossible in such a confined space. The beasts were adorned with leather saddles, and they growled, low and threatening, as their riders dug heels into their flanks, urging them into position at either side of their master.

The two guards were female and wore their hoods down. Both were startlingly beautiful—one with dark skin, the other with pale, milky flesh. Both were ritually tattooed like the men he had seen back in England. They carried long staffs, tipped with shining silver blades.

"Welcome to St. Petersburg," said the hooded man, "or at least, one of the many caverns beneath it. You are most honored to visit the tomb of our master."

"I presume you refer to Rasputin?" said the Ghost. "The founder of your order."

The man inclined his head. "Quite so. Here, he rests in undeath, presiding over us all, opening our minds to the vagaries of the universe."

"Does he teach you how to sound so pompous, too?" said Donovan.

"You should mind your friend, Mr. Cross," said the hooded man. "His blasphemy might put one in mind of a far more painful death than we had initially envisioned."

"See?" said Donovan, glancing at the Ghost." Pompous ass."

"Show yourself," demanded Rutherford, still pointing his gun at the man.

The man laughed. "As you wish." He reached up and, with a smooth gesture, cast his hood back to reveal his face.

"Boyd," said Regina. "Good God. You're supposed to be dead."

"And so are you, Regina. Things are rarely as they first appear. I was plucked from the wreckage of that car by my brothers, and revivified."

"*You're* the traitor," hissed Rutherford.

Boyd inclined his head. "From my perspective, it is you who is in the wrong, Peter."

Rutherford was gritting his teeth. The Ghost could see his anger was about to boil over, his finger twitching at his trigger.

The Ghost tensed, preparing to move. If the polar bears came for them, they couldn't allow themselves to get pinned. He rocked forward, his trench coat billowing open. A single movement, and he'd be airborne.

"I can see you want to, Peter. It's alright. Let it out." Boyd spread his arms, mocking Rutherford, making a target of himself.

Rutherford snapped. His finger depressed the trigger. The gunshot sounded like a thunderclap in the small chamber.

Boyd's eyes went wide, and he buckled, creasing forward, clutching at his belly and gurgling. Rutherford took a step forward, raising his gun again, preparing to finish him, but then Boyd took a sudden step backwards, and rose, laughing, as if he'd simply been taking a bow. He tossed something at Rutherford, which struck the flagstones by his feet with a metallic *ting*. The Ghost watched it roll to a stop by Rutherford's boot. It was a bullet.

"Well, I must say, this is all rather disappointing," said Boyd. "But there you are. That's the caliber of the British Secret Service these days." He waved a hand casually toward Rutherford. "Ladies, please dispose of the trash."

The women grinned as Boyd stepped back, spurring their beasts forward with a sharp jab to their ribs. The bears roared in unison, revealing cavernous jaws lined with deadly, blade-like teeth.

The Ghost yanked his ignition cord, soaring into the air as the polar bear on the right leapt off the platform toward him. He shot upwards, kicking out and striking the rider in the jaw with a well-placed kick.

She howled in rage as he twisted, spinning around behind her, spraying her mount with a wave of tiny flechettes. The beast bucked and roared as the blades opened scores of weeping mouths in its rear end, twisting around, gnashing its jaws as it tried to reach him. He moved again, darting sideways, showering the rider with another round of flechettes. This time, however, she was ready, and waved her arm, throwing up a defensive shield of crackling energy. The Ghost circled around, but the woman was swift in her retaliation, and whipped at him with her stave, slicing him smartly across the shin.

The Ghost grimaced, scudding quickly out of her reach as he felt the wound pucker, blood streaming down his lower leg, pooling around his ankle. He fired another burst of flechettes, targeting the polar bear's head, but she was ready for that, too, and slid her shield around, blocking the attack.

Across the other side of the chamber, Donovan, Regina and Rutherford were unleashing a hail of bullets at the other polar bear, aiming for its head, but its rider was sweeping all the shots aside, striding forward slowly, herding them into the far corner.

The Ghost fired another volley, this time into the flank of the other bear, and—catching the rider unaware—thudded into her back and side, too. She screamed, and the bear bucked, surging forward.

Donovan fired, catching it in the chest as it reared up, tossing its wounded rider to the ground, but coming back down on top of Regina, who barely managed to get her arms up in defense.

She crumpled beneath the creature as it came down, thrashing and rending with its claws. She screamed—a shrill cry of desperation—and then the bear bit down, and the scream was irrevocably cut off.

Rutherford roared, slamming the muzzle of his gun against the side of the creature's head. He pulled the trigger, once, twice, three times, and the creature bucked, and then rolled to the side, slumping across the flagstones. Rutherford and Donovan went immediately to Regina's side.

The Ghost didn't have time to see what had become of her, however, as the other rider was swinging her stave once again, trying to cut him down as he circled above her.

He needed a different tactic. He ducked low, swinging his feet around, dangerously close to the polar bear's jaws. He kicked out, and twisted, raking the bottom of his boot across its snout, searing its eyes with the flame from his boosters. It pulled back, screeching in pain, its eyeballs bubbling to jelly, as the Ghost pulled away again, rising into the air.

As he did, however, the woman swiped with her stave, catching the back of his left leg and bursting the fuel canister. Flame shot out in a hot stream, and the Ghost, caught off balance and unable to control his trajectory, went spinning toward the wall. He slammed into the granite at full speed, jarring his shoulder and causing his chest to light up in pain. He slid down the wall, grasping at the iron torch holder, but succeeding only in pulling it free, causing the torch, the bracket, and himself to tumble to the ground.

The woman on the polar bear was grinning. She knew

she had him now. The wounded bear, too, was at its most dangerous, swinging its head from side to side in abject pain, guided forward by its rider. It wrinkled its nose, panting. It could smell him. He shuffled back, against the wall, trying to figure out what he could do, to find a way out of it.

The bear surged forward, rearing up, and the Ghost threw himself to the left, scrabbling for the guttering torch he'd torn from the wall, still burning with its strange, unnatural fire. He twisted, swinging the torch around, and as the bear came down upon him, he jabbed it in the creature's mouth.

The flame took instantly, igniting the roof of the polar bear's mouth. The flesh around its nose began to blacken, and then suddenly wither, as if struck instantaneously by a thousand years' worth of decay. As the flames engulfed it, the head dissolved entirely, the skull folding in on itself, fluttering away like dust.

The remains of the creature collapsed under its own weight, tumbling sideways, sending the rider spinning to the ground, trapping her leg beneath its still-burning bulk.

The Ghost rose, still holding the torch. He considered sparing the woman, but then thought of Regina, and stalked forward, presenting the torch to her like a bunch of deadly flowers. She screamed as he jabbed it against her chest, and within seconds she was dead, her chest collapsing, her heart withered and decayed.

He dropped the torch, running over to join Rutherford and Donovan.

Rutherford was on his knees beside Regina. She was drenched in blood, with huge gouges ripped out of her side, and blood was still running freely down the side of her face and neck. Her shirt had been ripped open, and there were furrows right across her chest, where the polar bear's claws had raked her.

Donovan caught his eye, and gave an almost imperceptible shake of his head.

"Boyd," said Rutherford, through gritted teeth. He turned slowly, rising to his feet. He had his gun in his hand.

Boyd was strolling casually down the steps toward them, amidst the carnage of his dead followers. "Well, I must say, that was highly amusing," he said. "And here I was thinking they'd shred you apart in no time at all."

Rutherford rounded on him, emptying the chamber of his gun with a roar. Boyd laughed, waving a hand before him, brushing the bullets aside with a flash of fizzing energy. "You'll pay for this, Boyd. She was one of us. *You* were one of us!"

"I was never *one of you*," snapped Boyd. "Only you were too blind to see it. And now you've paid the price." He grinned. "Oh, I don't mean *her*. I mean London. Even now, the master is opening more portals. He sustains them with his power. Soon, the city will be awash with our followers. And you, Peter? You'll be dead." He waved his hand, and Rutherford clutched his throat, gasping for breath.

He was still walking toward them, so close now that he could almost sneer directly in Rutherford's face as he sucked the very air from his lungs.

The Ghost stepped back, whipping his arm around, squeezing the trigger of his flechette gun, but Boyd had anticipated such a move, and the shards bounced harmlessly off another floating shield. He pointed at the Ghost, and a stream of electrical light shot from his finger, encasing the Ghost in its crackling strands. The Ghost fell back, unable to move, unable to do anything but watch in exquisite pain as Boyd choked the life out of his friend.

Donovan rose too, but before he could even fire a shot, Boyd flicked his wrist and sent him careening to the other side of the chamber, where he struck the stone steps and slumped to the ground.

Rutherford was beginning to turn blue, raking at his throat with his fingertips. He dropped to his knees, and Boyd stood over him, grinning with grim satisfaction. "It's hard to watch a city die, Rutherford. Consider this a mercy."

"Consider this *revenge*," said a voice, choked with blood. Boyd's head detonated, blood spraying in a wide arc as the bullet exited his skull. His body buckled, suddenly losing all coordination, and his knees gave out, his corpse crumpling to the floor. "*That's* the caliber of the British Secret Service," said Regina, before tottering over into a bloodstained heap.

Rutherford wheezed, gasping at the air, gulping noisily as the color slowly began to return to his oxygen-starved face. The Ghost sat up, the wards on his back burning fiercely. He climbed to his knees, and then forced himself up, staggering over to where Regina lay, her eyelids fluttering as she fought to remain conscious.

"Regina…" he said, brushing a loose strand of hair from her face.

"He always did talk too much," she croaked, her lips twitching in an attempt at a smile.

"We'll get you back to the Fixer," he said. "We can use their doors."

"No," she said, shaking her head. Her voice was faint now, as if she was struggling to draw enough breath to talk. "You heard Boyd. He said the master was opening more portals. He controls the doors. He's the source of their power. You need to see it through." She coughed, and blood welled out of her mouth. She looked up at him, panic in her eyes, and then suddenly she was still. Her final breath burbled from her lungs, bubbles forming on her bloodied lips. The Ghost reached down and closed her eyes.

Rutherford was standing behind him, looking down, still breathing erratically.

"I'm sorry," said the Ghost.

"So am I," said Rutherford.

They both looked round at a groan from the other side of the room. Donovan was stirring, sitting up, rubbing the back of his head and wearing a pained expression. His eyes widened as he saw the scene before him. "It's over?"

The Ghost stood, shaking his head. "Not yet. Not until we put a stop to the thing controlling the doors."

"Rasputin?" said Rutherford, his voice dry and cracked.

"Rasputin," said the Ghost. He walked over to the steps, and then looked back at Rutherford. "You coming?"

Rutherford's only answer was a grim smile.

TWENTY-TWO

Horwood could hardly breathe.

His chest burned, his vision was swimming, and all he could think about was getting back to his house, locking the door, and hiding away until all of this was over. Maybe a drink would help to settle his nerves, too. Something strong. Something *very* strong.

All around him, the world seemed to be falling to pieces. He couldn't hear himself think for the roar of the biplanes overhead, the chatter of machine guns, the crash of crumbling masonry. He watched as a nearby telephone box exploded in a shower of twisted metal and shattered glass, torn asunder by a stream of bullets. Closer by, a vine had shot from the ground, splintering the paving slabs, to grasp at a Koschei. It snaked around the man's legs, dragging him to his knees, before bursting through his chest, spreading his ribs like bony fingers. The flickering light of his spell died on his fingertips as the vine withdrew, and his broken corpse pitched heavily to the ground, blood pooling in the gutter.

Horwood sensed movement to his left, and ducked behind the corner of a building, pressing his back against the wall. A Koschei hurried past, blue light flickering as he summoned a portal, disappearing through it as if simply folding himself out of existence. There were more of them, too, sliding in and out of reality all around, sending streaming fistfuls of ethereal light in the direction of the Albion avatar. One of them was likely to spot him at any moment.

Horwood had no idea what to do. He'd never been able to hold his own in a fight. Even back in his school days, he'd taken regular beatings from the older boys, and had found his only solace in the library, whiling away all his free time amongst the dusty stacks, avoiding interaction with the other children. Even during the war he'd been given a desk job, deployed to a secret facility in Lincolnshire and tasked with investigating ways to counter the occult designs of the Kaiser. If he took on a Koschei—even just one of them—he'd be dead in seconds.

He looked up, suddenly aware of the sound of a biplane engine directly overhead. Its tail had been snagged by another curling vine, and Albion was forcing it into a steep dive. It was heading right for him, its propeller churning the air, its pilot frantically hammering the controls as it plummeted.

Horwood ran, throwing himself around the corner of the building and charging down the street, back toward the main crux of the battle. Behind him, the engine roar grew louder, more insistent, until the sound became a whining scream, and he thought his eardrums were going to burst with the pressure. It was coming down right on top of him. There was no way he'd be quick enough to get out of the way.

This was it. He knew then that he was going to die. He'd be dashed across the road as it struck the ground, or lacerated by the propeller as he tried to dive out of the way.

And then he was falling forward, arms flung out before him, as the biplane struck the road behind him, detonating in a sudden fireball, its propellers cutting grooves in the pavement as its burning undercarriage slid wildly across the tarmac and rebounded from another nearby building, causing the brickwork to crack and the roof to slump, slate tiles cascading to the ground in a crashing shower.

Horwood struck the pavement hard, his breath leaving his body. He flopped onto his back, and then rolled, wide-eyed, as a fragment of contorted wing flew overhead, so close that he could read the Russian markings on the paintwork. It clanged to the ground a few feet away, smoldering.

Horwood came to rest in the gutter, and remained there for a moment, trying to catch his breath. He was so close to the burning wreckage he could feel the warmth of the flames against his cheek.

He heard a voice, and looked up to see two Koscheis standing over him. The one on the left was a woman, her lips parted in a fierce sneer, her eyes only just visible beneath the hood of her robe. On the right, her male companion was levelling a weapon. It looked familiar—one of the flame guns, just like the one Regina had used in the Underground.

Horwood swallowed. What were the chances? He'd managed to escape a crashing biplane, only to find himself confronted by a man standing ready to conflagrate him in stream of elemental flames.

And then suddenly the two Koscheis were stumbling back, waving their arms before them in an attempt to ward off a flock of crows, which had descended from above in a flurry of stabbing beaks and disorientating wings.

Horwood scrabbled back on his elbows as the men screamed, trying desperately to bat the birds away. But the crows were relentless, and within seconds both Koscheis had collapsed to the ground, their faces and hands reduced to a bloody mess, their eyes pecked out to reveal empty, staring sockets, dribbling with blood. The crows cawed in triumph, fluttering off in search of their next victims.

Horwood picked himself up. To his left, the Albion entity was striding through the massed ranks of Koscheis, sword sweeping low, cleaving heads from shoulders with every swing. Around it, vines continued to erupt from the cracked paving slabs, knitting together to form a protective wall, a shield intended to pin the Koscheis in place, to shepherd them toward their doom.

He saw the avatar look up, and followed its gaze. Another biplane was droning overhead, sweeping low in a wide arc, preparing to make a run at the avatar with its machine guns.

The avatar waited, allowing the biplane to enter into its dive, before throwing out its arm, which extended into a whipping tendril, encircling the biplane even as the pilot tried to weave around it. With a flick of its arm, the avatar sent the biplane skywards, hurling it into a spinning trajectory for the nearest airship.

Horwood saw the pilot bail, flinging himself out of the cockpit just as the biplane collided with the silvery lozenge of the airship, twisting through the taut outer skin like a corkscrew and tearing a massive rent in the gasbags as it crashed through the interior. The entire vessel buckled, before erupting into a massive ball of flame, temporarily lighting the street below, columns of black smoke curling away into the evening sky. The airship shuddered, and then began its ponderous descent toward the rooftops of the city far below.

The avatar had already returned its attention to the Koscheis in the road, cleaving and lopping with its massive blade. The Russians were backing away toward the cathedral, concentrating their attacks on the avatar's chest. The wood smoldered and burned where the elemental flames splashed across the avatar's torso, and it writhed in pain, lashing out with even more ferocity, vines whipping from the ground to snare the unwary.

Horwood backed away along the road, looking for somewhere to take cover. To his right, the shimmering figure of Ginny floated, dreamlike, above the street, her arms held out by her sides, her hair stirred by a strange, unnatural breeze. She was cloaked in tattered ribbons, which fluttered as she moved, translucent and eerie. Before her, her ghostly lions bounded along the road, bursting through the bodies of Koscheis, silently consuming their souls.

Horwood ducked into the doorway of a baker's shop, catching his breath. His elbows were smarting, and he was certain some shrapnel from the crashed biplane had buried itself in his back. He could feel blood trickling down the crease of his spine. He had to get out of there. Had to—

He turned at the sound of the avatar screeching. It was a deep, inhuman sound, guttural and frantic; the sound of rending wood, amplified and distorted. A Koschei had managed to get behind the thicket wall, and had turned his flame gun upon the avatar's back. As Horwood looked on, he saw the blue light searing a fist-sized hole in its shoulder. He felt something twist in his gut. The avatar twisted, trying to turn around, but the Koschei was now adjusting the beam of the weapon, burning a deep groove into the avatar's back. It screeched again, staggering, the other Koscheis still bombarding it from the front. Horwood glanced around, searching for anyone who could help. There was no one—the soldiers he could see were all locked in battle with Koscheis, and Ginny had drifted out of sight. He gritted his teeth. There was nothing else for it.

Almost before he knew what he was doing, Horwood was running, feet pounding the concrete as he charged at the Koschei with the flame gun. His back was agony, now, but it barely mattered—he knew he had no chance of surviving this. There was no other choice, though—the avatar was the only thing that could save them, and he was the only one able to do anything to help. He couldn't allow the Koscheis to bring Albion down.

So intent was the Koschei on his target that he didn't see Horwood coming until it was too late. The man twisted, snarling, trying to bring his gun to bear, but Horwood was too close, barreling into him, lifting him from his feet and sending him crashing to the ground. Horwood sprawled too, going over inelegantly, slamming to the ground atop the writhing Koschei, barely able to believe that he was still alive. The flame gun skittered across the road, out of reach of them both.

The Koschei grabbed for Horwood's wrists, trying to heave him off. But Horwood, fired by a sudden surge of adrenaline, was having none of it. He bunched his hands into fists, squeezing until they hurt, and then unleashed a barrage upon the Koschei, pounding the man's face once, twice, three times, striking him over and over, until his nose was spread across his pale face in a bloody streak, and his jaw was hanging loose and broken. Some of his teeth had been knocked free, and bright blood was streaming from the corner of his sagging mouth. He'd stopped moving.

Horwood breathed, ragged breath whistling through his teeth. His fists were covered in blood, his palms stinging where he'd buried his own fingernails into the flesh. Sweat stung his eyes.

Slowly, he got to his feet. He glanced at the flame gun, just a few feet away. To his right, the avatar had resumed its battle with the Koscheis, and the wound in its back was already beginning to close, vines knitting together around the hole.

Horwood staggered toward the gun. If he could just figure out how to activate it... His fingers brushed the metal grip, just as something hard slammed into him from behind. He didn't have time to see what it was before he went over, shoved forward with incredible force, striking his head against the pavement.

Everything went black.

TWENTY-THREE

The ebony door yawned open.

The chamber beyond felt cavernous, although it was difficult to discern, even with the benefit of his night-vision goggles; the edges of the space here were dark and impenetrable, cast in unnatural shadow. It was frigid, too—colder, even, than the previous chamber. He felt his boots crunch ice crystals as he walked across the threshold.

To either side of him walked Rutherford and Donovan, both battered and bruised, but both determined to see it through. The traitor had been dealt with—now all that remained was to cut the Koscheis' network of portals off at the source.

"Straight ahead," said the Ghost. "I can see something that looks like a sarcophagus."

He led the others across the open space, their footsteps ringing out in the darkness. He could just make out a large stone structure in the center of the chamber—what appeared to resemble a large stone coffin, sitting upon a low plinth. Cables trailed from inside of its open lid, emitting the occasional flicker of low yellow light.

"Who goes there?"

The voice was eerie and disembodied, as if the speaker was standing right beside him, whispering in his ear. He could almost feel the ghost of their breath on his cheek, and despite himself, he felt his skin prickle with anxiety.

"Answer me."

He could hear that the words were being spoken in Russian, but somehow, a second, spectral voice was speaking simultaneously, translating the words into whispered, broken English. The sound of it made his brain itch, as if something were ferreting around inside his head.

"Show yourself," he said.

For a moment, there was nothing but silence. He wondered if his demand had angered the owner of the voice. Then, slowly, the corners of the chamber began to glow, igniting with the same corrupting blue flame as the torches in the previous chamber, only bigger, like burning pyres, columns of terrible flame.

Slowly, the full extent of the chamber resolved.

It was huge, at least fifty feet wide and a hundred feet long, carved from the natural bedrock, its walls and ceiling roughly hewn and encrusted with a thick layer of blue-white ice.

They were standing on a man-made platform or dais, and around the edges stood a series of upright booths. They took the form and shape of coffins, but were glass-fronted, and rimed with frost. Fat cables trailed from each of them, trailing across the ground, before snaking up the side of the stone sarcophagus, disappearing within. Soft light pulsed along each of the cables.

There were around twenty of the glass-fronted booths, ten on each side of the dais, and Donovan crossed to one, wiping at the hoary glass with his sleeve. He recoiled at the sight that greeted him—the withered form of a man, ancient and near-death. The end of the cable was buried in his chest, as though whatever was inside the sarcophagus was slowing drawing the light from inside of him, absorbing it into itself.

"They're all full of people," said Donovan, checking another of the booths. "It's grotesque."

"It is necessary," said the voice in the Ghost's ear. "It is the only way."

He watched as the thing in the sarcophagus stirred, slowly rising until it was sitting up. It had its back to them, and it twisted, turning to regard them.

It was like nothing the Ghost had ever seen—a living corpse, half rotten, its flesh peeling in tattered strips, jagged bones jutting from the end of its fingers where the skin had eroded. Its face was sallow and waxy, skin stretched thin across its skull, and its eyes were yellow and bulbous, protruding from their sockets as it glowered menacingly at him. It still wore a straggly gray beard, but its hair was almost entirely gone, with just a few wisps left upon its papery scalp.

What flesh remained on its back was covered in faint black markings—ancient pictograms and sigils; the language of the elements. Its elbows had been supported by mechanical servos that made a dry, grinding sound as it lifted itself up to its full extent, turning to provide them with a full and proper view. Servos also supported its hips and knees, and its chest was a mess of broken ribs and cables. Here, the opposite ends of all twenty cables were embedded, feeding this living corpse with whatever energy it was siphoning from the people in the booths.

"I am Rasputin," said the creature. "Master of this place. Chief Magus of the Tsarina. Saviour of all Russia."

"You are long overdue a proper burial," said the Ghost. He raised his hand and loosed a flurry of flechettes. They struck home, but pinged uselessly off the creature's hide, the black symbols on its necrotic flesh taking on a gentle glow.

The creature laughed. "Russia is eternal," it said. "So is Rasputin."

It walked forward, moving with surprising speed and grace, leaping down from the sarcophagus. It landed neatly on the dais and walked toward them, trailing cables across the ground.

"Sod this," said Rutherford. He snapped out a series of shots as he walked toward the thing, emptying the chamber of his gun at its head and chest. Once again, the bullets struck it, and fell harmlessly to the floor, the sigils on its flesh glowing brighter with every shot.

It flexed the dry, creaking ligaments in its neck, and then struck Rutherford in the chest with the flat of its palm. Light erupted, and he was tossed from his feet, tumbling back, wheeling his arms, until he collided with one of the glass-fronted booths. He slid to the ground, groaning.

"Death is everything," growled Rasputin. "Life is a mirage. Death is the only constant."

The creature swung, waving its arm and causing Donovan's gun to be whipped from his fingers, clattering away across the other side of the cavern. It closed its fist, and Donovan clutched at his chest, doubling over, collapsing to his knees.

The Ghost surged forward, closing the gap between them, swinging at the creature with all his might. It twisted, seeing him coming, and raised its hand, catching his fist as he came in to land the blow.

With a strength that belied its form, the creature squeezed his hand, twisting his arm so that he fell to his knees, wincing, as he tried to prevent his shoulder from popping out of its socket.

"This is only right. All shall kneel before Rasputin, for I have mastered death itself."

Panicking, the Ghost fought against the white stars of pain that were burning across his vision, trying to remain conscious as the creature pulled his arm ever further back, wrenching it until it dislocated with a loud pop.

Master of death… How could he kill a thing that was already dead? Where did he even start? What was it that Newbury had said to him? Only the opposing force could beat the Koscheis. Only light could beat darkness, only water could beat fire. And only life could beat death.

He understood it now. Understood everything. That was what Albion represented: rebirth, and new life. The avatar lived only so long as it was needed, before returning to the soil. Then, when it was called upon again, it would sprout anew, regenerating, taking on a new form. This *thing* before him, though, this walking corpse—it represented everything that Albion did not. It clung desperately to its tattered existence, even while its body decayed. It drew upon the life force of others simply to eke out another day, another year. It claimed to have mastered death, but all it had done was perpetuate it—inflicting death upon all those around it. That was why Horwood had insisted only Albion could help them beat the Koscheis. That was why Albion was the only thing that could destroy this monster—life versus death.

With a roar of effort, the Ghost reached inside his trench coat, dragging the thorn he'd taken from Albion from his belt. This was Albion's gift to him. It had known what he would face, and it had armed him for the battle to come.

He raised his head, screaming at the pain in his dislocated shoulder. "I shall *not* kneel before you!"

He pulled his left arm back, and plunged the thorn into Rasputin's chest.

Immediately, the creature released its grip on his arm, staggering back. Both hands were at its chest, trying to pluck the thorn from the wound, but it was as if its hands could not grasp the weapon. It glared at him, yellowed eyes filled with shock.

"But I... am... Rasputin," it stammered.

The sigils on its flesh had begun to glow. The Ghost staggered to his feet, right arm hanging useless by his side. He rushed over to Donovan.

"Felix? Felix?" He grabbed Donovan by the collar, feeling for a pulse. It was still strong and steady. "*Felix!*"

Donovan spluttered, and looked up to see the Ghost standing over him. "I haven't missed it all *again*?"

"Just get up and start running," said the Ghost. He crossed to Rutherford, preferring his good hand, hauling the British agent to his feet.

Behind them, the creature was still scrabbling at its chest, but now its entire body had begun to glow, wracked with an elemental energy it could no longer contain. It looked up, meeting the Ghost's gaze.

"Come on," said Rutherford, dragging him toward the door. "The portals are about to stop working, and we're still trapped in a tomb beneath St. Petersburg."

They barrelled toward the door, hurrying through into the adjoining chamber. Behind them, a sound like an erupting volcano marked the final moments of Rasputin, as his corpse-shell finally gave in, and the entire chamber was flooded with light.

The Ghost paused on the threshold for a single, satisfied glance back, before launching himself through the portal.

They fell out of the portal into the hallway of the house near St. Paul's, to find the portals all around them were beginning to blink shut, flickering to nothingness as if they had never existed.

The Ghost was barely conscious, the pain in his shoulder so intense that it was sending waves of dizziness crashing over him, threatening to take him down. He fought it back, desperate to know that Ginny and the others were still alright, to see if they needed his help.

He staggered toward the main entrance, reaching for the handle.

"Hold on, Gabriel!" said Donovan, from behind him. "What if there are still Koscheis out there?"

"Then damn well shoot them," said the Ghost. He yanked the door open and staggered out into the cold night air.

Out here, he could see that the battle was nearly over. Above, the two airships burned like twin suns, their gasbags ignited, their biplanes all lost. Vines curled from several holes in the ground, and the corpses of Koscheis littered the street. At the end of the road, British soldiers were still fighting a small pocket of hooded figures, but with nothing to power their portals, they were finished—stranded in London, and facing the might of the armed forces.

The Ghost took a step toward them. Maybe he could help round up the last of them while he searched for Ginny and Flora. But suddenly the world was spinning, and he was listing, scrabbling for something to grab hold of. He felt someone catch his elbow, and Rutherford was by his side, righting him.

"I think I might need to pay a visit to your Fixer friend," said the Ghost, before pitching forward onto the cobbles as the blackness swam up to greet him.

TWENTY-FOUR

Horwood was running, but no matter how hard he tried, it wasn't fast enough.

He pushed himself harder, his feet striking the paving stones until they hurt, until he was sure he was wearing them down to bloody stumps. Yet still he ran, and still he could hear it behind him—the roar of the biplane coming in at a dive, the burr of its propeller, so close that he could feel it stirring his hair.

He cried out, throwing himself forward, just as the biplane struck the ground behind him, lifting him from his feet...

He sat bolt upright on the sofa, dripping with sweat. For a moment, he had no idea where he was. He licked his gummy lips, wiped his forehead on the back of his sleeve. The front of his shirt was damp. He took a deep breath.

He was in his living room. He was home. It was over.

He swallowed, but his mouth was dry. He was desperate for a drink. On the floor before him was an overturned bottle of red wine. It was almost empty, but there were still dregs in the bottom, enough to wet his palate. He grabbed for it and gulped it down thirstily, then discarded the bottle. Perhaps he'd be better off fetching some water.

Slowly, he got to his feet. His back was still agony, and his hand went involuntarily to the wound. He'd have to get the bandages changed soon. The piece of shrapnel he'd had removed at the hospital was the size of his thumb, and he'd been lucky it had missed his vital organs.

His left eye was still swollen shut too, from the trauma he'd received to his head during the fall. Flora Donovan had told him afterwards he'd been caught full force from behind by a Koschei, tossing him almost ten feet up the road. He'd been knocked unconscious in the fall, and the Koschei had left him for dead. Flora had come to his aid as soon as the coast was clear, dragging him to safety. She'd sat with him for nearly two hours, taking pot shots with her pistol at anyone who came close.

He'd woken briefly in the ambulance, and again just before surgery, but all he remembered was the stuttering of bright lights and Flora's worried face.

Now, he was home. He was supposed to be getting some rest, but every time he closed his eyes, all he could see was the biplane coming tumbling out of the sky, heading directly for him.

There was a rap at the door. He sighed, massaging his temples. He was in no fit state for visitors. He'd had a stream of telephone calls demanding statements and interviews, from the police, the Secret Service, even a newspaper journalist who'd somehow managed to get hold of his details. He'd told them all they'd have to wait. And now one of them had found out where he lived.

"I'm not here," he called. "You're wasting your time."

"Roland? Open the door. It's Flora. I've brought the others to see you."

"Flora?" Bemused, he crossed to the door and opened it. There she was, standing on the step. She was smiling. Behind her were Donovan, Gabriel and Ginny. "Why are you here?"

"We came to see how you were doing," said Flora.

He frowned at her for a moment.

"Well, are you going to show us in?"

"Oh, yes, sorry," he said. He turned and wandered back into the living room, leaving the door open behind him. "I wasn't expecting guests."

"And you weren't expecting to have a biplane dropped on you, either," said Gabriel. "We just wanted to say thanks, and see if you needed anything."

Horwood smiled. "I don't know… I mean, I haven't really thought about it. I haven't thought about anything much, to be honest." He started for the kitchen. "I'll put the kettle on."

"I'll see to that," said Donovan. "You sit down. You're supposed to be resting." He disappeared into the kitchen. Moments later, there was a clatter of mugs.

"What you did," said Gabriel. "It made a difference."

"If it hadn't been for you, the Koscheis might have won," added Ginny.

Horwood shrugged. "I couldn't let them destroy it. Without it… well, I hate to think."

"What happened to it?" said Gabriel. "By the time I'd come out of the Fixer's operating theater, it was gone. We passed by there earlier today, too. They've already burned away all evidence of the vines. There's nothing to say it was ever there, save for the terrified accounts of a few locals."

Horwood grinned. "It came home," he said.

"Home?"

He nodded. "Come on, I'll show you." He beckoned them down the hall, and out through the rear door into the garden. The cool air felt fresh and welcome, clearing his head of the alcohol fug. He led them to the hollow at the bottom of the garden.

"Here," he said, indicating what remained of the avatar, nestled amongst the trees. It had already begun to break apart, its limbs unraveling and turning to mulch. The light had gone out of its eyes, and the rose that had served as its heart had withered and dried, petals flaking. It was returning to the soil, just as it always had; ready to grow anew when it was needed.

"It was here all along?" said Ginny.

"Yes. I'm sorry I kept it from you. I didn't know if I could trust you. Not at first," said Horwood.

"And that's it," said Flora. "It's gone? Just like that."

"For now," said Horwood.

They were silent for a moment.

"Come on, let's go and see about that tea," said Flora. "I don't trust Felix in a kitchen." She looped her arm through Ginny's, and started off, back up toward the house.

Horwood turned to Gabriel. "You did it. You ended it. I heard about what you did to Rasputin."

"Oh, I fear it's only just beginning," said Gabriel. "There'll be reprisals. Your queen won't allow this to pass. It's the excuse she's been looking for. I fear another war is brewing."

"Will you stay? Help out when it comes?" said Horwood.

Gabriel shook his head. "No. I'm needed back in New York. But you should take those calls." He started up toward the house, following after Flora and Ginny.

"Calls?" Horwood hurried to keep up.

"You know which calls I mean," said Gabriel. "From the Service. They need good men like you. And if you don't mind me saying—it might give you the sense of purpose you're clearly looking for."

"You mean they want *me*? To work for *them*?" Horwood could hardly believe what the American was saying.

"I mean you should take their calls," said Gabriel, pausing in the doorway. "Talk to them. I meant what I said—you made a difference. Maybe you can do it again." He ducked into the house.

Horwood stared after him, stunned. "Maybe I could," he said, quietly. "Maybe I could."

TWENTY-FIVE

"Where the devil is he?" said Absalom, whiskers twitching in irritation. He took a sip from his brandy, regarding the others around the table with a furrowed brow.

They were back at the Savoy, having finally rearranged their dinner date with Rutherford, along with a few additional guests. Rutherford, however, was running late... for a second time. They'd been at their table for over an hour, and Donovan was beginning to think he was a no-show. "Perhaps he just doesn't like goodbyes," he said, flicking ash from the tip of his cigarette into the cut-glass tray.

"Nonsense," said Absalom. "He's just a bugger for getting waylaid, is all. Never has been able to keep a date. It's why he has such a terrible love life. He'll be here, if he knows what's good for him."

Donovan laughed. He turned to Flora. "I'll be glad to get home," he said, "but I'll miss this place, for all its quirks."

Flora smiled. "You know, I think what we need is a vacation," she said. "A *proper* one. Just you and me."

Donovan frowned. "I'm not so sure I'm very good at vacations."

She laughed. "No. I don't suppose you are."

Gabriel was sitting across from him, holding Ginny's hand

beneath the table. He'd been through a lot, but he was almost back to his usual self: cocky and talkative, and keen to impress.

Ginny had been quiet since they'd found her, tired and disheveled, in the shadow of St. Paul's. She barely remembered what she'd done during the battle, but the rumors amongst the soldiers were that a beautiful, ghostly spirit had come to their aid, smiting scores of Koscheis and saving their lives from the Russians' devastating elemental attacks.

Newbury sat beside Gabriel, sipping quietly at his glass of red wine. He'd spoken little since arriving, but Rutherford had hinted that he'd played a significant role during the battle, although to what end, nobody seemed to be clear. It didn't seem appropriate to ask.

The last of their guests was Hargreaves, who had sat in sullen silence since arriving. Donovan wondered if perhaps he'd taken umbrage at the fact he'd been excluded from the final stages of the mission, but in truth, he suspected he was simply mourning the death of his colleague. Regina's death had been a grave loss, to all of them, and in addition, she'd died at the hands of Boyd, her former colleague and friend. It had left something of a sour taste in Donovan's mouth.

"So, you're heading back to New York tomorrow," said Newbury. "Are you feeling rested?" He cocked a knowing half smile.

"Hardly!" said Gabriel. "In fact, I've been considering demanding a refund. London isn't at all like they said in the brochure."

Newbury laughed. "No, I don't suppose it is."

They lapsed into silence, looking to the door.

"What do you think will happen now?" said Ginny. "Will

there be reprisals? Are we looking at another war?"

Absalom shrugged. "I fear so. The Tsarina has already issued a formal apology to the nation, claiming it was the work of a rogue element in her military, that they're being weeded out for trial and summary execution. She's also offered to pay for all the repairs to the city, but it won't be enough. Rumor has it Alberta is already hatching plans for a retaliatory strike." Absalom sighed. "No doubt my agents are going to be busy. Eh, Hargreaves?"

Hargreaves nodded, but didn't answer. Absalom had told them earlier that Hargreaves had led a search of the Underground tunnels used by the Russians. He'd found scores of bodies down there in various states of decomposition. It seemed the Koscheis had been using them as a gruesome repository for some months. At least it went some way to explaining the bodies they'd encountered beneath City Road.

"And besides, there's a few of the blighters still loose in the city. Someone'll have to hunt them down, and I can't see the boys at the Met being up to it, what?" Absalom glanced at Gabriel. "Which reminds me, if any of you—and I mean *any* of you—would like to stay on, my agency is always on the lookout for good people. There'd be no problem with paperwork. I can see to all that. You just need to say the word."

Gabriel grinned. "Thank you, Major. It's a tempting offer, but my home is in New York. I find myself pining for the place when I'm not there."

"Ah, well," said Absalom. "Can't blame a man for trying, now can you?"

"What's this? Not trying to replace me already, are you? I'm only, what, ten minutes late?"

They all turned to regard Rutherford, who stood huffing beside the table as he fought to regain his breath.

"Ten minutes!" roared Absalom. "See! I told you!"

Sheepishly, Rutherford pulled up a chair beside Ginny. Behind him, the waiters—who'd been patiently awaiting the cue to serve—moved in, hastily placing bowls of soup before each of them, now that the last of them had finally arrived.

Rutherford took a swig of water. "Look, I'm sorry I'm late. You should have started without me. It's just, there's this albino count I've been tracking for weeks, and one of my informants had word, and well... you know how it is."

Gabriel smiled. "We know how it is. But it's good to see you, Peter." He raised his glass. "And now you're here, I'd like to propose a toast," he said. The others reached for their glasses. "To Regina, for giving her life in the pursuit of what she believed in."

"To Regina," came the echoing reply.

"Now, what's *this*," said Gabriel, taking his spoon and running it through the soup. His face fell. "Oh, no. This won't do at all. What *is* it about this place and the soup. Waiter? *Waiter*! Over here!"

Donovan glanced at Flora, and sighed. It was going to be a long journey home.

ABOUT THE AUTHOR

George Mann was born in Darlington and has written numerous books, short stories, novellas and original audio scripts. *The Affinity Bridge*, the first novel in his Newbury and Hobbes Victorian fantasy series, was published in 2008. Other titles in the series include *The Osiris Ritual*, *The Immorality Engine*, *The Casebook of Newbury & Hobbes*, and the forthcoming *The Revenant Express* and *The Albion Initiative*.

His other novels include *Ghosts of Manhattan*, *Ghosts of War*, and *Ghosts of Karnak*, mystery novels about a vigilante set against the backdrop of a post-steampunk 1920s New York; *Wychwood*, the chilling first novel in a new thriller series; and an original *Doctor Who* novel, *Paradox Lost*, featuring the Eleventh Doctor alongside his companions, Amy and Rory.

He has edited a number of anthologies, including *Encounters of Sherlock Holmes*, *Further Encounters of Sherlock Holmes*, *Associates of Sherlock Holmes* and *Further Associates of Sherlock Holmes*, *The Solaris Book of New Science Fiction* and *The Solaris Book of New Fantasy*, and has written two Sherlock Holmes novels for Titan Books, *Sherlock Homes: The Will of the Dead* and *Sherlock Holmes: The Spirit Box*.

ACKNOWLEDGEMENTS

The usual round of thanks go out to Cavan Scott, for enduring friendship and support—and for kicking around ideas for this one between panels at San Diego Comic Con; to Miranda Jewess, Cat Camacho and Gary Budden for superb editorial support; to my agent Jane Willis; and most of all, to my family, in all its many guises.

WYCHWOOD

GEORGE MANN

When a local woman is found murdered in her own home, slashed viciously across the throat, the police begin a manhunt of the surrounding villages, unsure exactly of whom or what they are looking for. Elspeth May, a young journalist accidentally first on the scene, finds her interest piqued, and sets out to investigate the details surrounding the crime. More murders follow, each of them adopting a similar pattern. What links the victims? And why are some of the local people trying to cover things up?

"A sleek serial-killer mystery in the knotty vines of English folklore"
James Lovegrove

"The perfect blend of crime thriller and supernatural horror"
Eric Brown

SHERLOCK HOLMES
THE WILL OF THE DEAD

GEORGE MANN

A young man named Peter Maugram appears at the front door of Sherlock Holmes and Dr. Watson's Baker Street lodgings. Maugram's uncle is dead and his will has disappeared, leaving the man afraid that he will be left penniless. Holmes agrees to take the case and he and Watson dig deep into the murky past of this complex family. Is it connected to the robberies being committed by the enigmatic iron men?

"Mann clearly knows his Holmes"
Crime Fiction Lover

"A proper tribute to Doyle's earlier works"
Horror Novel Reviews